DARK ANGEL

A Ryan Weller Thriller

EVAN GRAVER

ALSO BY EVAN GRAVER

Ryan Weller Thrillers

Dark Water

Dark Ship

Dark Horse

Dark Shadows

Dark Paradise

Dark Fury

Dark Hunt

Dark Path

Dark Prey

Dark Fraud

Dark Drone

Dark Country

Dark Order

Dark Cover-up

Dark Angel

Stand Alone

Liberty Brigade

John Phoenix Thrillers

Rising Phoenix

Target Phoenix

Dark Angel

www.evangraver.com

ISBN-13: 979-8-9876681-7-7

Cover: Wicked Good Book Covers

Editing: Novel Approach Manuscript Services

This is a work of fiction. Any resemblance to any person, living or dead, business, companies, events, or locales is entirely coincidental.

Printed and bound in the United States of America

First Printed March 2024

Published by Third Reef Publishing, LLC

Hollywood, Florida

www.thirdreefpublishing.com

CHAPTER ONE

Harbour Towne Marina
Dania Beach, Florida

"Mail for you, Mister Weller."

Ryan glanced over at the teenage girl standing not far from him in shorts and a polo shirt bearing the marina's logo. The wind teased her brown hair, and she looped it behind her ear. She held out a small stack of white envelopes and what appeared to be two magazines.

Rolling his eyes, Ryan flicked off the orbital sander and pulled down his respirator mask. He placed the sander on the makeshift worktable beside him, constructed from a couple of sawhorses and half a sheet of plywood. His catamaran, a Fountaine Pajot Saba 50 named *Huntress*, was up on blocks in the marina while he sanded off the old antifouling paint so he could apply a fresh coat before he and his wife Emily set sail for the wild Pacific.

He took the mail from the girl and thanked her. With a

quick flash of silver braces, she turned on her heels and headed for the marina office.

Ryan glanced at the mail. His personal correspondence went to his mother-in-law's house in Hollywood, and he picked it up every couple of days. All the envelopes and magazines he now held in his hand were for some guy named Dennis McGuire.

"Not again," Ryan moaned.

He'd been getting McGuire's mail since moving *Huntress* from her mooring at Hollywood Marina a few weeks ago. No one in the Harbour Towne office had ever heard of McGuire, nor did they know why Ryan received his mail. Even the USPS seemed mystified when Ryan had taken the mail to the local post office to return it. The postal service was excellent at delivering the mail, but everything else about it seemed mired in bureaucratic madness. And despite his objections, the USPS kept delivering McGuire's mail to Ryan at the marina.

He wiped the sweat from his brow with a nearby rag and then shuffled through the stack of envelopes. There were credit card bills, offers to refinance a mortgage, a sailboat magazine, and another about motorcycles.

After retrieving a bottle of water from his cooler, Ryan sat in the shade of his boat hull and flipped through the sailing magazine. There was a nicely written article about the Cook Islands and another about inspecting and replacing standing rigging. After reading through it, Ryan tossed the magazine onto the makeshift workbench and grabbed the motorcycle rag. It contained a spread on Honda's newest adventure machine, the XL750 Transalp.

Putting the magazine back on the workbench, he checked his watch and saw it was almost five p.m. He wasn't in the mood to pick up the sander and go back to work. What he wanted was a cold beer and a thick steak. And while he wanted to share both with his wife, he couldn't. Emily had gone to Tampa to do one last job as a freelance insurance investigator for Ward and Young.

He was really beginning to hate Kyle Ward and his damned company, but he couldn't say anything to Emily about it because his job thrust him into danger with every turn. He consoled himself with the fact that she at least worked in an office.

Ryan was a freelance troubleshooter with ties to Dark Water Research, a commercial dive and salvage company with deep connections to the U.S. government's many intelligence agencies. His job, when called upon, could entail anything from fixing deep water oil rigs to recovering top-secret military technology from the hands of foreign actors.

He hoped sailing away on their next voyage would change all of that. Tired of all the running and gunning, Ryan wanted to be a boat bum, spending his days sipping beers and chasing the wind.

Climbing the rickety wooden ladder tied to the stern of the catamaran, Ryan stripped off his clothes in the cockpit, which he'd enclosed with a series of cloth and plastic panels. He stepped into the salon and then descended the steps into the port hull.

The master stateroom was more spacious than any other sailboat Ryan had ever owned. He loved being able to spread out, and he loved the oversized shower with its glass door and posh five-star hotel feel.

He spun on the hot knob and waited for the instant water heater to provide scalding water with which to cleanse the sweat and dust from his body. While the heater worked its magic, Ryan found his cellphone and started to send a text message to Greg Olsen, one of his closest friends and his boss at DWR, asking if he wanted to get steaks and beer. Just before Ryan hit send, he remembered Greg was *way* out of town—thousands of miles away, in fact, working a salvage job near the island of Dominica.

There weren't many people in the greater Fort Lauderdale area Ryan wanted to have dinner with. Since most of them were on board *Dark Ocean* with Greg, he settled for calling his mother-in-law, Melissa Hunt.

Once the call connected, Ryan asked if she wanted to join him for dinner at Tropical Acres Steakhouse. He liked the restaurant and its grill-fired steaks. The steakhouse was one of the oldest in South Florida, established in 1949 by Gene Harvey. At any given time, patrons could see anything from a Yugo to a Ferrari in the parking lot, while inside, happy diners enjoyed delicious, hand-prepared meals.

Melissa readily accepted his invitation and asked if she could extend it to her son, Paul, Emily's younger brother, who was a computer programmer and still lived at home. Even though Ryan wasn't a fan of Paul, he told her it was fine. They agreed to meet at the steakhouse at seven. Ryan called the restaurant, made a reservation, and hopped in the shower.

When he stepped out, he dried off and wrapped the towel around his waist. Wiping the mirror clean with his hand, Ryan stared at his reflection. Inside, he felt like he was still twenty years old, with the energy and stamina to match, but looking in the mirror, he could see the reality. He was closer to forty than twenty.

The sun and the wind had weathered his tanned skin, and his crow's feet extended farther down his cheeks from his green eyes when he smiled. Even his brown hair was retreating, leaving him with a broader forehead. Suddenly, he felt exhausted, and he yawned deeply.

"You're not a kid anymore," he muttered to himself.

Ryan pulled on a white button-down shirt, dark blue slacks, and a matching blue blazer from Brooks Brothers. It was the only suit he owned. Ryan called it his "marry-them-

and-bury-them" suit, as it seemed he only wore it on those occasions, but for some reason, he wanted to dress up for dinner tonight.

He didn't have a Ferrari, but he did have Emily's four-door Jeep Wrangler. He pocketed his wallet, phone, and car keys, ready to head out the door.

With time to kill, Ryan grabbed a beer from the fridge and sat on the couch in the salon. He texted Emily to tell her he was having dinner with her mother and brother. Within seconds, she texted back, telling him she'd already heard and that she loved him for taking the time out of his day to have dinner with her family.

You owe me one, he texted back, then added a winking emoji followed by an eggplant, which was as close as Ryan came to sexting. Emily replied with a laughing emoji, meaning he wasn't getting laid anytime soon.

Ryan climbed down the ladder and surveyed the boatyard. The military had drummed situational awareness into him since his first day of boot camp, and it had become deeply ingrained after years of working as one of the U.S. Navy's elite explosive ordnance disposal technicians and then as a free-lance troubleshooter. Ryan scanned the other boats sitting on the hard in cradles that made them look ungainly and hideous. Land was not where these fiberglass creatures roamed free.

The yard was rectangular, surrounded by a high chain-link fence on three sides. Blue mesh fabric had been interwoven into the metal strands to offer a sense of privacy. On the fourth side of the marina was a boat ramp that led into a canal, connecting the yard to the Intracoastal Waterway and the Atlantic beyond. Marina workers had arranged the yachts in a semi-circle in the small yard. Some had been wrapped with blue or white shrink wrap, while two motor yachts underwent extensive mechanical retrofits and interior remodeling. Only *Huntress* and a Beneteau Oceanis 40 were owned by guys who liked to work on their own vessels. Conrad Shultis waved from his lawn chair under his Beneteau as Ryan headed for the Jeep.

Ryan walked past the check-in shack, cutting across the manicured lawn toward the parking lot. Just as he clicked the unlock button on the Jeep's door remote, a black Chevy Tahoe came screaming into the lot and slammed to a stop, blocking the Jeep from leaving.

Two men in suits dismounted the vehicle—one from the front passenger seat and one from the rear while the driver remained behind the wheel. Typical for the State of Florida, there was no license plate on the front of the Tahoe, but Ryan didn't need to read the plate to know these minions worked for the government. They reeked of bureaucracy, from their cheap suits to their aviator shades.

The FBI must have a tailor at Quantico.

"What the hell, guys?" Ryan asked as the two suits formed up around him.

"Mister McGuire?" the front passenger asked. He wore a tan suit coat to go with his blue slacks.

"No," Ryan replied firmly.

"You need to come with us right now, Mister McGuire," Black Coat from the back seat said forcefully.

"How about you guys get your facts straight?" Ryan countered. "I am not, nor will I ever be, Dennis McGuire. Now, move your vehicle. You're trespassing on private property."

He glanced around to see if anyone was watching the confrontation.

It was after regular business hours for the marina, and most of the employees, yard workers, and salesmen had already gone home for the evening. A breeze rustled the palm fronds above their heads as the setting sun cast long shadows on the pavement.

Tan Coat produced a pair of handcuffs from behind his back. "Let's go, McGuire. We're not asking."

"Well, I'm telling you, you've got the wrong guy," Ryan insisted. "McGuire's mail gets delivered to my boat, but I'm *not* Dennis McGuire. Here, let me show you."

He reached for his wallet in his back pocket. Black Coat stepped back and jerked his pistol from its holster on his belt.

Ryan threw his arms out, wallet in hand. "I'm getting my ID, asshole."

"I don't care if you claim to be Bigfoot, you're getting in the vehicle, Mister McGuire," Tan Coat said. "*Now*."

Ryan opened his wallet. "My driver's license is from North Carolina. It says 'Ryan Weller.' Now, leave me alone!"

"Get in the Tahoe," Tan Coat said, enunciating each word as if it were its own sentence.

When Ryan made no move to enter the SUV, the driver got out and came around the front of the sports utility vehicle. It wasn't just that he was a giant of a Black man with a shiny bald head and shoulders as broad as a yardstick that made Ryan nervous. It was the black HK416 battle rifle with a suppressor, EOTech optics, and a collapsible stock that he carried—a much more persuasive method to convince Ryan to get into the vehicle.

"Get in, Mac," the driver ordered. "I hate paperwork, but I don't mind perforating your ass with some five-five-six."

"Why didn't you lead with that?" Ryan asked, keeping his hands up.

"Get in!" Black Coat held the rear passenger door open.

Before Ryan entered, Tan Coat held out his hand and ordered, "Cellphone and car keys."

Reluctantly, Ryan handed them over, knowing he had no choice. Tan Coat opened the door to the Jeep and tossed the phone and keys onto the driver's side floorboard, then locked the Jeep and slammed the door. By the time he finished, Ryan was in the back seat of the Tahoe beside Black Coat, and the driver had the SUV in reverse. Once Tan Coat was inside, they headed out of the parking lot.

Ryan glanced over at the boatyard, catching sight of *Huntress*'s mast rising into the sky. He was being forced to leave at a time when disappearing could bring an end to his already fragile marriage. Not so long ago, he had taken an op without telling his wife, and it had led to some severe trust issues. Being swept up by these goons and disappeared by them would only make matters worse.

The driver navigated through the maze of residential streets to U.S. 1. Ryan was glad they hadn't blindfolded him.

Hazarding a chance, Ryan asked, "Can I borrow one of your phones? If you all are kidnapping me, I need to call my wife with your ransom demands."

CHAPTER TWO

Twenty minutes after leaving the parking lot at Harbour Towne Marine, the black Tahoe entered the complex of private aviation terminals and businesses at the western end of Fort Lauderdale International Airport.

The driver pulled up to a security gate and entered a code into the keypad. As they drove onto the tarmac, Ryan began to reevaluate his earlier belief that these pussies were FBI agents. While they dressed the part, their mannerisms made them appear more like trained shooters, and they'd come at him with the hammer instead of flashing their badges and threatening to arrest him.

After passing several airplanes, the driver stopped the Tahoe near the rear of a low-slung hangar with multiple hangar doors facing the apron and smaller walk-in entry doors leading inside. Each had a sign displaying the business logo and contact information. However, there was only one steel door with a keypad and no logo. It wasn't hard for Ryan to guess which door he'd be entering. Sitting not far away on the tarmac was a white private jet with no tail markings.

Freaking CIA.

Ryan shook his head in consternation. He was in deep with spooks.

Tan Coat and Black Coat got out of the SUV and came around to Ryan's door. They opened it and motioned for the troubleshooter to get out. Once his feet were on the ground, the two men pushed Ryan toward the unmarked security door.

Tan Coat punched in the code, opened the door, and shoved Ryan into a darkened hallway.

By the time Ryan recovered his balance, the door had slammed behind him. He still turned back to the door, trying the handle and finding it locked. There was another keypad on the wall beside him, but Tan Coat had been too quick when entering his code for Ryan to have seen it.

Turning to look down the dimly lit hall, Ryan faced a narrow corridor with a single door instead of a massive hangar bay.

Before Ryan could decide what to do next, a slim, balding man in dark slacks, a white dress shirt, and a white lab coat stepped through the door and said, "Mister McGuire, glad you could join us. In here, please."

"I am not McGuire. My name is Ryan Weller."

"It's okay, Mister McGuire. We understand your reluctance. Please step this way." The bald man took Ryan by the arm, led him into the room, and turned Ryan to stand with his back against a wall. "Stand straight."

Reflexively, Ryan did as the man told him. A green light stabbed out of a machine in front of him to scan his face, and then a flash popped, causing stars to dance before his eyes.

Ryan realized the bald man had placed him in front of a blue background like he was having a driver's license photo taken—or a passport.

This is getting worse by the second.

"What the hell is going on here?" Ryan demanded.

"Nothing to concern yourself with, Mister McGuire. Is it okay to call you Dennis or Denny?"

"No!" Ryan said exasperatedly. "You're not listening to me. I am *not* Dennis McGuire. Look, I can prove it." He extracted his wallet from his pocket and opened it again to show his driver's license. Pointing at it for emphasis, he said, "It says 'Ryan Weller.'"

The bald man took the wallet from Ryan and turned it to examine the license under better lighting. "Hell of a reproduction. Who did this quality work?"

"Edith at the New Hanover County DMV."

"I think this is the work of the Art Dealer."

"Who?" Ryan asked.

"The Art Dealer. He's a master forger." Baldy slipped Ryan's wallet into his pocket. "Damn shame you wasted your money on it. The facial recognition scan proves you are, in fact, Dennis McGuire."

"How in the hell did a facial recog scan prove I'm McGuire?" Ryan demanded. "I'm Ryan Weller!" He was starting to feel like a broken record as he extended his hand, palm up. "Give me back my wallet."

"Sorry, Mister McGuire. I can't let you keep it. You'll get a new one later."

"Later? What about that one? It's got my driver's license and credit cards in it."

Baldy patted his pocket. "I'll hang on to it for now. It won't do for you to leave here with this."

Realizing he wouldn't get his wallet back, Ryan changed tack. "Can you at least tell me what's going on? Why am I here?"

"You'll have to talk to Grady about that?"

"Where's Grady?" Ryan asked.

"He's out."

"Who are you?" Ryan demanded.

"Phillips. Now, come on. You're late." He took Ryan firmly by the elbow with his right hand and snagged a briefcase off a shelf with his left. "I'm glad you're already wearing a suit. We'd have made you change otherwise."

"I suppose you would have kept my clothes, too," Ryan muttered as Phillips steered him toward the door to the hallway.

Moments later, both men were outside and headed for the white jet.

"Where are we going?" Ryan asked.

"You're getting on the plane," Phillips said. "I'm staying here."

Halfway to the airstairs, another man ran out and handed Ryan a passport. The troubleshooter flipped it open to find his picture with the name "Dennis McGuire" beside it.

Son of a bitch!

Ryan snapped it closed and tried to hand it to Phillips. "Here, you dropped this."

Phillips took the passport and kept hustling Ryan toward the plane.

Ryan glanced at his watch. It was seven-thirty. Melissa Hunt and her son would be seated at a table at Tropical Acres by now, listening to the live piano music and wondering why he hadn't arrived yet.

At the door to the plane stood a man in a pilot's uniform. He took the briefcase from Phillips, and once again, Ryan pleaded his case with the bald man. "I'm not getting on that plane. I'm not Dennis McGuire. My name is Ryan Weller. You have my wallet. At least call Grady or someone above him and verify my identity. They can run a background check on me or call my buddy Larry Grove at the Defense Intelligence Agency and ask him who I am. Hell, run another facial recognition scan if you have to because the one you ran in there was complete bullshit."

"Sir, if you have to ask if I know who you are, then the answer is: I don't know, either. My job is to provide you with a passport and get you on the plane. Grady was supposed to be here to brief you, but he's not."

"Come on, man!" Ryan shouted over the jet's engines. "Just make a damn phone call. I'm not going anywhere until you do."

Phillips withdrew Ryan's wallet from his coat pocket, studied the photo on the driver's license, and then glanced up at Ryan's face. He raised his eyebrows and dipped his head to the left as if unsure.

"Let me speak to Grady," Ryan shouted.

"I told you, he's not here. Now, please get on the plane."

"Not without some answers," Ryan replied. "Call Grady. Call my buddy Larry Grove. Call anyone and confirm that I am *not*, nor have I ever been, Dennis McGuire."

"Sir, the case file is in the briefcase. A change of wardrobe and toilet kit are waiting for you on the plane. We have everything prepared for you. I don't understand your reluctance."

"I'm reluctant because I don't know what the hell is going on here," Ryan decried. "Frankly, I'm getting tired of this Three Stooges act. Now, call Grady."

"That's not necessary," Phillips replied curtly. "Please, get on the plane, Mister McGuire."

"Just make the call! There must be a computer error. I've been getting McGuire's mail at my boat for some reason and now you guys think I'm him."

Phillips studied Ryan's earnest face and then looked at the driver's license again, his features betraying a slight puzzlement. Reluctantly, Phillips agreed. "Fine. I'll make a call, but I need you to wait on the plane. You're too exposed."

Ryan closed his eyes and shook his head. He knew it was a trap. If he got on that plane, he was going wherever it was spooled up to go, to do whatever dangerous mission Dennis

McGuire had ducked out of by getting the CIA to believe Ryan was him.

Phillips extended his hand toward the open plane door. "Please, sir, just wait inside."

"How about I go back into the building with you?" Ryan suggested.

Phillips jabbed his finger at the plane. "Get on, or I'm not making the call."

Reluctantly, Ryan climbed onto the plane, and the captain followed, closing the door behind him.

Ryan knew he had just sealed his own fate. He'd made a crucial error. Ryan realized he should have taken out Tan Coat and Black Coat and fled the scene before the driver had gotten out with the gun, but Ryan couldn't argue with a thirty-round lead spitter in a three-on-one situation.

The pilot climbed into the cockpit beside his co-pilot, and amid the shudder of the engines, the plane began to move.

Cursing under his breath, Ryan stared out the window and waited for the plane to slow as it taxied toward the runway. When the pilots were preoccupied with flipping switches and checking gauges, Ryan moved toward the door and tried the handle.

The pilot glanced over his shoulder. "Hey, buddy, it's locked. I'm not opening it until we land."

Blowing a heavy sigh through puffed-up cheeks, Ryan returned to his seat and fastened his belt. At least he was traveling on a private plane in the lap of luxury.

"Does this crate come with meal service?" Ryan asked. "You guys caused me to miss dinner."

"Yeah?" the co-pilot asked. "What were you going to have?"

"Steak at Tropical Acres," Ryan replied.

"No shit? You did miss a great meal," the co-pilot said.

The pilot turned in his seat. “Catering didn’t load us up for this flight. Plenty of booze, but nothing to eat.”

“Might be some saltines,” the co-pilot called over his shoulder.

“Great,” Ryan mumbled to himself as his stomach growled. He was about to get up and rummage through the cabinets at the back of the plane when the jet lurched forward. It began rolling toward the end of the runway, bypassing several waiting commercial passenger jets. Ryan couldn’t help but grin. He bet the people on board were angry that they had to wait even longer to accommodate a little commuter jet with priority take-off status. Such were the privileges of government.

Moments later, the plane rocketed east down the runway toward the dark Atlantic Ocean. Suddenly, the nose came up, and the plane was airborne, climbing into the atmosphere. Below them, the lights of South Florida glowed between the dark swaths of open ocean and Everglades National Park—the River of Grass.

“I’m sorry, Emily,” Ryan said, pressing his forehead against the plexiglass window.

Half an hour later, the pilot climbed out of his seat, entered the cabin, and handed Ryan the passport Phillips had given him.

“Where are we headed?” Ryan asked around a mouthful of Ritz crackers he’d found in a cabinet at the rear of the plane.

“Saint Kitts.”

Ryan shook his head in wonderment. He’d been to the island before but hadn’t spent much time there, remembering it was more for the jetsetters and trendsetters than a broke young sailor.

"What's your name?" Ryan asked.

"Johnson," the pilot said.

Ryan shook his head at the vagueness of their names. "Look, Johnson. You guys need to come to grips with the fact that I'm not Dennis McGuire."

"He's on the passenger manifest."

"Maybe he is, but I'm the one on the airplane. Turn around and take me back to Fort Lauderdale."

"I can't do that, sir," Johnson said. "You've been shipped, and my order is to get you to Saint Kitts. There's nothing I can do about it."

"Get on the radio and tell them I'm not Dennis McGuire."

"I can't do that, either," the pilot said.

"Johnson, what the hell is this all about?"

The pilot shrugged. "Pardon my ignorance, sir, but maybe there's some answers in the briefcase."

Ryan retrieved the case from where he'd tossed it on the floor. He'd discovered in his search for food that it was the only piece of luggage aboard the plane other than a leather valise that contained extra clothing and a toilet kit.

He set the briefcase on his lap and unfastened the clasps. Inside was a new wallet with two credit cards and a Florida driver's license for Dennis McGuire. Beside the wallet were five banded stacks of crisp, new twenty-dollar bills—ten grand in total. The only other item in the briefcase was a tan file folder.

Ryan placed the file on the seat, then put the wallet, money, and passport in his suit coat pockets before closing the briefcase.

The pilot walked to the rear of the plane and fixed himself a cup of coffee. On his way back to the cockpit, he said, "We'll be landing in ninety minutes. We have clear skies all the way to Robert Bradshaw International in Basseterre."

"Roger that," Ryan replied. He opened the manila folder. "Are you my support on this mission?"

"I'm just transport," the pilot replied. "We're a government contractor. They give me the coordinates and tell me when to fly. What's in the file?"

Holding up a photo from the folder, Ryan said, "What this is about, Johnson, is Megan Babcock."

"You know her?" Johnson asked.

"No," Ryan said. "I've never met her, but I have *heard* of her."

"I think everyone has heard of her. Maybe McGuire knows her—if you're not McGuire like you say."

"What burns me is that I was supposed to be eating medium-rare New York strip at Tropical Acres, but instead, I'm here, choking down these crackers." Ryan held up another photo, then turned it toward Johnson. "And here, we have the hard news: Babcock in an almost nude dress at some awards show."

"She has a nice rack, though," Johnson said, then added, "When we land, someone will be along to pick you up."

"When we land, I'm catching the first ride back to Fort Lauderdale," Ryan said adamantly.

"That's your prerogative, sir," Johnson replied, then turned toward the cockpit with his cup of coffee.

"Hey," Ryan called out. When Johnson turned around, he asked, "Can I borrow your phone? I want to call my wife."

"You'll have to do that on the ground, sir. FAA regs. No in-flight calls."

With a snort of disgust, Ryan continued to sift through the file. Babcock was a beautiful woman who made Paris Hilton's wild partying days look tame in comparison. Even her wedding to Blake Babcock had been a multimillion-dollar extravagance that saw Megan walk down the aisle alongside her father, Charles Gaspar, and two white Bengal tigers—the evening capped by a fireworks display that would rival many small towns' Fourth of July budgets.

After Charles Gaspar passed away some years later, Megan became the heir to Charles' fortune. As a teen, Gaspar had started as a lowly machine operator in Massachusetts. Then, in his late twenties, Gaspar moved to Texas and started a small firm that provided specialized equipment to the oil service industry. From there, the man turned his fortune into Gaspar Industries. The conglomerate now consisted of machinery, manufacturing, packaging, agriculture, military development, electronics, engineering services, and data analytics, serving over thirty countries with an average annual income estimated at nearly one hundred billion dollars.

Megan Babcock had the money to be extravagant. But according to the file, she'd settled down after meeting her husband, proving her worth as a philanthropist and concentrating on running her father's corporation with Blake's help.

Ryan put down the file and turned to stare out the window into the darkness. Occasionally, he could see lights on the islands far below, while above, the Milky Way stretched out in an endless display of twinkling stars. Ryan wondered how Dennis McGuire knew Megan Babcock and what their relationship had been like. Ryan supposed he would have to ask her.

But on this mission, finding out the extent of McGuire and Babcock's relationship would be the least of Ryan's worries.

CHAPTER THREE

Core Tek Shipping
Basseterre, Saint Kitts

CIA case officer John Phoenix didn't like that Headquarters had sent a civilian to help him.

But the paper pushers in the Latin American Division seemed to think they knew how to do his job better than he did. In fact, he'd argued long and hard with his handler that he didn't need Dennis McGuire for this operation.

Phoenix stood in the office of Core Tek Shipping, in an industrial district off the Pond Road roundabout, watching the clock. The shipping company was a legitimate asset of the U.S. government, set up and run by the CIA as a cover to move their officers in and out of Saint Kitts and Nevis. He hoped they'd use it as a cover for McGuire, assigning him NOC status or non-official cover. The Company would consider McGuire a deniable asset, unlike Phoenix, who had diplomatic cover and a black passport to match, which was the equivalent of a get-out-of-jail-free card if his host country caught him spying. A NOC, on the other hand, would rot in jail before the CIA lifted a finger to help.

He glanced at his Rolex Submariner and then checked the time difference between it and the clock on the wall—mere seconds. Phoenix only wore an expensive watch as it could be used as a bargaining tool to grease the skids of law enforcement or to butter up an asset.

He was the only person in the building. All the local employees had gone home for the evening. From his vantage point behind the security desk in the second-floor office suite, Phoenix could see the clock and the two computer monitors displaying the security feeds from the cameras placed around the exterior of the shipping facility.

The building was a large white steel complex that reminded Phoenix more of an automotive repair shop than a shipping company, with its multiple garage bays to park delivery vans and a warehouse space that housed packages to be shipped and the secret offices of the CIA officers who worked there.

Phoenix rubbed his chin as he stared at the cameras. The shipment was overdue. He knew he should be used to the waiting game by now, but he still hated it. As a professional soldier for twelve years, with both the 75th Ranger Regiment and then with Special Forces, better known as the Green Berets, he had done his share of "hurry up and wait."

After joining the CIA, Phoenix had to learn a different kind of patience. Instead of sitting on his ass, waiting for the brass to send him into danger, Phoenix had to supervise his own mental clock. Walking a surveillance detection route for hours could be tedious, and waiting for a potential asset to show could take even longer, but Phoenix had adapted like the chameleon he'd learned to be long ago.

While the CIA wanted to use McGuire to push Megan Babcock to block the sale of her cutting-edge submarine technology company, MCG Marine Defense, to Subsurface Kinetics, an Iranian front company, Phoenix thought it would be best to do the job himself. He was no slouch when it came to coercing information from both hostile personalities and foreign assets. It was his damned job.

But McGuire had a history with Megan Babcock. The two had dated intermittently since meeting between classes at The University of Pennsylvania, where they were both Business Economics and Public Policy majors. While Megan had gone on to get her master's from the Ivy League establishment, McGuire had taken a job in Washington as a senator's aide before being recruited into the Department of Homeland Security in 2003. Phoenix figured McGuire was one of those bureaucrats for life, sucking on the government teat and never really doing anything to affect change or policy.

While Phoenix could also be accused of sucking on the government teat since all of his paychecks had some form of government seal at the top of them, he knew he was the tip of the spear, making real change. He also knew the consequences all too well if he screwed up. It wouldn't be a slap on the wrist or a cross-promotion to a new job. His reward would be a bullet in the back of the head in some dark alley.

Phoenix had studied McGuire's file extensively and wondered why the schmucks on the Seventh Floor thought McGuire could sway Megan Babcock's mind. Clearly, she had moved on from him, marrying a lawyer from the Department of the Treasury where he'd sat on the Committee on Foreign Investment in the United States and worked at the private think tank known as the Council on Foreign Relations, which, unbeknownst to most Americans, shaped the country's foreign policy.

Blake Babcock was a tall, handsome fellow who reminded

Phoenix of an Abercrombie and Fitch underwear model with wavy brown hair and sky-blue eyes. The guy was obviously batting above his average by landing a wealthy heiress like Megan Gaspar. Phoenix thought it was interesting that she had a weakness for wussy government types. He idly wondered if he had a shot at being her paramour.

Rechecking his watch, Phoenix tapped a couple of buttons on the computer keyboard, switching one bank of cameras from the exterior view of the shipping facility to the feed from the CIA's private hangar at the Saint Kitts airport.

Through the camera lens, he saw a white Bombardier Challenger 350 glide into view and stop outside the hangar. The jet's door opened, and the airstairs deployed. A man came to the door, looked hesitantly outside the plane, and then glanced over his shoulder. Slowly, the new arrival descended the airstairs and stepped onto the hangar's apron.

John Phoenix swore. The facial recognition program that had been running in the background pinged when it zeroed in on the face of the new arrival, but the data window that popped up said the man was not Dennis McGuire. Bending closer to the screen, Phoenix read the information.

Ryan Weller was a known asset of both Homeland Security and the Defense Intelligence Agency.

Phoenix scanned Weller's biography. The man had an excellent curriculum vitae and an already established cover in the Caribbean as a marine hardware salesman named Bob Parker.

"What the hell are you doing here?" Phoenix wondered aloud.

The case officer turned his attention back to the security screen as a white Ford Transit van with the Core Tek company logo on the side stopped beside Weller, and two men got out. He watched as the three of them had a lengthy conversation, and then an exasperated-looking Weller threw his bags into the backseat and climbed in through the sliding door.

With a shake of his head, Phoenix picked up his encrypted phone and dialed Headquarters in Langley, Virginia. The line rang on the other end until a man finally answered by saying, "Core Tek Shipping, how can I help you?"

"This is Bowie," Phoenix said. "I'd like to speak to my normal representative, please."

A minute later, the line clicked, and Leslie Connelly came on the other end. The woman Phoenix knew as Nightingale asked, "What's going on, Bowie?"

"We have a problem."

"What is it?" Nightingale asked, sounding frustrated.

"The Irishman you sent to talk to The Pirate is not the man who just arrived."

"What are you talking about?" Nightingale asked, the confusion evident in her voice.

"According to my facial recog scan, this dude goes by the code name Dark Horse. He's a freelancer tied to Homeland and the DIA."

"How did this mix-up occur?" she asked.

"I'm not sure," Phoenix said, "but you better send someone to the Irishman's place to check on him."

"I'll get someone down in Sunshine to do it," Nightingale said. "Call me after you speak to what's-his-name ..."

"Dark Horse," Phoenix confirmed.

"Yes," Nightingale replied. "Call me after you speak to Dark Horse."

Phoenix ended the call and put the phone back in his pocket. From a desk drawer, he pulled out a Glock 19 pistol and press-checked the slide to confirm there was a nine-millimeter hollow point in the chamber. He reseated the slide and tucked the gun into his waistband, ready to confront Dark Horse the moment he came through the door.

CHAPTER FOUR

The troubleshooter kept his head on a swivel as the van left Robert Bradshaw International in Basseterre and headed south. The two guys up front didn't speak to Ryan again after he'd gotten into the van. He figured they were a couple more spooks, and they wouldn't feed him any more information than he'd already learned. Someone had to be running this cluster of an operation, and hopefully, he got to speak to the head spook soon so he could find out exactly what was going on.

Six minutes after leaving the airport, the driver pulled the van into the parking lot of a shipping company, hit the remote for the garage door, and waited for the door to open with the engine running and the transmission in gear. Moments later, the van rolled inside, and the door slid closed behind them as the driver switched off the engine.

Ryan saw no one else in the building but figured the head spy awaited their arrival. He paused to allow the two spooks to dismount first, and one of them opened the side door for him to get out. Ryan stepped onto the grease-stained concrete floor, carrying the briefcase and valise in his left hand, and glanced around at the empty loading bays.

Before he could react, a man stepped out from a nearby door and leveled a pistol at him. "You've got fifteen seconds to tell me who you are and what you've done with Dennis McGuire."

Ryan dropped the valise and briefcase and raised his hands. He noticed the men from the van slowly edging out of the kill zone—no sense getting splattered with blood and brains if they didn't have to. Ryan assumed the guy with the gun was the leader of the Stooges.

"You, Grady?" Ryan asked.

"No," the stranger replied. "But you're going to tell me who *you* are."

The gunman was around five-ten, and Ryan guessed he tipped the scales at one-hundred-ninety pounds of solid muscle. He looked in top physical condition, and his brown eyes had a wary gaze that told Ryan the man had seen combat. His black hair was long but neatly trimmed, like his beard and mustache. The suspected CIA operative wore khakis and a white dress shirt with brown Doc Marten leather oxfords—good heavy soles for kicking the shit out of someone.

"McGuire's mail kept getting delivered to my boat slip, and then a couple of your Ground Branch goons snatched me up and put me on a plane to here. Their facial recog said I was McGuire, and I told them I wasn't." Ryan glanced at the two guys who had picked him up at the airport and then returned his glare to the dude with the gun. "Apparently, you don't think I'm McGuire, so let's call it a day, and I'll be on my way home. I don't want to be here anymore than you want me here."

The pack leader holstered the Glock behind his back. "I'm Peter. That's Paul and Mary."

"Which one of you is Mary?" Ryan asked flippantly.

The men pointed at each other, and Ryan snorted in derision at the comedy routine. "I guess that makes me Puff, the Magic Dragon."

"It makes you is an unwelcome guest," Peter said.

"I didn't ask to be here," Ryan said. "I've told everyone I met since this ordeal started that I am *not* Dennis McGuire, but no one seemed to care. And some guy named Phillips back in Fort Lauderdale took my wallet, or I'd show you my ID."

Ryan eased his hand inside his suit coat and pulled out the passport created for him in Florida. "All I have is this do-it-yourself forgery with my picture and McGuire's name on it."

"They didn't check your ID?" the gunman asked.

"They seemed to think I was using a fake driver's license to avoid doing whatever you all want McGuire to do here. Now that we all know I'm not McGuire, maybe Mary can drive me to the airport so I can catch a flight back to the States?" Ryan exaggeratedly checked his watch. "I'm *way* overdue for a dinner reservation."

"What a freaking mess," the man who'd introduced himself as Peter lamented. "We finally have a shot at contacting Megan Babcock, and they've sent me the wrong man. Did they even brief you?"

"Your men gave me a folder with some background information, but they didn't tell me what I should do with it. But I'm not interested in Megan Babcock. I want to go back to the States. I'm supposed to be leaving on an extended trip with my wife, and you guys are fouling it up."

"Mister Weller, you have every right to be angry and very little reason to help us," the gunman said.

Ryan shouldn't have been surprised that this guy *finally* knew his name, but he was. And the fact he had addressed him by name was intriguing. It meant this guy,

Peter—or whatever the hell his real name was—knew Ryan's true identity and wasn't afraid to let it be known.

"Now that I know who you are, Weller, I need your help," the man said. "McGuire would have been perfect for this part. Megan trusted him, but who knows what happened to him."

"Then find him and get him down here," Ryan said.

"There's no time to do that. We have to move on Megan Babcock in the next two days. Otherwise, who knows when we'll get a chance to speak to her again."

"What's so important about the next two days?" Ryan asked, intrigued.

"As you might have read in the file, Megan Babcock is selling MCG Marine Defense to Subsurface Kinetics, a company registered in Miami, Florida."

"How is that a problem?" Ryan asked.

"Subsurface Kinetics is a front. They have an office space, but the company doesn't manufacture anything or even do R&D." The gunman walked down the stairs. "Before you ask who owns Subsurface Kinetics, I'll tell you. Maybe this will sway your opinion."

Ryan felt like they were finally getting to the crux of the matter.

"Iranian MOIS operatives own Sub K, and it's a front for their Ministry of Intelligence and Security to do bad shit in our own backyard."

The idea that a sworn state enemy owned property and ran a business in the United States wasn't a new concept for Ryan. He knew the Chinese had been buying up U.S. farmland and food production companies for years. The Russians owed a significant stake in the Canadian firm Uranium One, which, in turn, mined uranium in the United States. And there were probably a thousand small businesses that were fronts for other countries, drug dealers, criminals, and smugglers.

Capitalism and open borders at their finest.

Peter continued. "MCG has developed a new stealth hydrodynamic propulsion system for submarines. The problem with the sale is that not only is Iran our sworn enemy, but China has a strategic alliance with them. China provides the Iranians with military, economic, and technical assistance, so any tech that Iran gains from MCG will go straight into the hands of the Chinese."

"If it's not there already," Ryan countered, thinking about an encounter he'd had on an earlier mission with a high-tech Chinese submarine.

Ignoring Ryan's jab, the CIA officer continued. "Megan Babcock is in Saint Kitts for a photo shoot for a new perfume line for her cosmetics company. Once she's done, I don't know when her husband will let her out in the open again."

Ryan leaned against the side panel of the van and crossed his arms, thinking about the problem. Since he'd signed a non-disclosure agreement with the DIA, Ryan couldn't tell this spook about the underwater tech he'd seen China using to power their submarines, and he doubted whatever tech MCG had developed was any more advanced than what Beijing already possessed—but Ryan's assumption was completely wrong. MCG's tech was lightyears ahead of anything the Chinese had developed, and Blake Babcock was trying to hand it to them on a silver platter.

"Why doesn't Congress step in?" Ryan asked. "Don't they have oversight of strategic military sales to state enemies?"

The man Ryan assumed was a CIA spook just snorted. "It's a private corporation being sold to another U.S. corporation, so Congress really has no say, but if you ask me, yeah, it's a huge security breach, and we're here to stop it." He put his hands on his hips. "I know your record, Weller. I know you've done this type of thing before. I can't go in because Blake Babcock knows who I am, so I'm asking you."

Ryan's stomach grumbled. He held up his hands to pump the brakes. "First, Case Officer Whatever-Your-Name-Is, you guys made me miss a very nice steak dinner and a couple of cold beers, so if you're going to pitch me on doing some dangerous shit, then you need to put some food in my belly so I can think straight. And second, I need to call my wife."

"You're a trip, Weller." The man stepped forward and held out his hand. "I'm Bowie."

"Bowie? Is that a code name?" Ryan asked as he shook his hand.

"How about I call you Ryan, and you can call me Jim?"

"You make any good knives lately?" Ryan joked. "Or should I be concerned about dying at the Alamo on this job?"

"Neither. Bowie is my code name. I can call you Dark Horse if you'd like."

Ryan smiled. "I see you've been reading my DIA file."

"Like I said, you're no stranger to this kind of thing. Come on. Let's get you something to eat. I could use a good steak myself." Bowie turned to the other two men. "I'll see you boys later."

Ryan followed the man he now knew as Jim Bowie through the back door of the shipping facility. Bowie ensured the door locked behind them and then pointed toward a four-door sedan.

"We're overdressed for a beach bar, but the locals are used to seeing well-heeled tourists," Bowie explained after the two men were in the car, heading for the restaurant.

"We're going for food, which is the first thing on my list. What about the second?" Ryan asked.

Bowie pulled a phone from his pocket and unlocked it with a pattern combination. "It's encrypted, but keep it short."

Ryan nodded. He opened the phone app and dialed Emily's number, praying she would answer the unknown number. Ryan figured she would, assuming her mother had already called her to find out why he hadn't shown up for dinner. He breathed a sigh of relief when his wife answered.

"Emily, it's me," he said.

"Where are you?" she exclaimed. "Mom called and said you didn't make it to dinner, and your cellphone goes straight to voicemail."

"I'm safe," Ryan said, glancing skeptically at Bowie and wondering just how much he should or could share with his wife. "I'm helping some Caspers with a mission."

"'Caspers?'" Emily asked, questioning his vague statement. She thought it through and said, "Oh, I get it. The friendly ghost. Spooks."

"Exactly," Ryan said. "Sorry to leave you hanging, babe."

"I know. Thanks for calling. I was worried you'd wandered off again."

"Not by choice," Ryan replied. "It was a case of mistaken identity. You know I've got no plans other than to sail away with you."

Bowie made a motion for Ryan to wrap up the call.

Ryan shot him the bird but said to his wife, "I gotta go, Em. I'll call you as soon as I can. Love you."

He ended the call and handed the phone back.

Leaning his head against the seatrest, Ryan stared out the window at the buildings as they rushed past. Several of the businesses were well-lit, outside of which people milled about, drinking beer and enjoying the beautiful night, blissfully unaware of the danger around them.

Ryan tried not to reflect on the meal he'd missed and instead focused on what lay ahead. Once again, he'd become embroiled in a situation concerning national security. While he was naturally reluctant to start a new job, he considered himself a first-rate troubleshooter, and stopping the sale of top-secret technology to a hostile nation seemed like a nail worthy of being pounded.

They drove the rest of the way to the restaurant in silence. Ryan tried to study his new minder discreetly, but it wasn't easy in the darkened vehicle. The man obviously knew how to handle himself and had been in situations like this before, but Ryan wondered what his bona fides really were. It was one hell of a SNAFU for Ryan to have been mistaken for Dennis McGuire back in Fort Lauderdale, after all.

Ryan had worked closely with CIA case officers as an EOD tech in Iraq and Afghanistan. The taciturn case officers were not known to be forthcoming with personal information and often only shared mission-critical specifics when absolutely necessary. Some were excellent at their jobs, while others, like the COs Ryan had encountered while foiling a plot to rig the Haitian presidential election a few years ago, were downright nefarious. Only time would tell on which side of the fence Bowie sat.

The case officer brought the car to a stop outside Boozies on the Beach, a restaurant on what was known as the Frigate Bay Strip. The place looked like an old shack from the outside, reminding Ryan of buildings he'd seen in the American West. It felt like Wyatt Earp could ride up on his horse at any moment and burst through the swinging saloon doors. Inside, the place was modern and clean, with exposed wooden beams that held up a cathedral ceiling covered by weathered tin. Cozy tables and lounge areas provided intimate settings in which to dine or to watch one of the televisions mounted on the walls around the bar.

Smelling the cooking meat and vegetables made Ryan's stomach growl again. The Ritz crackers hadn't satisfied his desire for protein.

The hostess seated them at a table on an outside veranda

that extended to a deck with an open firepit surrounded by plush chairs.

Moments later, Ryan finally had a cold Carib in his hands. He drained half of the bottle in several long swallows, enjoying the coolness as the beer slid down his parched throat.

After the waitress had delivered a second round of beers and both men had ordered the medium-rare ribeye steaks, Ryan leaned in closer to the spook. "Since we're going to be working together, I'd at least like to call you by something other than a code name."

Bowie looked Ryan dead in his green eyes. Ryan stared back, noting the man's eyes were brown. Despite fully seeing the case officer's face, it was wholly unremarkable. The man's skin was brown as if he had a touch of Latino in his background—maybe Native American, based on the cheekbones. But in the right light, Bowie could have been a Latino, an Arab, or an average white guy.

Ryan wondered how the man had become a spook and doubted he would ever know.

The intense staring contest ended abruptly when Bowie smiled. "You can call me John."

Ryan snorted. "Jim, John, James ... I guess it doesn't matter, does it? You're probably so used to having a code name that you've forgotten your real one."

Bowie glanced out toward the water, took a long pull from his Carib, and then looked back at Ryan. "Despite what you might think, my real name is John."

"Good to know," Ryan said.

The two men sat in silence, sipping their beers. Ryan turned to sit sideways in his chair with his back to the wall. Beside him, light from an open window spilled out onto the deck. Above them, colorful lantern-style lights swayed in the evening breeze.

He wished he was sitting there with Emily instead of the brooding spook. Ryan closed his eyes and imagined holding her hand as they walked barefoot along the curve of the beach, watching the silent breakers wash across the sand and run back out to sea, the grainy sand between their toes.

Opening his eyes, Ryan asked, "How long will this job take?"

John shrugged. "Couple of days."

Ryan sipped his beer without comment. He was going to hold Jim-John Bowie to his word. Two days max, and he was getting on a plane home. The CIA could handle their problems without him.

John's cellphone rang as the hostess delivered their steaks on sizzling metal platters. The spook stood and walked away with the phone pressed to his ear.

Ryan didn't wait for him to return before cutting into his steak. The juice ran out of the meat as he took a bite. He put down his knife and fork, leaned back in the chair, and closed his eyes, savoring the steak as he chewed.

It wasn't the best steak he'd ever eaten, but it ranked right up there with the best, if for no other reason than because he was hungry. After that first bite, he ate ravenously, watching John pace near the water's edge and talk on his phone well out of earshot of anyone who might overhear.

When John walked back up on the deck, Ryan saw something had changed in his demeanor. The spook sat down across from Ryan and began cutting his steak, shaving off pieces of meat and stuffing them quickly into his mouth. The guy could rival Ryan with the speed and efficiency of his eating habits. Ryan knew it stemmed from the military. Eating quickly was a habit ingrained from day one.

Still, Ryan could sense the urgency with which John ate had more to do with wanting to get out of the restaurant than old habits. Before the spook had finished eating, Ryan signaled the waitress for the check. When she brought it over, Ryan pulled out the wallet meant for McGuire and handed her cash from the stacks he'd taken from the briefcase. The official currency of Saint Kitts and Nevis was the Eastern Caribbean dollar, better known as the EC. However, American currency was still used interchangeably, although the exchange rate for the EC was almost two EC to the dollar.

"Put your money away," John said. "You said this was a stipulation of helping me."

Ryan shrugged. "It's not my money. Your people handed me a stack of cash. We'll consider it on the house."

John thanked Ryan for paying for the meal, and both men stood from the table, but instead of heading for the car, John led Ryan toward the shoreline.

Out of earshot of anyone else on the beach, the case officer said, "McGuire is dead."

CHAPTER FIVE

Ryan felt a wave of disbelief wash over him as the CIA case officer he now knew as Jim-John Bowie filled him in on the death of the real Dennis McGuire. The tension had just ratcheted up.

"After you got off the plane, I knew they'd brought the wrong man," John explained. "I called my handler at Headquarters and filled her in. She sent an officer to McGuire's place in Fort Lauderdale, and they found his body in his apartment. Apparently, the guys in Fort Lauderdale just scooped you up by following McGuire's mail. How they missed it on facial recog scan, I don't know, but it happened. However, I'm glad you're the one who got tangled up in this mess and not some civilian."

"I am a civilian, John," Ryan protested.

"That may be true, but you also happen to be a covert operator with the highest clearance. We have to proceed with this mission, and I need your help now more than ever."

"How does Blake Babcock know you?" Ryan asked.

"Blake and I worked together. That's part of why I was

assigned this operation. Headquarters figured since I knew Babcock, I might be able to find out his end game."

"Where did you work together?" Ryan asked.

When John didn't answer, Ryan wondered if the man was afraid he might do some digging and find out exactly how the two men knew each other. If he did that, he would probably be able to figure out John's real name and his path to the CIA. It was an interesting idea—one Ryan considered tasking his intelligence contacts with so he would have a leg up on the CIA man—but he shelved the idea for now.

"What's Babcock's game?" Ryan asked.

John shrugged. "I don't know, but I can tell you that after he married Megan, Blake suddenly had more money at his disposal than he knew what to do with. He tried the playboy lifestyle, with Ferraris and jets and yachts, but after old man Gaspar passed, Blake and Megan settled down to run her company. The longer he and Megan have been married, the more he keeps her under his thumb."

"So, what's the plan?" Ryan asked.

"I want you to meet with her and see if you can get her to open up about the sale of MCG. We need to see if there's a way we can put a stop to it. Letting that tech fall into the hands of the Iranians puts the U.S. farther behind in the arms race, especially if they pass it to the Chinese."

"Don't we already have the tech?" Ryan asked. "Obviously, MCG has shared it with DARPA or the Navy."

"I don't know. My job—*our* job—is to prevent the sale of MCG."

"How does McGuire tie into this?" Ryan asked.

John turned in a slow circle to see if anyone had crept up on them while they had been talking. Ryan had kept an eye on his half of the beach and had seen only an elderly couple strolling hand in hand and well out of audible range, considering the noise of the gentle surf and the wind and helping to mask their conversation.

"McGuire and Megan Gaspar got engaged after she graduated from The Wharton School, but it didn't last. Luckily for us, they stayed in regular contact despite their failed engagement. Megan trusted him and often asked McGuire's advice about business arrangements and contracts. When news about the sale of MCG hit the wires, McGuire immediately emailed her and tried to convince her to stop it. She responded that Blake had brokered the deal, and she had no renegotiation power. Once the company I work for read their email chain, they went digging and found out that Megan had signed over a seventy percent stake in Gaspar Industries to her husband."

"Do I want to know how you guys figured that out, or do I just assume you're reading all the emails of everyone in the national security business?" Ryan asked.

"I'm just the tip of the spear, Ryan. Whatever happens back at Headquarters stays at Headquarters."

"Kinda like Vegas," Ryan added sarcastically.

"Exactly like Vegas," John said. "Only there's no photographs turning up on social media a week later."

"Do you think McGuire is dead because he opposed the sale?" Ryan asked.

"That's a good guess and the best one Headquarters could come up with, too."

"What was the forwarding date on his snail mail?" Ryan asked.

"They didn't say."

Ryan stared out at the black waves rippling in the moonlight. He scratched the back of his neck as he pondered the situation. "Do we know McGuire's time of death?"

"My handler was waiting on the coroner's report when she called me," John replied. "Why? What are you thinking?"

"I'm just kicking the can around a little here, so bear with me. What if McGuire knew someone was targeting him?"

"Why forward the mail?" John asked.

"How much did you learn about me with a basic search?" Ryan asked.

John was quick to reply. "You're a freelance troubleshooter tied to several high-profile news stories about stopping terrorists and rescuing hostages."

"Okay. Kick the can a little farther. McGuire knows more about me because of his government connections. He thinks something is wrong with the MCG deal, and he wants to get my attention in a nonthreatening way. He sends the mail to me, but I ignore it instead of looking into it. McGuire gets killed, and you guys sweep me up by accident."

"It's a stretch," John admitted. "How did McGuire know we'd go to him to help stop the sale?"

"Maybe he was already in touch with your people," Ryan suggested. "Or he knew you were reading his mail."

It was John's turn to ponder the statement. After a few silent moments, he said, "Let's say everything we just discussed is true. Who silenced him?"

"It has to be Blake Babcock," Ryan surmised. "He made the deal to sell MCG. If McGuire was whispering in Megan's ear, Babcock might have felt like his deal and marriage were about to fall apart."

"You're one shrewd operator," John said admiringly. "I like how you think. Conspiracies within the conspiracy."

"Isn't that how you guys operate?" Ryan asked.

"Sometimes," John said, "but we try to back the RUMINT up with HUMINT."

Ryan knew the spook meant verifying rumors intelligence with corresponding human intelligence. Analysts at Headquarters in Langley would forward questions to the case officers in the field, who would, in turn, query their assets for more information and then report back. He'd seen it happen numerous times during his time in the Navy. When assets couldn't provide answers, the military was sent out to find them. Sometimes, that meant reconning by fire or using enhanced interrogation techniques on captured hostiles. The goal was to produce actionable intelligence, conduct covert action, and safeguard the nation's secrets—according to the CIA's mission statement Ryan had read while overseas.

"Why is Babcock all fired up to sell MCG?" Ryan asked.

"That's the million-dollar question, isn't it?" John replied. "One, you'll hopefully find the answer to tomorrow."

CHAPTER SIX

The next morning
Timothy Hill Overlook, Saint Kitts

Ryan held up the press pass gifted to him by Spooky Jim-John Bowie, and the policeman at the checkpoint allowed him to enter the roped-off area at the edge of the overlook on Timothy Hill.

Normally, the overlook teemed with tourists, and today was no different, but the police had erected barricades to separate the peasants from the elite. Some of the onlookers had their cameras out and were acting more like marauding paparazzi than fresh-off-the-cruise-ship bumpkins.

Ryan ignored the cluster of people around Megan Babcock as they primped her gown and makeup for the photoshoot. He instead focused on the breathtaking view before him. Timothy Hill Overlook was one of the most photographed landscapes on Saint Kitts, allowing for breathtaking views of the narrow neck of land that led to the Southeast Peninsula.

Facing south on the 587-foot summit, Ryan could see the zigzag of black tarmac snaking off Timothy Hill and down the length of the neck before rising through the mountains on the far side. The Atlantic rolled in from the east, restlessly washing white waves on the rocks, and on the left, just a couple hundred yards away, the placid Caribbean nibbled at the sand on the beaches, looking like a flat lake compared to the frothing ocean.

Ryan could understand why Megan Babcock's cosmetics brand had chosen this spot for the shoot. With his camera around his neck, Ryan, dressed in cargo shorts and a guayabera, began photographing everyone on the set. As he watched through the lens, Ryan saw Blake Babcock hovering near his wife, and when he stepped away to answer his phone or attend to other business, two beefy security goons closed in on Megan. The goons alone weren't a problem, but the pistols they had holstered on their hips were an effective deterrent.

Since Ryan traveled extensively and his job often entailed handling firearms, he made it a point to know the laws of the countries he visited. Like most Caribbean Island nations, Saint Kitts and Nevis had outlawed firearms except with special written permission from the Commissar of the Police. Ryan doubted the guys guarding the Babcocks gave a tinker's damn about the commissar or the laws of their host nation. In fact, Ryan was more than willing to bet that Babcock had paid a special "fee" for his men to carry their guns.

Ryan smiled as he thought of his buddy Scott Gregory, who would have said, "Ryan, you dumbass, you mispronounced the word *bribe*."

"What I wouldn't give to have you here now, Scotty," Ryan muttered.

Ryan needed to bump Megan Babcock and cause a meeting, but he was unsure how to do that with her minders sticking to her like smell on a skunk.

Suddenly, one of Megan Babcock's entourage stepped away from the group and clapped his hands above his head. "Listen up, people! Clear the staging area. Let's *go*!"

People scurried away from the edge of the cliff to make way for Megan, and Ryan got his first good look at her. Until a few minutes ago, Ryan had only seen his target in pictures. While her file had contained her particulars—she was five feet, six inches tall, with blonde hair, blue eyes, a net worth of billions, the number of companies she held in her portfolio, and her charitable efforts—it hadn't given Ryan a sense of who Megan Whitney Gaspar née Babcock actually was—and *none* of the photos had done her justice.

Of course, the "artists" had plastered her with makeup, her hair having been curled and teased to within an inch of its life, and she wore a stunning white off-the-shoulder dress ruched around the midsection. The asymmetrical hem allowed a nearly full view of her tanned and toned left leg. On her feet, she wore white sandals with four-inch heels, the matching straps wrapping halfway up her calves.

Perched on the edge of the cliff, Megan Babcock looked absolutely stunning. She didn't need a wind machine to toss her hair. The natural breeze from the Atlantic ruffled everything in sight. Ryan snapped photos of the men and women around Megan, trying not to focus solely on her, but like everyone else looking her way, it was difficult not to stare.

After a half hour of posing in various positions, with Megan's team constantly fluffing the dress, adjusting the hemlines, and the off-the-shoulder placement, the photographers had what they wanted. They moved on to shooting Megan in a white bikini she'd been wearing under her dress. A muscled hunk with rippling abs and gelled hair stepped into the frame to hold Megan from behind, making the two models appear cozy and intimate.

Once the shoot wrapped, Megan stood at the edge of the cliff while her assistant brought her a pair of canvas shoes, sweatpants, and a T-shirt. Megan changed right there, removing her heels before pulling on the sweatpants and shoes.

As Ryan snapped a candid photo of Megan taking the T-shirt from her assistant, he saw a man rushing toward the heiress out of the corner of his eye. Not knowing what was happening or if Megan was in danger, Ryan reacted by shovel passing his camera straight at the running man's head. It wasn't until the bulky Canon Rebel had left his grasp that Ryan noticed the knife in the man's hand.

Years of target practice on various shooting ranges and over a decade in combat had honed Ryan's instincts as to how to lead a target when said target was in motion. He had instinctively thrown the camera slightly ahead of the man's head, and as the attacker ran forward, the camera smacked him square in the temple, breaking off the long lens and shattering the LCD viewing screen.

The assistant screamed, and Megan stood stock-still, staring at the attacker as he fell at her feet, the knife sliding from his hand and skittering over the edge of the cliff with Ryan's camera.

Ryan sprang forward and placed his knee in the man's back, wrenching his arm around to immobilize him further.

Suddenly, there was commotion all around. The goons rushed forward to escort Megan away from the scene of the failed attack while paparazzi and tourists snapped Ryan's picture as he subdued the knife-wielding assailant. Ryan tucked his chin to his chest and turned his head to prevent the cameras from getting most of his face.

Then, in seconds, the police were there, pulling Ryan off

the attacker and cuffing the man where he lay on the ground. One officer held Ryan's arm behind his back until they could sort out the details of the failed attack.

"He had a knife," Ryan explained to all the cops around him. "It slid over the edge."

Inspector Browne, the Royal St. Christopher and Nevis Police Force officer in charge of the protection detail, ordered two of his cops over the edge of the precipice to search for the weapon.

"Grab my camera while you're down there," Ryan called to the officers. He knew the impact had probably damaged the Canon beyond repair, but the memory card would still be intact.

While the officers searched, the inspector paced along the edge of the road. He was a tall man with a pot belly and a round face made comical by his tiny rectangular glasses and the way he pulled his service cap down so low that the brim practically sat on the bridge of his nose. Ryan noticed the officer had pressed military creases into his uniform, and he had plenty of medals and ribbons on his chest. What action the man had seen to earn them, Ryan didn't know, but he doubted the inspector had ever seen combat or drawn his sidearm in the line of duty.

Moments later, one of the police officers found the camera, and the other located the knife. With gloved hands, he held it up by the tip of the blade for all to see, and flash strobes lit the air in conjunction with the rapid clicking of shutter-release buttons.

"What a freakin' circus," Ryan muttered.

"You need to come to the station and give us a statement, sir," Inspector Browne informed Ryan.

Blake Babcock walked over and extended his hand to Ryan. "I want to thank you for saving my wife's life."

"No big deal," Ryan replied. "Any of these good officers would have done the same."

"But they didn't," Babcock insisted. "You did." Turning to the officers, he said, "I think this man is a hero."

"Even heroes need to make statements," Inspector Browne said.

"When you get done at the police station, please join us at the Park Hyatt in Christophe Harbour," Babcock said to Ryan. "We're in the villa. I'll leave instructions at the front desk."

"Thank you," Ryan replied.

"What's the name I should use?" Babcock asked, glancing down at the press pass.

"Ryan Weller," he replied. He and John had decided Ryan should use his real name, figuring that if Babcock ran a background check, he would discover any false names Ryan tried to use, thus making Babcock suspicious of him.

And now Ryan was pretty sure he was going to have his picture plastered on the front page of every tabloid rag from Saint Kitts to Luxembourg for saving Megan Babcock from being stabbed. All his life, Ryan had shied away from the media as much as he could, but given the scale of some of the threats he had faced over his troubleshooting career, he knew it was impossible. And intervening in the potential stabbing of one of the most recognizable women on the planet was never going to go unnoticed.

He shook his head as he watched Babcock walk away. Despite the media attention, at least one good thing had come from the morning's events. Ryan had scored a better way into the Babcocks' inner sanctum than he could have ever hoped. It was certainly better than his previously planned method of bumping Megan at the next photoshoot location in front of the #StKitts sign at Port Zante, where all the cruise ships docked.

"Sir?" the police inspector said.

Ryan turned to face the island native. "Yeah?"

"We need to go to the station."

"He's innocent," a short man with a video camera on his shoulder said. He looked like a typical aping tourist except for the massive professional camera used for filming the perfume commercial. "I have it all on video."

The videographer turned the camera so the inspector and Ryan could see the viewing screen and reran the footage. Ryan watched himself throw his Canon and bean the assailant in the head with an extremely lucky shot.

"It seems you made an excellent judgment call, Mister Weller," Inspector Browne said. "But we still need a statement. And we'll need a copy of your video, sir."

"I'll email you a copy as soon as possible," the cameraman said.

Ryan rode in the police inspector's cruiser to the station in Basseterre, his damaged camera in his lap. The SD card was secure in his pocket, along with several others in a plastic case.

Once at the police station, Ryan identified the attacker in a lineup, then drafted a detailed report about his encounter with the man on the edge of the cliff. Satisfied with Ryan's answers and his written testimony, the inspector declared him free to go.

"Can I ask you a question, Inspector?" Ryan said.

The man shrugged. "I don't see why not."

"Did Babcock obtain a permit for his men to carry firearms?"

The inspector frowned. "That is not a question I have an answer for, Mister Weller. You will need to speak to the Commissar about that. But he's on vacation right now."

"Of course he is," Ryan muttered, then headed for the exit.

Being free to go meant Ryan had to find his own way back to his hotel. He had no vehicle at his disposal since he had taken a bus to the top of Timothy Hill. His watch told him he'd spent several hours being questioned by the cops and had missed the remainder of Megan Babcock's photoshoot and the cocktail hour in a local bar that had followed. He hailed a cab and had the driver stop at an electronics store, where he purchased another Canon Rebel camera, a burner phone, and a cheap laptop. He pocketed the receipt for the CIA expense account.

Ryan then directed the driver to take him to the Bird Rock Beach Hotel.

After touring the hotel room last night, Ryan had decided he'd slept in worse, although the brilliant yellow accent wall made his eyes ache even when they were closed. Overall, it was a decent place, cheaper than most on the island, and since Spooky John was chipping in the government's dime, Ryan didn't have much of a choice unless he wanted to cough up his own dough.

He showered and pulled on his suit, which he'd had dry-cleaned and pressed by the hotel last night. Ryan checked himself in the mirror and decided he looked close enough to James Bond.

Pulling out his new laptop, Ryan copied the photos from the SD card to one of the other empty cards in the plastic container. He used a blue ballpoint pen from the suite's bureau to mark it with an exclamation point on the tiny label, then tucked it safely into a pocket of the leather valise he'd carried off the jet.

As Ryan walked toward the taxi stand, carrying his camera bag, Jim-John Bowie appeared at the edge of the hotel property and motioned the troubleshooter over. Ryan joined Spooky John in a secluded spot and gave him a full report of the events on Timothy Hill and the interview at the police station, even though the case officer knew most of it already.

"Do you have the photos you took?" John asked when Ryan told him he'd destroyed the camera.

Ryan handed over the original SD card and said he'd thrown the camera away since it was now useless junk.

"Did you get a chance to speak with Megan?" John asked.

"No, but I received an invitation to their suite at the Park Hyatt," Ryan replied. "I'm headed there now."

"We don't have much time before the handover takes place, Ryan," John said. "We need to stop it."

CHAPTER SEVEN

"Trust me. It's good," Blake Babcock said as he handed Ryan Weller a Skol beer.

They stood on the extended pool deck of the Babcocks' three-bedroom presidential villa at the Park Hyatt Saint Kitts Christophe Harbour where they had a stunning view of Banana Bay. Just two and a half miles away was the mountainous island of Nevis, rising green and glorious from the sea, formed eons ago by volcanic activity.

Ryan looked down at the beer's label to see it had been crafted by the same brewery as Carib, but after just one swig, he decided it was the better beer.

Behind them, the Babcocks' private chef prepared an outdoor grill to cook steaks. Megan Babcock lounged nearby, chatting quietly with a pretty blonde Babcock had told Ryan was his wife's assistant. Ryan didn't think the girl was much over eighteen. He wondered if it was just a trick of the light, but she looked younger and even her giggle made her sound like a schoolgirl.

"What brings you to Saint Kitts?" Babcock asked conversationally.

"I decided to try my hand at photojournalism," Ryan replied. "Your wife made the perfect subject."

Babcock glanced over his shoulder at Megan. "She is beautiful. Remember, you're here to take her picture, not try to bed her."

Ryan chuckled. "Why? Are you jealous?"

"Jealous of what? You're a penniless photographer. I have wealth and power at my fingertips." Blake lowered his voice and leaned in closer to Ryan. "I could make you disappear."

Ryan shook his head as he tried to choke back a hearty laugh. "What is it about me that threatens you, Mister Babcock? I'm just a guy who happened to be in the right place at the right time and saved your wife from being stabbed by a lunatic."

Babcock regarded him with furrowed brows as if puzzled that this peasant would have the audacity to do anything but kowtow to him. Then he smiled, his whole face beaming, but Ryan could read the deadly shade of suspicion lingering in the man's brown eyes.

"How did you get into photojournalism, Ryan?" Babcock asked.

"I've tried my hand at a lot of different things, but I was always good with a camera. You look at that sunset and see the magnificent colors. I look at it and think f/16 aperture, 1/30 second or longer shutter speed, and single shot, daylight mode for best white balance."

Babcock chuckled. "I've got no idea what you just said, but I guess it seems right."

Ryan sipped his beer. Truth be told, he didn't know if it was right, either. Being an excellent bullshit artist was part of the game. "But to answer your question more fully," he said, "I got tired of shooting weddings and babies and family portraits and decided to become a freelancer. You know, going wherever trouble is and trying to make a difference."

The best lies had grains of truth sprinkled in for authenticity, hoping the mark would be more willing to believe the lie.

"What difference are you making by photographing my wife?" Babcock asked.

"Well, I did save her life," Ryan said. "And I just happened to be passing through Saint Kitts and heard about the photo shoot. I figured, what the hell? I've always wanted to rub elbows with the paparazzi."

"I have some other guests coming tonight," Babcock said, seemingly satisfied with Ryan's answers. "Do you have your camera?"

"Of course. It's in my bag." Ryan motioned to the camera bag on the table just inside the massive sliding glass doors. "I never go anywhere without it."

"Excellent." Babcock slapped Ryan on the shoulder. "I want you to be my guest photographer. Take pictures of Megan in her natural environment, so to speak."

Now Ryan understood the invitation. This wasn't a party for the hero. It was Babcock's way of securing Ryan's services.

Babcock walked over to where Megan lay on the lounge chair. He knelt beside her as Ryan edged closer, trying to eavesdrop on their conversation. He couldn't hear what Babcock said to his wife, but he did hear Megan's reply.

"Do we have to, Blake? I'm not feeling well, and I have a headache."

"Take some of your pills, Megan," Babcock replied. "They always help."

Ryan saw Megan roll her eyes at her husband's response.

Blake's tone was brusque and businesslike. "The gentleman who saved you today will be taking pictures of us tonight, so get buttoned up. The guests will be arriving soon."

Ryan retrieved his new camera and returned to the deck, snapping photos of the Babcocks together. When Blake finally walked away, he captured Megan leaning back in the lounge chair, looking peaceful. The woman beside Megan got up and went inside, allowing Ryan to photograph Megan alone.

Seizing his chance, Ryan said, "Mrs. Babcock, would you mind standing by the railing, please? I'd love to get some shots of this sunset behind you."

Megan rose and walked to the railing, posing instinctively for the camera as Ryan snapped photographs. Before he could finish his impromptu session, the blonde assistant returned with a glass of water and some pills. Megan dutifully swallowed them down, then rubbed her temples with her fingertips.

"Are you all right, Mrs. Babcock?" Ryan asked, concerned.

"I'm fine. I just get these headaches and feel tired most of the time, no matter how much sleep I get." She stiffened and put on a plastic smile. "I need to change for our guests. Come on, Karen—let's get ready to put on a show."

As Megan walked away, Ryan asked Karen, "What did she mean 'by put on a show?'"

Karen offered him her own plastic smile that barely lifted her thin lips. "She hates these meet-and-greet sessions, but Blake insists upon them to help sell the beauty products."

"I thought she was a party girl," Ryan said.

Karen sighed. "She was, but not anymore. Megan would rather spend her days in solitude than go traipsing about like Blake wants her to."

"And how do you feel about Blake?" he asked.

The mention of Blake Babcock's name brought a twinkle to Karen's eye and a sly smile to her lips as she said, "He's the best thing to happen to Megan. He loves her very much." The look faded, but something in her smile made Ryan think there was more to the relationship between Karen and Blake Babcock than met the eye.

"Now, if you'll excuse me, I have work to do," Karen said.

"Please, make yourself at home, but stick to the photography. Don't bother the guests."

"Yes, ma'am."

Karen walked away, leaving Ryan to wonder what the marital dynamic was like behind closed doors.

As the evening progressed, more guests arrived. Most were movers and shakers on Saint Kitts, some were businesspeople from Gaspar Industries, and others were wealthy, jet-setting entrepreneurs and influencers like Megan and Blake, there to party lavishly and spend their lives and fortunes in the lap of luxury. Ryan photographed them all, trying to memorize their names and occupations. When he could step away, he jotted notes on index cards he kept in a compartment of his camera bag.

After Ryan had eaten dinner on the deck with the other guests, he resumed his rounds with the camera. He was biding his time until he could sneak away, bored of listening to rich elitists assholes talk about money and privilege and chatting about balance sheets and investments. However, he did pick up some excellent stock tips that he figured would be considered insider trading if he acted upon them.

Ryan moved through the villa, now just a background fixture for the guests. As a working-class stiff, he was someone to be ignored. He felt like a ghost, moving through the crowd with the camera up to his eye. If someone looked away or demurred to be photographed, Ryan moved into another position to capture their image. It became a game for him, discreetly targeting his prey.

But in the back of his mind, Ryan had another destination to reach in the villa. When no one was looking, he slipped upstairs to the bedrooms. All three showed signs of occupation, two by women and one by a man. Moving quickly through the first bedroom, which had two queen beds, Ryan found luggage with tags for Karen Friar, the assistant. Letting the tag drop from his hand, Ryan looked down into the wastebasket beside the suitcase rack. There were two used condoms in the half-full can. Ryan hadn't seen another man around when he'd arrived, so his thoughts naturally gravitated toward Karen having an affair with her boss' husband.

Ryan moved on to the next bedroom. This one contained a king-size bed, and the luggage belonged to Blake Babcock. A glass wall looked down on the pool below, which meant Ryan had to be careful not to be seen. In the dark, his flashing camera would undoubtedly draw attention to himself.

He quickly shut off the flash, hoping there was enough light to snap photos by, and quickly swept the camera over the room, capturing it and its contents.

Moving on to Megan Babcock's bedroom, Ryan found it to be a mirror image of her husband's. Once again, he investigated the suitcase. Then he moved into the adjoining bathroom, finding the pills Babcock had ordered his wife take and administered by her assistant. He clicked a shot of the label, then opened the bottle and pocketed two pills, curious as to what the heiress was taking.

After replacing the bottle on the counter, Ryan returned to the bedroom. He quickly moved toward the stairs, squatting at the top to get a wide-angle view of the party scene, and continued to snap pics as he descended.

Near the base of the steps, Ryan froze.

A new guest had arrived, and his face was all too familiar to Ryan.

Larry "Iceman" Grove stood amongst the other guests in charcoal gray slacks and a matching jacket, his cream-colored dress shirt open at the collar. The former SEAL Team Six member had aged since Ryan had last seen him over a year ago. His blond hair was graying at the temples, and laughter lines crinkled around his icy blue eyes. Larry looked a lot like

Val Kilmer's character in the original *Top Gun* and even had spiky hair to match.

The last time the two men had worked together, Larry had been assigned to the Defense Intelligence Agency, ostracized from the Navy community for violating his chain of command while helping Ryan to stop a freighter turned suicide bomb laden with diesel fuel and ammonium nitrate on a collision course with Fort Lauderdale.

Transferring to the DIA meant Larry wouldn't achieve his lifelong dream of becoming an admiral in charge of Naval Special Warfare Command, but the active-duty SEAL had come to realize his current work was just as important, especially when helping Ryan to recover a top-secret satellite stolen by the Chinese. During that operation, Ryan had seen the Chinese submarine technology that he hadn't been able to share with Spooky John. Ryan supposed the DIA agent was there for the same reason he was—to stop the sale of MCG Marine Defense.

Larry made eye contact with Ryan. It didn't show on the man's face if he was as surprised to see Ryan at the villa as Ryan was to see him. Iceman—cool under pressure, the second reason behind his nickname.

Ryan maintained his casual demeanor and decided it was time to leave Blake Babcock's villa while Iceman mingled with the crowd. He was ready to call his wife and go to bed.

Walking back to where he'd left his bag, Ryan put his camera inside and checked to ensure no one had tampered with the contents.

"I expect you to email those photos to me this evening," Babcock said, coming up behind Ryan and clapping him on the shoulder again like they were old friends.

"Just as soon as I get back to my hotel," Ryan promised.

Babcock reached into his pocket and withdrew five crisp

East Caribbean one-hundred-dollar bills, equivalent to one-hundred-eighty-five bucks U.S.

"Wow, that's mighty generous of you, Blake, but let's try that again. Make those U.S. dollars, and I'll go away happy."

"It's this or nothing," Blake replied resolutely. "I gave you free food and drink and exclusive access to my party."

"You and I have a different definition of exclusivity, but if you want to give me exclusive access, let me have Megan tomorrow afternoon for a photo shoot and an interview."

Babcock snorted.

Ryan plucked the money from the man's hand before he could put it back in his pocket and added, "I'll send a car for her."

"You've got some nerve, Ryan, but I respect a man who takes what he wants and makes no apologies about it."

Ryan squared up to Blake Babcock. "Tomorrow at one."

He picked up his camera bag and left the villa, forcing himself to move casually across the resort grounds. Ryan wanted to run as hard and fast as possible from the strange vibe between Megan Babcock and her husband, but he knew he couldn't. Spooky John wanted him to dig deeper into the puzzle.

Ryan found a taxi and rode across the island to his hotel, staring into the darkness. While he hadn't been able to speak privately with Megan tonight, he now had the opportunity to do so tomorrow if Blake didn't flake and stop the meeting from happening.

And he wondered how many other intelligence agencies had taken up residency on the island. The CIA and now the DIA were keeping tabs on the Babcocks. Ryan figured the Iranians and the Chinese also had people nearby.

None of which boded well for Ryan.

Once he was back in his room, Ryan copied the photos from his camera's SD card onto the hard drive of his new laptop, then uploaded the party photos, minus the ones he'd taken in the various bedrooms and of Megan's medication bottle, to DropBox and sent the photos to Blake Babcock.

He stared at the photo of the pill bottle, clasping his hands behind his head.

After a long moment of contemplation, Ryan leaned forward and typed arsphenamine—the name of the pills on the bottle—into an Internet search engine.

According to the first link Ryan clicked on, in the spring of 1909, German scientist Paul Ehrlich had discovered arsphenamine, a derivative of arsenic, which he then successfully used as an antibiotic to treat syphilis. Later, medical professionals used the drug as a chemotherapy treatment for several types of cancer and leukemia. Ryan also read that advancements in antibiotics had led to the discontinuation of the use of the drug.

"Well, she's either going blind from syphilis, has cancer, or someone is trying to kill her," Ryan muttered to himself.

Shutting down the laptop, Ryan took out his phone and called Emily. She answered on the second ring.

"Hey, babe." Ryan stifled a yawn.

"How's the job going?" she asked.

He rubbed his chin as he thought about his upcoming meeting with Megan Babcock. Not wanting to bother her with details, he said, "Stress-free so far, but who knows what tomorrow will bring."

CHAPTER EIGHT

By one p.m. the next afternoon, Ryan had a plan.

Instead of sending a car for Megan Babcock, he went to pick her up himself. He pulled his rented Jeep Wrangler to a stop outside the Babcocks' villa and climbed out. In Ryan's estimation, the Wrangler had to be one of the most rented vehicles in the world, and he was familiar with its handling characteristics since he frequently drove his wife's whenever he was in Fort Lauderdale or rented one during his many adventures throughout the Caribbean. When picking a vehicle, he wanted something he was comfortable driving if things got out of hand, but the problem with every Jeep he'd ever driven was that the suspension was so stiff Ryan could drive over a quarter and tell which side was up.

After collecting the Jeep from the rental agency, he'd driven to the Core Tek Shipping office to talk to Spooky John and sketched out the plan. John had quickly approved, and the two men had consulted a map to scout the best location for a meeting.

Once they had a fully formulated game plan, Ryan headed across the island to pick up Megan.

Outside the villa, Ryan jogged up the short flight of steps to the front door. Before he could knock, Karen opened the door. She carried two large bags, one slung over either shoulder. "These are for Megan and I," she said curtly.

"I was hoping to get Mrs. Babcock alone for this interview," Ryan said pointedly. "Maybe you can stay behind and entertain Blake the way you normally do."

Karen's head jerked back in a gesture of denial, fear flooding her eyes.

"It's okay, Karen," Ryan said, lowering his voice. "I'll take the bags. You go keep Blake occupied for me."

"But ... but ... how ...?"

"It's pretty obvious, Karen. You gotta stop mooning over him. Oh, and stop leaving used condoms in your trashcan. That's a dead giveaway. Now, I can either tell Mrs. Babcock about your indiscretions, or you can stay here and keep your lover boy, Blake the Flake, company. What's it gonna be?"

Before Karen backed out of the doorway, she took a pill bottle from her pocket and handed it to Ryan. "She needs those for her headaches," then added, "I'll get Mrs. Babcock for you."

Moments later, Megan Babcock stepped through the front door of the villa, wearing a black sleeveless pencil dress with matching high heels and sunglasses.

Ryan escorted her down the steps and led her to the Jeep. She tried to climb into the rear passenger seat, but Ryan insisted on her sitting in the front. "It's safer this way," he said.

"Now, why would a photographer think about something like that?" she asked.

"Well, there's more airbag protection up here, and my wife has a Jeep similar to this, so I'm accustomed to driving with someone in the front seat beside me. Besides, you deserve all the protection you can get."

"You're married?" she asked, accepting his answer.

The troubleshooter grinned. "Her name is Emily. We've been married for a couple of years now."

Ryan shut the door once Megan Babcock was inside, then walked around to the driver's side. He slid behind the wheel and fired up the engine.

"If you don't mind, we're headed for Basseterre," Ryan informed her.

Megan remained silent, content with staring out the window.

As they left the Park Hyatt resort, Ryan repeatedly checked his mirrors for a follow car he was sure would tail them across the island. If Babcock was traying to control Megan, then the goons wouldn't be far behind.

Rounding Great Salt Pond and heading out onto the narrow neck separating the Atlantic from the Caribbean, Ryan glimpsed a black SUV speeding up from behind. He kept his pace leisurely as he drove, but he was nervous about the timing of their plan.

Before leaving the Core Tek office, Ryan had enabled the sharing function on his phone so Spooky John could track him via his GPS coordinates. John's fellow spooks would distract Babcock's goons during the drive, allowing Ryan to slip away.

Cresting the top of Timothy Hill, Ryan slowed, and the follow car closed in on him. He kept the SUV in sight as they wound down the hill toward the roundabout at the bottom. The goons made it easy, staying a couple of car lengths back.

Just as Ryan entered the roundabout, he saw the orange Volkswagen Spooky John had pointed out to him in the Core Tek parking lot approaching from the road to his left. The car was a mid-nineties rust bucket with plenty of dents and dings.

The little car hesitated just a beat to give the goon's vehicle a chance to enter the roundabout, then charged out between the follow car and Ryan's Jeep. In a screech of tires, the orange Volkswagen rammed into the side of the black SUV, slamming it into the high curb surrounding the center of the roundabout and forcing the SUV to come to a stop.

Ryan kept his foot on the gas, not bothering to check his mirrors as he headed for the meeting with Spooky John.

CHAPTER NINE

Park Hyatt Villa

"Why did you let her go alone?" Blake Babcock demanded.

"What else could I do?" Karen asked. "That photographer guy said he knew about us and would tell Megan. I had to let her go."

Babcock swore and tilted his head back, pinching the bridge of his nose in consternation. He didn't have time for this nonsense, and letting Megan disappear with a stranger, even one who had saved her life, was absolutely out of the question. She might say something that could endanger his whole scheme to sell MCG Marine Defense.

He had hoped to be alone in the villa while he met with the buyer's agent for Subsurface Kinetics. He hated the thought of selling the company to the Iranians, but they had him over a barrel.

MCG Marine Defense raked in good money from the Pentagon, which contracted with the company to develop new propulsion systems for submarines. MCG's claim to fame was the development of the magnetohydrodynamic propulsion drive.

In Tom Clancy's book, *The Hunt for Red October*, the technothriller author had called it a "caterpillar drive." Although the concept had been around since the 1960s, MCG had perfected the design. The basic concept was to apply magnetic forces to an electrical conducting fluid, namely saltwater, and force it to flow through a tube to thrust an underwater vehicle forward. An engineer had once explained it to Babcock as using opposing magnets to make the water inside the tube spin and pass over a propeller. The faster the rotation of the water in the tube, the faster the submarine would travel. MCG had been able to force the water through a waterjet nozzle instead of using a propeller, thus making the submarine more efficient and extremely quiet.

The concept had intrigued Babcock, and he'd spent time working with the engineers to develop and test the latest version. He'd even gone so far as to learn to pilot it, so Babcock was reluctant to hand his baby over to America's enemies. It wasn't that he had no allegiance to the United States. He had been raised a red-blooded American patriot, served as a Ranger in the Army, and then used his G.I. Bill to go to college, earning a Bachelor of Arts degree in Criminology from the University of South Florida. Upon leaving college, the CIA had recruited Babcock and flown him to D.C. for training, but the case officers who ran the Farm didn't believe Babcock was a good fit for the clandestine service and had washed him out.

Disgruntled, Babcock had spent a year abroad, backpacking through foreign countries and experiencing the variety life had to offer outside the States. Upon his return, he'd settled in Washington, D.C., and began law school at Georgetown. After passing the bar, Babcock had taken a job at Treasury. The work was mundane, but it had allowed Babcock to continue to travel—and he'd met Megan Gaspar on one of those government junkets. She had been smitten by his naturally good looks, charm, and wit, as had many of Babcock's past conquests.

In the early days of his relationship with Megan, a man named Xerxes Adi had approached Babcock. Adi was an Iranian agent working for the Ministry of Intelligence and Security, or MOIS. Initially reluctant to hand over any U.S. intelligence or provide access to his new lover's company, Babcock found himself in a dilemma as the Iranian laid out photograph after photograph of him in the most compromising positions with a girl whom he had known was no more than fourteen at the time. Babcock had been in Turkey, spending time in the resort city of Antalya, when he'd come across the young girl. In a lustful haze, he had paid handsomely to spend the evening with her, reasoning no one would ever know.

Babcock smiled to himself as he thought about that night. There was no denying he had enjoyed himself. At first, he'd tried to pass off his dalliance as a drunken mistake, but as the Iranian had supplied him with more girls to sleep with, Babcock had been forced to admit the truth to himself: he had a fetish for very young girls.

It was a secret that he kept well hidden from Megan and Karen, bedding the assistant whenever he needed a quick sexual fix. Megan, despite her reputation as a party girl, was an ice queen when it came to sex, especially since he'd started feeding her the arsphenamine pills laced with extra arsenic. Despite their sexual incompatibility, Babcock had married her anyway because the Iranians had plans for Gaspar Industries. They had supplied Babcock with the pills to keep drugging his wife, and he had coerced her into signing over seventy percent of Gaspar Industries to him in the belief that her health was failing.

Now, at the height of his deception, Babcock controlled wealth and industry, but whenever Xerxes Adi walked into the room, Blake Babcock knew he was no more than a puppet on the Iranian's string.

"Take the car and go shopping in Basseterre," Babcock instructed Karen.

The young assistant flung her arms around his neck and pecked him on the lips. "But I was hoping to spend the day with you ..."

Babcock wrapped his arms around the girl and squeezed her tight. "I know, babe, but I have a meeting and need everyone out of the house." He let her go, pulled his Amex Black card from his wallet, and handed it to her. "Buy whatever you want."

Karen didn't hesitate, snatching the card from his hand before turning on her heels and heading for her car.

Babcock watched Karen go down the steps, hungrily observing how her butt swayed under her tight-fitting midi dress. It would have been nice to spend a leisurely afternoon screwing her silly, but he had more serious matters to attend to.

THE IRANIAN ARRIVED in a black Mercedes. He was fit and handsome, with wavy black hair and clean-shaven olive skin. He wore a black Armani suit and matching shoes. He never drank alcohol and never partook in the sexual delights he consistently provided to his American puppet.

Xerxes Adi entered the villa without knocking. He strode to the pool deck, where Blake Babcock sat with a cold Skol beer in his hand.

"*As-salaam alaikum*," Babcock greeted, holding up his beer.

"*Salaam*," Adi replied automatically, not wanting to give this infidel the benefit of the longer greeting which bestowed peace, mercy, and Allah's blessing to a believer.

He sat across from Babcock in the shade of an umbrella and unbuttoned his suit coat.

Babcock always felt uncomfortable in the Iranian's presence. Adi exuded grace and confidence in a way that Blake wished he could emulate. While he'd never lacked confidence, Babcock often came across as a pompous ass, more aloof than cool.

"Everything is set," Babcock said, eager to hurry the meeting along so he could revel in the delight he knew the Iranian had brought for him.

"Excellent," Adi replied impassively. "Where will we take possession?"

"The submarine is still at MCG's headquarters in Guyana," Babcock replied.

While Guyana was rural and lacked critical infrastructure, the country was making progress as an oil producer and a tech hub, hoping to become a new Silicon Valley. Gaspar had spent millions building a factory in New Amsterdam and training Guyanese workers to staff the facility, including sending young locals to college to learn the latest in science, technology, engineering, and mathematics. Old man Gaspar had spent his own money to develop a local pool of laborers and scientists to draw from, but those same college graduates were being offered jobs in the burgeoning oil industry at much better pay.

The oil giant ExxonMobil had discovered massive offshore oil deposits capable of producing over a million barrels daily. Guyana was on the cusp of transforming itself from one of the most impoverished nations on earth to one of the wealthiest. Despite the claim of sharing oil profits with the Guyanese people, the only trickle-down economics the people saw were the occasional infrastructure project or social program.

Adi pondered Babcock's revelation that the submarine was not in Saint Kitts. "That's not the deal we made, Blake," he said. "You were supposed to deliver the goods to me here."

Babcock shrugged. "I can hand you a USB drive with all the technical schematics on it, but the submarine is more difficult to transport."

Adi sighed and glanced out at The Narrows with Nevis beyond. "Then I'll send my ship to Guyana, but I don't like this change in our plans."

"It was too difficult to justify moving the submarine."

Adi stood and buttoned his suit coat, then walked to the rail at the far end of the infinity pool. Turning back toward the house, he scanned all the doors and windows.

"There is another troubling development that I wish to discuss," Xerxes Adi said. "I believe our deal may be in danger."

"What do you mean?" Babcock asked, frowning.

"The man you invited here last night—Ryan Weller. He is not the photographer he represents himself to be."

Blake Babcock sat up straighter in his chair, setting aside his beer. "Then who is he?"

Adi casually examined the fingernails of his left hand, running his thumbnail over the edge of each manicured nail. He took his time answering his puppet. "Weller is a known associate of both the DHS and the DIA. I also believe he has met with a CIA case officer here in Basseterre, known to us as Bowie."

"Wait," Babcock said, holding up his hand. "He took Megan on a photo shoot this afternoon."

"I assure you, he is not a photographer. My guess is that he'll take your wife to meet with Bowie since you had her old lover McGuire killed for trying to interfere in the sale of MCG."

Babcock picked up his phone from the table beside him and opened the tracking app he used to monitor Megan's whereabouts and those of her security team. Megan's location showed her heading into Basseterre, while the dot representing the security team blinked unmoving at a roundabout at the base of Timothy Hill.

He immediately called Boris, the team leader.

"Why are you not with Megan?" Babcock asked when the former Russian Spetsnaz soldier answered.

"We were in a car accident. A Volkswagen hit the side of our vehicle."

"Megan is in danger," Babcock stated. "I need you to get to her right now. The man she is with is a threat to her life. Kill him."

"Yes, boss," Boris said and ended the call.

Moments later, the security team's blinking dot began to move. Weller had a head start, but wherever he was taking Megan, his men would be right behind him.

"My men are on their way to pick her up now," Babcock informed the Iranian.

"Excellent," Xerxes Adi replied. "It is good you are handling this. We cannot afford any distractions. We must get to Guyana as soon as possible to complete the transaction."

"Why can't you wire the money to my account now?" Babcock complained. "The tech is there, I promise."

"I want you to be there when we take possession," Adi replied. "I have a special surprise for you after the sale."

Babcock felt his pulse quicken as hormones flooded his

bloodstream. Typically, Adi's "special surprises" came in the form of young flesh. He couldn't wait to complete this transaction, and handing over the submarine meant more than just another girl to fulfill his desires. He would finally be free of the Iranians.

Come to think of it, he would be free in more ways than one. Megan would be incapacitated by the pills by then, if not dead, and he would be free to do as he pleased. He could sate his desires in the wilds of Guyana, plucking young girls off the street and turning them loose when he'd finished with them.

At times, Babcock often wondered what was wrong with him that he had such a fetish, but when the lust overtook him, he lost all control. The excitement he felt right then at the prospect of deflowering a young kidnappee was all-encompassing. He needed it like he needed to breathe.

"Call me on the secure line when you have your wife under control," Adi said as he stood.

"What about my reward?" Babcock asked.

"There is no reward today," Adi responded. "Weller has made you look like a fool. Your mistake has possibly jeopardized our entire operation."

"But you always provide me with a reward," Babcock whined.

Through hooded eyes, Xerxes Adi peered at the American with disdain, and Babcock reflexively blanched under his scorn. He knew he'd screwed up.

At the front door of the villa, Adi turned to Babcock, his hands clasped behind his back. "It's a shame. She was a pretty young thing, too. Maybe I will bring her to Guyana, but only if you handle this situation. And I don't want to hear anything in the news about tourist deaths. Handle this quietly."

"Of course, Mister Adi. I will handle it with the utmost discretion."

Adi nodded. "I trust that you will."

With nothing further to say, Adi slipped on his sunglasses and headed down the steps toward the waiting Mercedes.

Blake Babcock glanced at the tracking app again. His men were closing in on his wife's location. Megan would soon be back in his possession.

CHAPTER TEN

Basseterre, Saint Kitts

"What was all that banging about? Did someone have an accident?" Megan asked, turning in her seat to look out the back window.

"Just a little fender bender," Ryan replied with a slight smile. "I guess some people aren't used to driving on the left side of the road."

Megan turned back to stare out the windshield and crossed her arms. "Where are you taking me, Mister Weller?"

"I want you to meet an acquaintance of mine," Ryan replied.

"Another photographer?" she asked.

"Not exactly," Ryan said. "I'd like you to call me Ryan instead of Mister Weller. The 'mister' makes me feel old. But here's the score. I'm a freelance troubleshooter who's been swept up in this situation just like you."

"Since we're being friendly, you may call me Megan. But I'd still like to know what we're both caught up in."

Ryan glanced over at her. She was staring right back at him, her arms crossed and her back pressed against the door. "I'll let my friend do the explaining."

"I think I'd rather go back to my villa," she insisted.

"I can't do that, Megan. I need you to speak to my friend."

Turning and hooking her fingers in the door handle, Megan said, "If you don't turn around right now, I'm going to jump out of this Jeep and sue you for kidnapping."

"I wouldn't advise it," Ryan said, digging his passport out of the center console before handing it to Megan, open to his photo and the fictitious name beside it. "Tell me what you think of that."

Releasing the door handle, Megan took the passport from his hand. "What's so special about a passport?"

"Read the name."

Ryan glanced over just in time to see her eyes widen and her nostrils flare as she read the name on the inside page.

"Where did you get this?" she hissed, anger in her voice as she tried to keep herself in check.

"It's a CIA fake," Ryan explained. "They thought I was McGuire and scooped me up. Once I got to Saint Kitts, they asked me to help them."

"What does the CIA want with Denny?"

"He was on his way to see you," Ryan said. "He hoped to convince you not to sell MCG Marine Defense."

Megan rolled her eyes as if she'd been through it all before with McGuire. "If they picked you up by mistake, where's Denny?"

Ryan gritted his teeth. He hadn't wanted to tell her, but it was the easiest way to get her to meet with Spooky John. If she saw all the cards on the table, then there was a chance she might do something to stop her husband. "Local PD found his body in Fort Lauderdale. Someone murdered him."

"What?" she exclaimed. "I just talked to him two days ago! How can he be dead?"

"I don't know the specifics," Ryan told her. "I didn't want to break the news of his death to you like this. I'm sorry."

Megan covered her mouth with her hand and stifled a sob. Tears flowed freely down her cheeks as she cried silently in remorse at losing her former lover and friend.

Ryan tenderly patted her knee. "It's going to be okay, Meg. The agencies have good people on the case. They'll find Denny's killer."

Consumed with her grief, Megan didn't reply as she stared out the side window. Ryan withdrew his hand and kept both on the wheel.

Their destination was an abandoned building formerly known as the Fort Thomas Hotel. Ryan drove past Core Tek Shipping and then skirted the tourist traps around the cruise ship port, navigating into a residential neighborhood before coming to the old hotel on a peninsula that jutted into the tranquil Caribbean Sea between Limekiln and Basseterre Bays.

Ryan pulled past the open chain-link fence that someone had thrown up decades ago to keep out the prying public. When Spooky John had told Ryan the location of where they would meet, the troubleshooter had attempted to use Google Maps to scout the location, but there was no Street View and no Photo Spheres he could use for reference. Ryan had to rely on some publicly posted photos on two pins, one from a landscaping company and the other from a paintball club that used the old hotel grounds as their mock battlefield. Ryan would have liked to have explored the tan, three-story hotel and its overgrown grounds, but he hadn't even had time to drive-by before picking up Megan.

Fortunately, Spooky John had arrived early enough to open the gate in the fence. Ryan drove the Jeep under the old porte-cochère and parked on the circular drive beneath it. The whole place had a post-apocalyptic feel to it, from the rusted metal on the porte-cochère, stairwell railings, and massive hurricane shutters to the peeling paint on every surface of the building.

"What are we doing here?" Megan asked.

"Hopefully, the guy we're about to meet will have some answers for you," Ryan said as he slid out of the seat. He went around to Megan's door and opened it for her.

The two of them walked along a brush-choked sidewalk to the rear of the hotel, entering the building through the partially open door. Inside, the place looked even more rundown than the exterior. Tiles had fallen off the walls or worked loose from the floor. Debris littered almost every square inch of the place, with old light fixtures dangling from the ceiling by their wiring and ancient appliances left to rust. The stench of decaying mattresses, mold, mildew, and rat droppings added a putrid funk to the air.

"This place is disgusting," Megan commented. "Why does your friend want to meet here?"

"It's away from prying eyes," Ryan replied, glancing at the multi-hued graffiti on the walls, hoping the old hotel wasn't the territory of some violent transnational gang.

John's voice floated back to them from the terrace. "Out here, guys."

Ryan followed the voice, leading Megan by the elbow. Her high-heeled shoes weren't the best footwear for negotiating the hazardous building. In fairness, she hadn't expected to be clandestinely meeting a CIA case officer in the middle of the junkyard. There wasn't a better way to classify the hotel other than a general danger to the public, and Ryan wondered why the government hadn't torn the building down long ago.

Stepping out of the building, they found John leaning against what Ryan thought was an old bar beside an overgrown plot with palms and various other bushes sprouting from it. Not far from where they stood, Ryan could see the old stainless-steel ladder of a pool extending into the ground in the middle of the thicket. At some point, the pool had been filled with dirt, and nature, as she always did, had taken care of the rest.

"Who are you?" Megan asked John. "And what can you tell me about Denny's death?"

The case officer glanced at Ryan, uncertain of why she was ambushing him over the death of her friend.

Ryan shrugged. "I had to tell her something to get her here. She threatened to jump out of a moving car."

John extended his hand to Megan. "You can call me Jim. I asked Ryan to bring you here because we need to talk about the sale of MCG Marine Defense."

"What about it?" Megan asked sharply after shaking the spy's hand. "Is that why Denny was killed?"

"We don't know why," John admitted. "But we do know that your husband is selling MCG to the Iranians."

Megan shook her head in disbelief. "What are you talking about? Blake showed me the paperwork. He's selling it to a company called Subsurface Kinetics for a small fortune. I had to sign off on the deal."

"Whatever you signed is not the deal your husband is making," John said flatly.

Megan put her fingertips to her temples and massaged them. "This is giving me a headache. Ryan, can you get my pills from my luggage?"

Ryan glanced at the CIA case officer, who raised his eyebrows. He hadn't told John about the pills. Since they were springing all this information on Megan at once, Ryan decided now would be an excellent time to dogpile her. "What're the pills for, Megan?"

"Stop asking so many questions and just get me my pills," Megan snapped. "I need them for my headaches."

Ryan pulled the bottle from his pants pocket. "These pills?"

"Yes," Megan said, reaching for the bottle. "Do you have any water?"

"I didn't bring any with me," Ryan replied, stuffing them back in his pocket. "But there's some in the Jeep."

"Then go get it!" she snapped again when he didn't move.

Ryan met her gaze. "Can I ask you a question?"

"This place is atrocious, and you're being a bore, but fine, if it will get me some water ask away."

"Do you have syphilis?" Ryan asked.

Megan stopped rubbing her temples and looked up in bewilderment. "Why do you think I have an STD?"

"What about leukemia or some other form of cancer?" Ryan probed.

"I'm not sick!" Megan cried out. "I just get headaches, but I might throw up if we have to spend another minute in this God-awful dump."

Ryan took her by the elbow and steered her toward the open lawn, where paintballers had erected small barricades to hide behind during their war games. "Who gave you these pills?"

"Blake gets them for me," Megan admitted. "I saw a doctor about a migraine I was having, and suddenly, he came home with pills."

"How long have you been taking them?"

"A couple of years, I guess. Why?"

"I think Blake is trying to kill you with poison," Ryan said. "These pills are arsenic-based. Long-term exposure can lead to severe side effects and even death."

Megan jerked out of Ryan's grasp and stopped in the ankle-high grass. "Don't be ridiculous. Blake isn't trying to kill me."

She rubbed her temples again while staring at the ground. Megan Babcock seemed to sway in her high heels, and Ryan steeled himself to catch her should she fall.

"This whole thing is ridiculous," Megan said, sighing. "Blake is *not* trying to kill me."

As the words left her mouth, Ryan heard John shout, "Gun! Get down!"

CHAPTER ELEVEN

Ryan dove for the ground, pulling Megan Babcock with him.

He landed on top of her and immediately began assessing the best way to move to cover. They were in the open, near a dirt road that led to the waterfront cliffs. The closest cover was the hotel among the concrete walls of the time crypt.

In the stillness of the afternoon heat, a suppressed shot zipped through the air. Dirt and grass exploded just inches from Ryan and Megan's faces.

Megan screamed.

"Ryan!" John shouted. "Two shooters. Move east toward the end of the pool."

Without hesitation, Ryan sprang to his feet and grabbed Megan by the arm. He hoisted her to her feet and started dragging her across the lawn.

The ground sloped from the hotel proper down toward the sea, and the resort's builders had constructed an eight-foot-high retaining wall around the ocean end of the pool to ensure the pool deck remained level with the rear patio of the hotel. At the end of this deck, wide wooden stairs descended to the ground, with a small landing halfway down. As Ryan and Megan drew closer, he could see half the stairs were missing, those that remained were rotten and splintered, and the railing at the top appeared ready to topple in a strong wind.

"What's going on?" Megan asked, breathless and wide-eyed as they ran.

"I think your husband has switched from arsenic to lead poisoning," Ryan commented dryly as he peered around the end of the pool deck.

"Why do you insist on blaming Blake?" she demanded.

"Because, in my book, he's a piece of shit," Ryan replied. He glanced over his shoulder at her, huddled with her back against the rough blocks of the retaining wall. "Let's move."

"I'm not going anywhere," Megan insisted.

Another muffled gunshot flattened Ryan to the retaining wall. The sound came from behind him, and he could tell it was a different gun than the one that had fired the first two shots.

"Move!" Spooky John shouted.

Move where? Ryan wondered.

He had no idea where the shooters were. The last time he'd seen John, the spook had been by the pool bar, waiting for Megan to clear her head with fresh air.

More suppressed shots riffled the air, followed by two more from the other gun—dueling pistols.

"Let's go." Ryan grabbed Megan's hand and tugged her away from the wall beside the steps. They charged through the high weeds at the base of the pool's retaining wall, coming to the far side. There, the grass had been mowed flat for the paintball field. Stacks of old tires, pallets standing on end, and odd bits of timber or doors stolen from the old hotel rooms were spaced at various intervals across the field for the paintballers to hide behind. While the barricades would stop the air-powered paintballs, they wouldn't stop real bullets, but ducking and dodging between the obstacles seemed like the best way to avoid taking a round from one of Blake Babcock's goons.

Ryan gripped Megan by the arm and forced her to look at him. He could feel the fear radiating off her, the quickness of her pulse in the vein in her arm, and the pinprick pupils that said she was in shock. "We're going to be fine, Megan. We're going to race across this field, using those barricades as cover. Stay low and move when I move. We can get out of here once we get to the Jeep."

Megan nodded vaguely.

Ryan wondered if she was still suffering from the effects of her headache or if the adrenaline of being shot at was enough of a remedy.

He started forward, his hand still gripping her arm to guide her. When Megan didn't move as he did, he had to stop short, turning back to face her.

"I can't do this," she said, on the verge of tears.

Ryan glanced down at her high heels, realizing they would complicate matters. Without another word, Ryan bent and hoisted her over his shoulder, then bolted across the paintball field. A bullet struck a nearby pallet as he ran past, sending splinters of wood into the air. Megan bounced unceremoniously on his shoulder. This wasn't the first time he'd carried a woman out of a precarious position. The last one had been stark raving mad, trying to shoot a trespasser on her island. Megan was a docile creature in shock, more at ease giving orders like some television general than being shot at.

Another bullet thudded into the stack of rubber tires just ahead of them. Ryan cut to his right, running toward the gunmen. He caught a glimpse of one of the goons he'd first seen guarding Megan during the photoshoot at the top of Timothy Hill. The man swung his gun toward Ryan, and the troubleshooter zigged in another direction, breathing hard from carrying an extra one-hundred-ten pounds on his shoulder.

“Shoot somebody, John!” Ryan roared.

Two more gunshots thudded into barricades near Ryan, the last of the cover as he broke out of the paintball playing field and angled toward the porte-cochère. If he could just get to the Jeep, he could get himself and Megan out of harm’s way.

He didn’t know if John had heard him or if the spook had shot either of the goons, but Ryan made it into the bushes near the hotel’s entrance without further incident. He paused at the edge of the paved circle for a moment, checking to see if more goons were guarding his vehicle. He saw only the black SUV that had followed him from the Park Hyatt villa, parked across the opening in the fence and blocking the exit. The SUV had a long scrape down its left flank where the Volkswagen had banged into the side of it before forcing it into the high curb of the roundabout.

At the door of the Jeep, Ryan realized he’d made a time-critical mistake. The Jeep was right-hand drive, and he had automatically taken Megan to that side. He ran around to the left side and plopped Megan unceremoniously into the passenger seat. She tumbled in without offering a fight, and Ryan fastened her seatbelt, cinching it tight to keep her from moving around.

He jumped into the driver’s seat and fired up the V6 engine. Through Megan’s side window, he could see the goons coming around the back of the hotel and taking aim at him without bothering to change their stride. He jammed the shift lever into Reverse and backed straight toward the black SUV. He turned the wheel slightly, aiming for the front fender, and mashed the accelerator as soon as he straightened the wheel.

“Brace yourself,” he shouted at Megan.

The woman turned her head to stare blankly at him.

Just before impact, Ryan braced his hand against the steering wheel, thrusting himself back against the seat and throwing his left arm across Megan's chest. The Jeep slammed into the nose of the black SUV, pitching Ryan and Megan hard against the seatbacks, then immediately forward as the Jeep's momentum slowed. Ryan took his hand off Megan and grabbed the wheel, spinning it to the right while pinning the gas pedal to the floor. Metal screeched as the Jeep pushed past the goons' vehicle and broke free of the chain-link fence.

Once on the street, Ryan completed his reversing turn to the left, lining up the Jeep with the roadway and slamming on the brakes. He slipped the transmission into Drive and accelerated smoothly away from the scene of the action.

As they drove through the narrow streets, Ryan wondered how Spooky John had fared during the shootout. Obviously, he had known the hotel's layout and had directed Ryan on how to move, so Ryan reasoned he should have been able to get away quickly. And the two goons had come after him, leaving John an opportunity to escape the dangerous situation.

Ryan slowed, watching for another tail. He observed the speed limit and stopped at all stop signs and yellow lights.

"You can breathe, Megan. We're out of danger," Ryan said.

"Out of danger?" she blurted. "Just how do you figure that?"

Ryan shrugged. "At least there's no one shooting at us."

"You just told me that my husband is trying to kill me with poison and has somehow manipulated me into selling my defense company to the Iranians. And you think I'm out of danger?" Megan rubbed her temples again. "This is all too much. I need a drink."

"You and me both. Lucky for you, I know just the place," Ryan said. "But it'll take a couple of minutes to get there."

Megan arched her eyebrows and took a deep breath. "I am so tired of surprises."

"This is about the only place I know on this crazy island, but I'm with you. I'm tired of surprises, too. I'm thinking about retiring after this op."

Megan's laughter was a surprise to Ryan.

"You're going to retire?" she said.

"Yeah," he said, her infectious laugh causing him to join her. "I'm going to get on my boat with my wife and set sail for distant horizons."

"You know the horizon moves with you, right?" Megan asked.

"That's the beauty of it," Ryan said. "You're always chasing it."

"Sounds boring."

Ryan smiled. "Maybe to a woman who walked down the aisle between two white tigers, but I kinda like it."

Megan laughed. "It was a little absurd, wasn't it? I thought it would be ostentatious, but one of the tigers tried to eat my dress, and the other nearly mauled one of the groomsmen. I bet that didn't make the news, did it?"

"It wasn't in my briefing packet."

With a snort, Megan continued, "Anyway, that was five years ago. Seems like a lifetime. I quit partying like a sorority sister with my legs spread and my dress over my head and concentrated on learning Daddy's business. I don't get out much anymore."

"Probably for the best," Ryan said.

"What about your wife?" Megan asked. "Does she like to sail?"

"She does," Ryan replied. "We've spent a lot of time sailing together."

"You're lucky to find a woman who shares your passions," Megan said wistfully.

"Yes, I am," Ryan said. "Yes, I am."

———

TEN MINUTES LATER, Ryan and Megan sat at a table at Boozies on the Beach.

By the time their drinks arrived, Megan seemed calmer, but Ryan could see the woman was still in turmoil. Her eyes had been bright and clear when he'd picked her up earlier in the afternoon, but now, they were clouded with worry and suspicion. Given his knowledge of her situation, Ryan figured she had every right to fear for her life.

The hostess brought two margaritas in pint glasses with sugar on the rim instead of salt a few minutes later.

Megan took a long drink and closed her eyes as if savoring the delicious beverage.

Ryan sipped his drink and watched the surrounding patrons, eyeing the entrances and exits for hostiles.

"You know," Megan said, "it's been a long time since I've spent time with someone who hasn't wanted anything from me."

Ryan felt slightly guilty because he wanted her to stop selling her defense contracting company but remained silent, figuring she might open up more if he let her do all the talking.

After another drink, Megan said, "Thanks for saving me back there."

"It's my job," he replied.

"Maybe I should hire you to be my assistant instead of Karen," Megan said.

"At least I wouldn't be screwing your husband on the side," Ryan muttered.

Megan's eyebrows shot up. "Oh, this day just keeps getting better and better. I knew he was screwing around but not with Karen."

"I want to help you, Megan. Surely, you can see the mess you're in. Your husband is sleeping around, and he's trying to steal your company out from under you. And he's also prepared to kill you make it happen. It's time to make a change. Jim and I can offer you safe passage off the island, away from Blake. We can keep you safe."

"And what about my company?" she asked.

"What about it?" Ryan asked.

"How am I supposed to walk away from the company my father built and what I've worked so hard to expand, knowing Blake has conned me out of seventy percent of it?"

Ryan didn't have an answer for her.

"Despite the years I spent trying to blow my daddy's money, I did learn a thing or two about business from him. Things are running smoother than ever right now."

"Then why sell MCG?" Ryan prompted.

"Blake said it would be good for the company."

"Good for him, maybe," Ryan said. "How did he get control?"

"I signed over temporary control because of my health issues, but it was only supposed to be until I felt better. I can only assume Blake slipped the paperwork in with others I was signing. I didn't look at them closely. And those awful pills make my mind hazy."

Ryan nodded. He sipped his margarita and stared out at the sea. Megan was certainly in a quandary. Going back to live with Blake, knowing he was trying to kill her, made no sense, but wanting to protect her assets and her family name was something Ryan understood.

"I want to help in any way I can," Ryan said, producing a business card from his wallet. The imprint read:

MARITIME RECOVERY with the name Bob Parker embossed under it.

"What's this?" Megan asked.

"If you need assistance, give me a call. That number goes to an answering service that will relay a message to me."

Megan slipped the card into her bra. "Is that what you do? Rescue people?"

"Pretty much," Ryan confirmed.

Megan grunted in acknowledgment, then rubbed her temples. "I just want this headache to go away."

"Maybe it's time to see a real doctor and not that quack Blake is getting the pills from. There might be more to your ailments than the physical side effects of the arsenic."

She nodded and reached for her drink.

Ryan overheard a woman sitting at the front of the restaurant say, "What's with all the police cars?"

He and Megan both glanced toward the entrance just in time to see Blake Babcock stride into the restaurant with Inspector Browne of the Royal St. Christopher and Nevis Police Force right behind him. More cop cars arrived with lights flashing, and uniformed officers took up positions around the restaurant.

Babcock pointed to Ryan and said, "There he is. Arrest him for kidnapping my wife."

Murmurs rippled through the restaurant patrons as the police officers advanced.

Megan started to rise from her seat but was driven back by blinding pain that not only flashed through her body but across her face in a hard-set grimace. Ryan felt like punching Blake Babcock in the face and ordering the police to arrest him for the attempted murder of his wife, but he knew it wouldn't do any good. The cops would only arrest him for assault and allow Babcock to pass off his accusations as those of a deranged man.

Money has its privileges.

Inspector Browne walked calmly over to the table and asked Ryan to stand. The troubleshooter rose and placed his hands in front of him, knowing there was no use in resisting arrest. Browne snapped a pair of cuffs on Ryan's wrists and marched him past a smug-looking Blake Babcock, who hadn't moved to help his wife.

Ryan desperately wanted to throw a couple of verbal jabs in the man's face, but instead, he said to Inspector Browne, "Mrs. Babcock needs medical attention. Can't you see she's in terrible pain?"

Browne glanced over his shoulder at the woman still sitting at the table. "She looks fine to me."

With no other cards left to play, Ryan let himself be stuffed into the back of a police cruiser and driven to the station. Not so long ago, he'd been a hero, stopping a maniac from knifing Megan Babcock, and now he was the one in cuffs.

Inspector Browne led Ryan through the police station to his office and sat him in a visitor's chair. The overweight inspector dropped wearily into his creaky wooden chair and removed his uniform cap. He rubbed his nearly bald head and asked, "Did you kidnap Megan Babcock?"

"No," Ryan said flatly. "Did it look to you like I'd kidnapped her? I wasn't forcing her to sit at that table and drink margaritas."

"I can only say what I personally saw, and no, it didn't appear to me as if you were holding her against her will," the inspector said. "But still, charges have been levied against you, and it's my job to investigate them."

Ryan rolled his eyes and blew out a long breath through his puffed-up cheeks. In cop-speak, that meant he would be there for the duration.

"Do you have your passport on you?" Inspector Browne asked.

"Oh, shit," Ryan muttered. The inspector knew him as Ryan Weller, but his passport said his name was Dennis McGuire. He sighed again and said, "It's in my back pocket."

When Blake and Megan Babcock walked into the office, Ryan was explaining to Inspector Browne why his passport had a fictitious name on it.

"I hope you're pressing the maximum charges against this man," Babcock said to the inspector.

Ryan glared up at him while Megan remained docile beside her husband.

"In due time," Browne replied, his face still bewildered by the events unfolding in his office.

"I plan to sue him for kidnapping my wife," Babcock replied.

Ryan stood, his hand balled into fists. "Go ahead," he shot back. "I'll countersue you for reckless endangerment. Your two goons were shooting at us."

Megan inserted herself between the two men. "Please sit down, Ryan—and you can back off, Blake. We're not pressing charges against anyone. In fact, Inspector, I'd like you to release Mister Weller. He did nothing wrong."

Inspector Browne glanced from one Babcock to the other.

Megan turned and headed for the door, then said sharply over her shoulder, "Let's go, Blake."

Blake Babcock stared at Ryan, who was still on his feet, just a step away. "Don't ever come near me or my wife again," he seethed.

"Oh, I think we'll see each other again real soon," Ryan replied.

"Is that a threat?" Babcock growled.

"No, Blake, it's pretty much a promise."

Babcock shifted his gaze to Inspector Browne and said, "I want you to hold this man him until my wife and I have left the island."

"On what charge?" the inspector asked.

"You heard him threaten me," Babcock replied indignantly.

"I heard him say he would see you again," Browne said. "I heard no threat in his statement."

"It was implied," Babcock retorted.

"I'm not threatening you," Ryan said. "We just run in the same circle down here."

Babcock stared at him coldly.

"How soon will you and Mrs. Babcock be leaving our island?" Browne said.

"Within hours," Babcock said. "We have important business to attend to."

"I think you should reconsider your deal, Blake," Ryan said, sensing it might be his only opportunity to voice his opinion. "You know, so you're not a treasonous bastard."

"What the hell does that mean?" Babcock asked, advancing a step.

"Let's go, Blake!" Megan demanded.

"I think you know what it means," Ryan said. "But run along now before you get in trouble with your wife *and* your mistress."

Ryan hoped Megan would keep up the sassy attitude when she got home and didn't get kowtowed by Blake and her assistant into taking more pills or falling back into being a docile domestic creature under her husband's thumb.

He would see Blake Babcock again. Ryan was just as sure

of it as he was that Megan Babcock needed to be saved from her husband.

Babcock gave Ryan another threatening glare, then stalked out of the office.

Ryan took a seat across from Inspector Browne again and smiled politely. "Now, if you'll let me make a phone call, we can straighten out this passport business."

Browne turned the phone on his desk toward Ryan.

"I need my cellphone so I can get the number."

The inspector slid the cellphone across the desk, and Ryan picked it up. He didn't have Spooky John's number. All their meetings had been in person at John's convenience and place of choice. However, Ryan knew another high-ranking U.S. intelligence official on the island, so he dialed his number instead.

As the phone began to ring on the other end, Ryan glanced up to see a well-dressed man in a bespoke navy three-piece suit enter the police bullpen and make a beeline for Inspector Browne's office. He was American, above six feet in height and slightly chunky, with thick, wavy hair and a healthy tan.

Ryan ended his call before Larry Grove could answer and waited expectantly for the stranger to enter the office.

The newcomer stopped in the doorway and smiled, a self-assured gesture that lifted his left cheek only. Thrusting a hand into the pocket of his slacks, the man said, "Inspector, I'm here for Mister Weller-McGuire."

"Which is it?" Inspector Browne asked.

"Both, actually." He held up a brown leather briefcase. "May I?"

"Certainly. I'm eagerly awaiting an explanation," Inspector Browne replied.

The man set his briefcase on the desk and unsnapped the latches. "Dennis McGuire is the name of the man sitting before you, but he prefers to go by Ryan Weller." He pulled out a sheet of paper and handed it to the inspector.

Ryan saw the embossed raised seal of the notary stamp and the distinctive blue framing around the U.S. birth certificate.

Browne held the document closer to his face to examine it in minute detail and then slid it across the desk to Ryan. "Like your passport, I think it's a marvelous forgery."

"I wouldn't disagree with you," Ryan said, "but it's real. My full name is Dennis Ryan Weller-McGuire."

"We have a saying in my country, Mister Weller," Browne said with a glance at the well-dressed man. "All monkeys have the same face."

Ryan knew what he meant. The old saying indicated that he was exactly like the people with whom he associated, and based on the evidence of the fake passport and birth certificate, Ryan was just another American who thought he could fix his problems with plenty of money and U.S. government intervention. While Ryan knew that wasn't even close to the truth, Inspector Browne didn't have all the facts.

"I assure you, Inspector, Mister Weller-McGuire will be leaving your island post haste. He is, in fact, booked on a plane to Florida this afternoon."

Ryan's eyebrows shot up.

"If that's the case, then I will be happy to release Mister Weller-McGuire into your custody, Mister ...?" Browne's eyebrows furrowed.

"Friend," the man said. "Sam Friend."

Ryan almost laughed out loud but worked hard to keep his features stoic.

Sam Friend produced a U.S. Department of State identification card and showed it to the inspector and the troubleshooter. Despite Inspector Browne remaining unconvinced of the man's dubious background, he seemed genuinely amused throughout the entire proceedings. He handed back Ryan's passport and then looked up at Sam Friend. "I expect both of you will be leaving on the same jet out of my country."

"That we will, Inspector," Friend replied.

Ryan stood and extended his hand to the policeman. "I enjoyed my tour of the island. Thanks for having me."

Browne shook the proffered hand without standing and said without enthusiasm, "Enjoy your flight."

CHAPTER TWELVE

Park Hyatt Hotel
Saint Kitts

Xerxes Adi liked the idea of outsmarting the Americans almost as much as he enjoyed his power over Blake Babcock and the simple manipulations it took to keep him under his control.

However, as he listened to Blake and Megan Babcock arguing in her bedroom through the tiny listening devices planted throughout the couple's Park Hyatt villa, he wondered if the MCG deal would fall apart. It was Adi who had supplied Babcock with the pills laced with an extra dose of arsenic to help speed along his wife's death. He had hoped it would have happened already, clearing any obstacles for the sale of the submarine technology to his country. The president of Iran, Reza Soroush, had plans to build a fleet of submarines to control the Strait of Hormuz.

During her time with Ryan Weller, Megan Babcock had

learned the truth about everything. Now, she was working hard to convince her husband that the sale of MCG Marine Defense was against all her patriotic and moral judgment.

Babcock scoffed. "Since when have you ever been patriotic, Megan?"

"Our other businesses have multiple contracts with the U.S. government. If we sell MCG to the Iranians, we'll lose every contract with them and possibly more. The sale will be the death of Gaspar Industries."

"I realize that could happen, but what you're missing is the fact that you don't have control of the company," Babcock said. "I'm the one who owns seventy percent of Gaspar Industries."

Megan continued to argue her point. "Everything my father worked for, everything *we've* worked for, will be gone."

Adi smiled. He'd helped orchestrate the hostile takeover. As long as he had Blake Babcock in his hip pocket, he controlled Gaspar Industries. The corporation as a whole meant little to the Iranians, but securing MCG Marine Defense would be a significant advance for Reza Soroush's ambitions.

The sale was the only legitimate way to procure MCG's technology without being noticed by the U.S. government. Forcing Babcock to hand it over would attract even more attention than they were already generating. As far as Adi was concerned, it would have been much easier just to steal the plans for the submarine tech, but the decision to buy the company had been made above Adi's head. He was just the middleman, there to facilitate the transaction and to keep Blake Babcock in line.

The Iranian again scrolled through the photos Babcock had emailed to him. The MOIS had identified three U.S. intelligence operatives at the wrap party for Megan's photoshoot—and that number didn't include rogue operators like Ryan Weller.

A quick glance at the file MOIS had collated on Weller indicated he'd been a U.S. Navy explosive ordnance disposal technician in both the Iraq and Afghanistan wars. He'd been so successful at his job that the insurgents had placed a larger bounty on the bomb tech's head than the standard fifty grand every bomb tech received. Weller had been lucky to escape the war and return to his everyday life, but digging deeper into the file, Adi saw that Weller hadn't drifted far from his warrior roots. His name had been linked to covert operations across the Caribbean, and he'd even had an Interpol Red Notice placed on him by the SEBIN, Venezuela's intelligence service.

Adi took that with a grain of salt. Most countries ignored anything Venezuela had to say about criminals. Their country was rife with corruption from the top down, and putting a Red Notice on an American was like the pot calling the kettle black. Adi had dealt with Chávez and his successor, Michel Zarate, on several occasions and knew firsthand their corrupt and deceitful nature.

Turning his attention back to the fight between the married couple, Adi listened with mounting concern as they screamed at each other about the sale, the arsenic pills, and Babcock's infidelity with Megan's assistant. Adi snorted. If her husband's cheating appalled her, learning of his affinity for young girls might send her over the edge.

Adi heard the sound of shattering glass. Megan let out an anguished wail.

He grabbed what appeared to be a small diabetes kit that he kept on the nightstand and rushed out of his private suite, located not far from the Babcocks' villa. Running along the illuminated path, Adi knew he had to get the situation under control before other guests called the authorities. The black kit in his hand contained sedatives for just such an occasion.

Adi barged straight into the villa and took the stairs two at a time toward the bedrooms, passing Karen Friar, who stood shaking in the hall. Outside the door to Megan's bedroom, Adi unzipped the kit, checked the syringe he withdrew to ensure it contained the proper dosage, and then flicked the needle as he expelled trapped air from the plastic tube. Once the ketamine squirted from the needle, Adi prepared himself to enter the room.

Something crashed into the wall, and Megan screamed again. Adi heard the slap of flesh against flesh as he supposed Babcock had just struck his wife.

The Iranian stepped into the room to find Megan sprawled on the floor, jammed into a corner between the dresser and the wall. Blood seeped from the corner of her mouth, and her eyes were wide with shock and fear. Her glistening curly blonde in wild disarray.

After arriving back at the villa from her excursion with Weller, Megan had changed out of her black dress into plum-colored yoga pants, a white sports bra, and a loose tank top bearing the Gaspar Industries logo. While Adi harbored no special feelings toward the protection of women—they were second-class citizens in Iran, after all, and meant to tend the home, not own businesses—he did feel sorry for Megan Babcock. No matter his own sentiments about the role of women, he had been taught to honor them and never to strike them in anger.

Behind Adi, Babcock paced around the bedroom like a caged tiger. Megan ran her middle finger down the trail of blood on her chin. She stared impassively up at Xerxes Adi. The question in her blue eyes about who he was and what he was doing in her bedroom seemed to deepen her fright even more.

Adi bent over her, shoved the needle into her bare arm, and pressed the plunger, injecting her with the powerful drug. Seconds later, Megan Babcock's eyes fluttered, and her body went limp.

Rising to his feet, Adi placed the empty syringe back in its case, and zipped it closed. He turned to Babcock, who was still pacing frantically up and down the length of the bedroom.

"Pack your things," Adi instructed.

Babcock froze in midstride, then turned slowly toward the Iranian as if this was the first time he'd noticed the man's presence in the room. He glanced at his wife, lying limp on the floor.

"Pack your things," Adi repeated. "We must leave."

Stepping out into the hallway, Adi found Karen and beckoned her into the room. "Help them pack. I will have some men here shortly to escort you to your plane."

Babcock stared down at his wife's limp body and ran a hand through his hair. He let out a long breath and then nodded, confirming Adi's instructions.

"We'll go to Guyana," Babcock said. "We can finish the sale and be done with this business."

Ignoring the personal assistant frantically gathering Megan Babcock's clothes, Xerxes Adi stepped over to Blake Babcock and poked a finger into the American's chest. "This will never be over between us. You are my servant for as long as I choose—unless you want the world to know about your sexual proclivities."

Babcock backed up, but Adi moved with him, keeping his finger on the man's sternum. "I have a freighter headed for New Amsterdam as we speak. You will load the submarine onto it. Only then will I consider letting you live beyond your usefulness."

CHAPTER THIRTEEN

Robert L. Bradshaw International Airport
Saint Kitts and Nevis

"You're telling me you're not going to do anything to help that woman?" Ryan asked.

He stood in the cabin of another white Bombardier corporate jet with Sam Friend and Spooky John as it idled outside a private aviation terminal, ready to leave the two-island nation-state and return to the U.S. While the two men across from him appeared impassive, everything in Ryan's nature screamed at him to help Megan Babcock.

"Your cover is blown," John said. "There's not much else you can do here."

Ryan snorted. "I never had a cover. You guys mistook me for Dennis McGuire and then pawned me off as my real self when you wanted me to contact Megan. Everyone on this island knows I have a fake passport and two names," Ryan replied indignantly.

The words all came out in a rush, and he had to force himself to catch his breath. He was being benched and sent back to Fort Lauderdale, where he could resume his life and forget about being followed, shot at, and arrested on Saint Kitts.

Sam Friend handed Ryan the wallet Phillips had confiscated from him back at Fort Lauderdale International and his actual passport, retrieved from the safe aboard his boat, *Huntress*. Ryan wasn't even going to ask how they had managed that feat, knowing the CIA employed as many safe crackers and burglars as they did covert intelligence officers.

He rifled through his wallet to see if anything was missing and then shoved it into the pants pocket of his Brooks Brothers suit.

"Now you want to help?" John asked incredulously. "You weren't too keen about doing any of this when you got here."

"That was because I was being coerced," Ryan said. "But now I know the scope of the problem, and that woman is in deep trouble. Her husband is trying to poison her to death."

"Calm down, Ryan," John said. "We're doing the best we can. Our priority is to stop the sale of MCG to the Iranians and keep that tech in-house. If we can save Megan, we'll cross that bridge when we come to it."

"You're willing to put the good of the country over the life of a woman whose company is working to protect it?" Ryan asked.

"We understand where you're coming from," Sam Friend said, "but we must balance the needs of a nation—"

Ryan cut off his contrite snobbery. "Can I punch you in the face?"

Sam Friend recoiled. "Whatever for?"

"You know who needs her nation's help right now?" Ryan asked. "Megan Babcock. We just watched a video of her being loaded onto her private plane on a stretcher. Why? Aren't you guys interested in what happened to her between when she left the police station and when they stretchered her onto that plane? Obviously, someone is trying to prevent her from stopping the sale. Now, get off your high horse and send someone to help her."

"But we don't know if she needs help," Friend said. "The Babcocks are quite wealthy and could very well have a personal physician aboard that plane."

Ryan threw up his hands in frustration. "Her husband is *poisoning* her with arsenic. Those two goons followed us to the old hotel and shot at us indiscriminately. What more evidence do you need?"

"Your point is well made, Ryan, and I understand your frustration," Friend replied. "But what exactly do you want us to do about it?"

"Find out where her plane is going and send someone to check on her," Ryan replied.

"The plane is headed for Guyana," John said. "We have assets down there who can verify her safety."

"Why was that so hard to tell me?" Ryan asked. "If you'd said that from the start, we could have avoided half of this conversation."

"It's company policy to keep things compartmentalized," Friend replied.

"I hope your assets can get Megan to safety," Ryan said.

"How soon do you plan to leave on your sailing trip?" Sam Friend asked, changing the subject abruptly.

Ryan felt like he was being boxed out, but he knew the change in topic signaled the end of his protestations over the CIA's lack of care about Megan Babcock's life. He dropped wearily into the airplane's seat and leaned his head back. "Just take me home."

Spooky John shook Ryan's hand. "A pleasure working with you, Dark Horse."

"Same to you, Bowie," Ryan replied.

Moments later, the two CIA spooks were off the plane, and the Bombardier taxied out to take its place in the lineup on the runway. Inside the quiet cabin, Ryan stared thoughtfully out the window. He didn't like being sent home in the middle of an op. While he'd fought valiantly to stay out of it, Spooky John had dragged him into the middle of things, and Ryan couldn't shake the residual guilt of knowing Megan Babcock was still in immediate danger.

After nearly thirty minutes of sitting on the tarmac, the Bombardier finally lifted off into tranquil blue skies and turned northwest toward Fort Lauderdale. Ryan continued staring out the window until he felt his eyelids droop, then leaned back in his seat.

As he fell asleep, Ryan felt a small vindication at being able to return home, but he also felt there was a kettle about to boil over and that he would be the one to stop the whistling.

RYAN WAS MORE than happy to deplane in Fort Lauderdale. The aircraft dropped him outside the same building where Phillips had put him on a jet a few days ago. As soon as Ryan's feet were on the tarmac, the pilot closed the door, and the plane started rolling back toward the runway.

"So much for customer service," Ryan grumbled, glancing around at the empty parking apron. He walked over to the door with the keypad and beat on the metal, rattling the door on its hinges. No one answered, and waving at the peephole camera got no reaction, either.

"Ah, screw you, guys," Ryan muttered and pulled his burner phone from the leather valise that contained his laptop, camera, clothes, and the remainder of his ten K in cash the government had supplied him with at the beginning of the trip. Within minutes, he had a taxi headed his way, not wanting to take the time to download the Uber app and sign in.

He walked south to the end of the hangars and turned the corner, hoping a gate didn't also block this end of the drive. Ryan was unwilling to hop the fence, given that he would undoubtedly alert airport security and quite possibly shut down the entire airport just because the freaking spooks had decided to leave him hanging out to dry.

Thankfully, there was no fence blocking the road, and Ryan meandered up the sidewalk, peering into the windows of each business as he passed. The one he knew to be occupied by the fake passport-making Phillips and his mysteriously absent buddy, Grady, was empty, as he'd correctly assumed after getting no answer by beating on the service door. Unlike the surrounding business, the large window had no blinds drawn to block out the harsh western sun, and Ryan could see beyond the small front office into a spacious hangar. The hallway and room where Phillips had snapped his photo no longer existed.

Of course, it's gone—my tax dollars at work.

Ryan kept walking to the corner of the building and leaned against it in the slight shade of the overhanging roof. Dialing Emily's number, he put the phone to his ear.

"Hey, sailor. How are you?" she asked in greeting.

"I'm great. I'm back in Fort Lauderdale," Ryan said. "How soon will you be back here?"

"A day or two. Why?" she replied.

"Because I need to go to Guyana, and I want you to come with me."

"How soon are you leaving?" Emily asked.

Ryan glanced around at the empty parking lot, the parked cars baking in the hot sun. Sweat trickled down his back, soaking into his dress shirt. "As soon as I can get a plane ride down there."

"Are we going private or first class?" she asked.

"Probably economy. I can't imagine getting a flight for tomorrow will be cheap, but I'll make a few calls as soon as we're off the phone."

"Why are you going?" Emily asked.

"There's a woman who's in real trouble. I gave her my card and told her to call if she needed help—and I think she'll call soon. I also think you two would connect well. Maybe you can keep her from freaking out in the middle of a dangerous situation."

"You think it will get dangerous?"

"It already has, and there's some bigger issues at play." Ryan didn't want to elaborate on an unsecure line.

"Let me see if I can get free here," Emily said.

"I'd like you to be by my side on this, Em. We're a team, right?"

"Is she cute?" Emily asked dubiously.

"I'm not the judge of that. I'm married."

"Good answer, but who's the woman?"

"Megan Babcock."

"*The* Megan Babcock?" Emily asked a hint of excitement in her voice.

"Did that motivate you?" Ryan wanted to know.

"No," Emily said, "but it certainly spices things up."

"I think the bullets her husband's bodyguards were shooting at us were spicy enough," Ryan joked as he watched the taxi cruise along Lee Wagener Boulevard. "Hey, I need to go. My ride's here."

"I love you, Ryan. I'll call you later to see how horrible your airline reservation skills are."

"Probably as bad as you think they are," he replied before ending the call.

Stepping off the curb, Ryan ended the call, raised his arm to hail the taxi, and, once seated inside, gave the driver the address for Harbour Towne Marina.

TWENTY MINUTES LATER, Ryan paid the cabbie and walked over to the closed security gate of Harbour Towne Marina, where his sailing catamaran *Huntress* rested on the hard. He punched in his code, noticing the Jeep hadn't moved. Ryan pushed through the gate and went straight to the ladder tied to the stern of his boat.

"Glad to see you made it back safely," Conrad Shultis called from the shadows beneath his boat hull. "I figured when that guy pulled his rifle on you, you were a goner."

Ryan took his foot off the ladder and walked over to where Conrad sat, drink cold beer from a bottle. "You saw that?"

"I might have heard some commotion and peered through the fence." Conrad shrugged before lifting the beer bottle back to his lips. "I figured it wasn't my place to interfere."

"Probably best you didn't," Ryan agreed.

"Just glad to see you back. Although, I was thinking about trading up to your boat if you didn't turn up in another week."

"In that case, I'm glad I got back early," Ryan said. "Just one of those casual business meetings down in Colombia."

"I'm always down to party with a little nose candy," Conrad said.

"I'm just the middleman," Ryan joked. "I don't use my product or sell retail."

Conrad chuckled. "I always wondered how a bum like you could afford such a fancy boat."

"Hey, I'm just a working stiff," Ryan said, raising his hands good-naturedly, unfazed by the verbal jab. "I'll see if one of the dealers can come by and set you up."

"Mighty white of you," Conrad said.

"It's the least I can do for a guy who knows how to keep his mouth shut," Ryan replied, even though he had no clue where to buy cocaine nor any intention of supplying it to his marina neighbor.

Retreating to *Huntress*, Ryan climbed the ladder and entered the salon after unlocking the sliding door. In the master stateroom, he retrieved the spare keys for the Jeep and stood at a window to click the button, unlocking the Jeep's doors, then restored the spare keys. Going out the cockpit sliding door, Ryan locked it behind him. Now that he knew how nosy Conrad Shultis was, he couldn't afford to have him overhearing his upcoming phone conversations.

At the Jeep, Ryan tossed in the valise and climbed behind the wheel. His cellphone still lay on the driver's-side floorboard beside the keys where Tan Coat had thrown them after abducting Ryan from the parking lot.

Ryan started the motor and cranked up the air conditioning. Plucking his phone from the floor, he discovered its battery was almost dead, so he plugged it into the charger and then gunned the Jeep out of the parking lot. The hot sun had left Ryan parched, and one of the closest places to get a beer and a sandwich was at 3 Sons Brewing Company on U.S. 1.

It only took five minutes to get to the microbrewery and another five to have an amber ale in front of him and a platter of sirloin sliders on order. While he sipped his beer, Ryan moved away from the bar to a table in the corner of the bar as he dialed Larry Grove's cell number.

A moment later, the DIA agent was on the line.

"I need to get to Guyana," Ryan said, keeping his voice low. "Megan Babcock is in trouble."

"I saw them carry her onto the plane," Larry said. "What's it got to do with you?"

"You saw me at their villa, right? I was the guy taking pictures."

"Yeah, I saw you," Larry replied. "And it surprised me to see you there."

"You covered it well, Iceman, but seeing me there means you know I'm already involved," Ryan replied. "If you saw them carting her off, you know she's in trouble. I gave her my word that we could protect her. I want to get boots on the ground in Guyana as soon as possible."

Larry sighed. "Ryan ... you know I can't—"

"You read me into the drone op, Larry. You practically forced me to go. Now, I'm asking you to put me in place, and you're balking?"

"It's complicated ..."

"It's never as complicated as we think," Ryan protested. "Put me on the ground, and I'll be your eyes and ears, and maybe, just maybe, we can stop this MCG deal."

"Fine. There's a Gulfstream IV departing Homestead Air Reserve Base tomorrow morning at ten a.m. Be on time. Otherwise, you're flying economy with a twelve-hour layover in Puerto Rico."

"Put Emily's name on the manifest, too."

"Seriously, Ryan? You want to drag your wife into this mess?" Larry asked.

"I don't expect you to understand, Iceman. I just need to be there when Megan calls."

"I hope she doesn't call between now and then because that's the soonest I can get you there."

"What about you?" Ryan asked. "Are you in Georgetown?"

"Just keep your head down, Dark Horse."

The call clicked off as the bearded bartender brought Ryan's sliders to the table.

Ryan ate one of the sliders as the bartender retreated behind the counter, and then he dialed Emily's number as he finished chewing.

"First class?" she asked moments later.

"It's a Gulfstream IV," Ryan said.

"Whose paying for that?" she asked in amazement.

"The American taxpayers. Look, it's leaving tomorrow morning from Homestead," Ryan said. "That leaves me just enough time to drive to Tampa, pick you up, and get us to the plane."

"I've already booked a flight home tonight. In fact, I'm standing at the gate right now."

"Thank goodness," Ryan said with a sigh of relief. "I wasn't looking forward to driving all those miles."

"I get in at nine-thirty," Emily said. "I'll call you when I land."

"See you soon, hot stuff," Ryan said, ending the call. He drained the last of his beer and then went to the bar for another.

He was waiting for a refill when his cellphone rang again.

"Talk to me, Goose," Ryan said to Iceman.

"I think that's my line, dumbass," Larry replied wryly.

Ryan chuckled. "What's up?"

"Good news. When you get on the ground, I've got a guy down there named Slater Harden who will lend you a hand. He owns a company called SKY Security Services. He'll pick you up from the airport. I think you'll find them to be real friends."

"Okay. SKY. I'll keep that in mind."

"Just do me a favor and don't shoot any friendlies, Ryan. There are ghosts everywhere."

Ryan understood Larry's statement to mean there were members of other U.S. intelligence services on the ground in Guyana. "Thanks for the heads-up."

The bartender set the beer on a coaster on the poured concrete counter. Ryan thanked him as he pocketed his phone and handed over some of the CIA cash to pay his tab.

Carrying his beer back to his seat, Ryan wondered how things would play out. Guyana wasn't known for being a tourist garden spot, more like a backwater country used as a transshipment point for cocaine and illegally mined gold. The country was saddled with debt while gangs still roamed the streets. Despite the discovery of offshore oil, the profits were firmly seated in the pockets of the oil companies and the politicians who had made the deals, or so he'd read in Caribbean news journals.

While sipping his beer, Ryan pulled out his phone and typed "SKY Security Services" into the Internet search bar. The security company had a website advertising its services, such as armed patrols, cash escorts to and from banks, VIP escorts, unarmed security services, and alarm system installation and monitoring. There was no information about the owners and only a variety of stock photos besides the minimally detailed list of provided services and training. Another Internet search circled back around to the SKY website.

Ryan pocketed his phone and wondered why Larry had put him in touch with the security company. The only reasonable explanation was that SKY would have resources on the ground that Ryan would need access to himself. While Guyana allowed firearms in their country with strenuous background checks, there were a lot of illegal guns crossing the borders from Venezuela, Brazil, and, of course, the gun-friendliest country in the world, the United States. Ryan would need to source a lot of gear to mount a rescue operation for Megan Babcock, so partnering with SKY made sense in the abbreviated timeframe he knew he would have once the call from Megan came in—if it ever did.

He checked his watch. With a couple of hours to spare

before Ryan had to pick up his wife from the airport, he tried to decide what to do with himself. The time was best spent getting the lay of the land around the Babcocks' property and figuring out the best way to exfil the troubled Megan Babcock from Guyana.

With that in mind, Ryan went to the Jeep, retrieved his laptop, and then returned to his table in the restaurant, which was now filled with other patrons fresh from their workday, looking to unwind. The noisy conversations blended with the smells from the kitchen, but Ryan ignored them all as he nursed his beer and opened Google Maps.

The first thing he noticed was the jagged border lines, indicating Guyana's disputed territories with Venezuela and Suriname. Roads were scarce on the map compared to the neighboring countries of Brazil and Venezuela. Most of the roads had ferry crossings, which, in turn, meant time schedules. The two quickest ways out of the country were by airplane or boat.

Ryan ordered a third beer as he continued to study the map, spending time checking for Street Views or Photospheres that would allow him to get a better sense of the countryside, but Google hadn't gotten around to mapping the backwater country, leaving it to the locals to complete.

Frustrated by the lack of information on SKY Security and geographical knowledge from Google Maps, Ryan drained his beer, packed up his computer, and walked out to the Jeep. He got behind the wheel and started the motor, angling the A/C vents toward his chest. It seemed every day in Florida approached record heat. Even the evenings could be stifling hot.

Pulling out his cellphone again, Ryan dialed the number for Chuck Newland, Dark Water Research's chief pilot.

"To what do I owe the pleasure?" Chuck asked after they exchanged greetings.

"Where's the King Air?" Ryan asked.

"Straight to the point, as always," Chuck said. "Is this another Ryan Weller special operation?"

"I can't promise any party favors on this mission, Chuck."

"Well, since you asked, I'm in Texas. The King Air is undergoing yearly maintenance, and both engines are in tiny pieces."

"That sucks," Ryan said.

"What are you thinking about doing?" the DWR pilot asked.

"I've got an op brewing down in Guyana. I need options for a quick exfil routes."

"Then a clean plane would be best," Chuck replied. "Let me see what I can dig up. I've got a couple of pilot buddies down in South America."

"Thanks, Chuck, and, hey, I promise it will be margaritas and señoritas on the way home." He didn't know if that was true, but Chuck always liked the promise of a good time.

"Don't make promises you can't keep, Ryan."

The troubleshooter laughed. "I can tell you for sure that we're rescuing a pretty girl."

"Then I'm your man," Chuck boasted.

Ryan laughed. "I figured you would be."

"I'll get back to you and let you know what I find," Chuck said.

"Thanks. I'll talk to you soon."

Ryan ended the call and stared out the windshield, trying to gather the moving pieces into a coherent plan. Once again, he wouldn't know how things would work out until they fired the first shot, and even then, it was a dicey proposition.

CHAPTER FOURTEEN

Homestead Air Reserve Base
Homestead, Florida

The next morning, Ryan and Emily pulled up to the front gate of the air base at nine a.m.

When Ryan stopped beside the heavily armed guard in camouflage BDUs, he wondered how much fast-talking he would have to do to get through. But when Ryan presented their civilian IDs and explained they were on a plane to Guyana, the airman called the hangar and found their names were on the flight manifest.

"You'll have to park your vehicle in the lot across the road. Sergeant Flood will drive you to the airfield."

Ryan did as the guard instructed, and after having their bags searched, Sergeant Flood drove them across the base in an olive-green Humvee. The sergeant stopped at the gate to the tarmac, flashed his badge, and then drove them right out to the waiting Gulfstream IV.

An aircrewman stood beside the open door and showed Ryan and Emily where to stow their luggage in the plane's belly before taking them on board. After pointing out the two supple leather seats they would occupy for the flight, the aircrewman said, "General Hackworth and his staff will be joining us shortly."

True to his word, a staff car flying the general's flag pulled up next to the plane and disgorged a tall, fit man with salt-and-pepper hair and movie star looks. His uniform was immaculately pressed, and he had a tall ribbon rack with multiple campaign medals from hot spots around the globe.

Hackworth paused in the aisle when he saw the two civilians already on board, a momentary flicker of disgust passing over his face before he took his seat near the head of the plane. Moments later, a major and a lieutenant colonel, both carrying attaché cases, came aboard. They sat behind the general and didn't cast anything more than a glance at the two civilians at the rear of the plane.

The pilot swept through the cabin, ensuring everyone had buckled their seatbelts and all loose articles had been appropriately stowed. Then, the aircrewman buttoned up the plane and locked the door. Moments later, the jet was in the air, heading south toward Guyana.

Ryan looked down to see the reach of the Atlantic stretching to the horizon, a sight he never tired of. He was growing tired of these missions and the toll they took on his body and his relationship. He was getting older and starting to feel the physical effects of years of running and gunning.

Turning to Emily, he whispered, "What do you think about calling it quits after this?"

Her brow creased. "What do you mean?"

"You know," Ryan said, spinning a finger in the air. "All this. Let's make this the last mission and sail away forever."

"Are you sure?" Emily asked, knowing her husband

couldn't give up chasing purse snatchers and arms dealers. It was just who he was.

He turned into her a little more. "Yeah. We do this one, then disappear. We lose the phones, the GPS trackers—all of it. We sail by sextant and chart, just like the old days."

"I don't know," Emily said dubiously. "I think you'll miss your GPS chartplotter."

"Okay, probably—but what do you say?" Ryan prodded. "Let's call it quits and get out while we're both young and upright."

Emily laughed, subconsciously rubbing her belly. "I have no problem with that."

"Good." He kissed the back of her hand, glancing up to see the general glaring at them disapprovingly.

"What's up?" Ryan asked, not wanting to address him by "sir" or acknowledge his rank.

"I expect a little decorum on my plane," Hackworth stated.

"I didn't realize I wasn't allowed to show affection to my wife," Ryan said. He figured he'd never see this guy again and didn't want to spend time kissing his pompous ass. Ryan had always felt men achieved the rank of general or admiral with some hard work, but primarily by kissing ass.

The general sat on the armrest of the chair across the aisle. Hackworth had a rocks glass in his hand with two ice cubes and two fingers of what Ryan assumed was whiskey, although it was a little early for drinking. "Who are you, and what are you doing on my flight?" he asked.

"We're just a couple of civilians catching a ride to Guyana to conduct hostage rescue training for the folks down there."

The general's eyebrows rose. "Who are you working with?"

"A civilian outfit," Ryan replied.

"Civilians," the general grunted with disdain. "Should have

known you were CIA. Can't you people keep your fat fingers out of the pie?"

Ryan turned to look out the window, ignoring the general while still holding Emily's hand. He didn't care about some National Guard puke. He had other problems to worry about. But Ryan could see the man's reflection in the window, and he was just staring at Ryan as he sipped his drink.

"I was with EOD Mobile Unit 2 in Little Creek," Ryan said, meeting the general's gaze in the window and then turning to face the man in uniform. "Now, I'm a contractor for a few of the alphabet agencies."

"And you?" Hackworth asked Emily.

"Logistics and engineering," she said without missing a beat.

Hackworth eyed both of them over the rim of his glass. "We'll be running exercises with the Guyana Defense Force near the airport where we'll be landing. I expect you all to stay well clear of the area," the general said, rising to his feet. "Civilians complicate the battlefield."

"With pleasure," Ryan muttered. He wondered if the general had actually come under fire to win the honor of wearing a Combat Action Badge or if he'd just pushed the paperwork through for the medal.

Hackworth returned to his seat at the front of the Gulfstream.

"He seems nice," Emily said with a touch of sarcasm, her right hand resting on her stomach as she held her husband's hand with the other.

"The brass doesn't like civilians on their little planes," Ryan said, readjusting himself in the seat. "It's cool if retirees and their families fly on the big transports, but spooks fly on the little planes with the top brass, and you know how well the military and CIA play together."

"Not well," Emily murmured.

"Hackworth thinks we're spooks, so, naturally, he doesn't like us."

It was the last the couple said on the subject as the plane winged high above the Caribbean Sea, tracing the green islands through their arc to South America.

For Ryan, stepping off the plane into the humid air at Cheddi Jagan International Airport was a relief. The aircrewman was tending to another issue with the aircraft, so Ryan walked around to the cargo hatch and popped it open. He unceremoniously dropped duffels and packs on the tarmac until he came to his and Emily's bags, which he shouldered.

Walking past General Hackworth, who glared intently at the civilian interlopers, Ryan said to the major, "I guess you're part of the E4 mafia now. You better get the gear before old Hack starts kicking your rear."

The major's face turned beet red, and the light colonel smirked at Ryan telling the major he had to work as an enlisted man.

After clearing customs, Ryan and Emily made their way toward the front of the airport to meet with their contact from SKY Security Services.

Glancing around, Ryan observed that the reasonably new airport terminal was clean, modern, and empty.

"I guess we arrived between flights," Emily said, taking in the long rows of vacant, teal-colored seats, a display of Guyana's flag and coat of arms, and the unoccupied lines at the customs station. Their passports and visa requirements had apparently been met by someone yesterday, and there was no fee for them to get their stamp. Ryan made a mental note to thank Larry Grove the next time he talked to him.

A white SUV pulled up to the arrivals gate and stopped in front of Ryan and Emily. The decal on the side of the vehicle read "SKY SECURITY SERVICES" in bold red letters. The SUV rocked on its suspension as the driver jammed the transmission into Park and got out.

Ryan stopped short when he saw the woman who came around the front bumper. The duffel on his shoulder slipped from his grasp and fell to the ground.

"What's wrong?" Emily asked, pausing to glance between the woman beside the SUV and the stunned look on her husband's face.

"Nothing," Ryan said. "Just more ghosts."

CHAPTER FIFTEEN

Georgetown, Guyana

John Phoenix was glad to be back on what he considered to be his home turf.

South America had been his stomping grounds since the Latin American Division chief had picked him for his language abilities and the ease with which he could blend in with the local population.

Phoenix's father, an Anglo with Comanche blood, had been a hunting and fishing guide in Texas. On one of his trips into the wilderness, he had found a Colombian woman left for dead by the coyotes who'd smuggled her across the border. After nursing her back to health, the two had fallen in love, and a little Phoenix had risen from the depths after she had hauled his father's ashes.

Now, Phoenix was back in Guyana, where he'd been monitoring the rise of Venezuela's criminal elements, including the government-sanctioned actions of the Venezuelan Army. The corrupt military and other transnational cartels used Guyana as a transshipment point for illegally mined gold, human trafficking, and drugs headed for the United States or across the ocean to Africa and Europe.

Aside from their trafficking routes, the Venezuelans wanted access to Guyana's oil fields. After Guyana had discovered oil in the contested Essequibo Region, Venezuela demanded a piece of the action. International arbitration between Venezuela and Britain had awarded the Essequibo Region to Guyana in 1899, but Venezuela didn't see it that way. In fact, the current dictator, Michel Zarate, was making life difficult for Guyana by obstructing oil exploration and drilling and ratcheting up military activity along the current international boundary. Zarate wanted to reclaim almost three-quarters of Guyana's territory back to Venezuela.

Phoenix reported to his handler, Leslie Connelly, anything he'd observed by drafting more reports than any one man should have been forced to write. Yet reports were the lifeblood of the CIA, and he figured if they dried up, it would cripple the agency. He often wondered if anyone read his reports besides his handler.

Leslie Connelly had once been an active case officer in South America, and she and Phoenix had a brief but torrid affair. While she had moved on, seeking to rise to the Seventh Floor, where she would dictate missions and policy instead of getting her hands dirty running assets, Phoenix still carried a torch for her. He wondered if Nightingale's insistence in getting back to Washington, D.C., had backfired on her since the LA Division chief had given her the perilous job of being his case officer after he'd pissed off a couple of his previous handlers. Phoenix didn't know whether the posting had been intentional or just a coincidence, but it was always nice to know a beautiful, intelligent woman was on the other end of the line when he called.

Phoenix sat behind a desk in the office of SKY Security Services, one of the many contractors the CIA routinely employed to help their case officers complete their missions. While he traveled under the diplomatic cover afforded him by his black passport, it was often easier to source weapons and gear in his host country through contractors like these.

He listened through the phone receiver as Nightingale gave him an update on several projects he'd previously been working on before being redirected to Saint Kitts to deal with the Megan Babcock situation. There wasn't much to report: oil production was up, the politicians were diverting money earmarked from infrastructure projects into their pockets, and a fuel shortage denied critical operations in Guyanese hinterlands—none of which Phoenix or the CIA could do anything about unless they wanted to affect another regime change in the small country.

"One final word," Connelly said, her voice smooth and creamy. Phoenix liked to listen to her talk, and he pictured her now. Leslie had long black hair that she normally kept straight, but he loved it when she curled it. As a Black woman, she described her skin as "espresso." Phoenix missed the feeling of her body pressed against him. She had once been warm and receptive to him, but now she was aloof, cold, and distant, as she should be as his handler.

"What is it?" Phoenix asked.

"The DIA wants in on this op. They're sending a rep down to work with you."

"Shit," Phoenix muttered. "That's not good."

"You'll need to pick him up from the airport. His name is Larry Grove. You might have seen him on Saint Kitts."

"Only in pictures," Phoenix replied. "I never met him in person."

"Now's your chance," Connelly said. "Pick him up from

the airport in an hour. And your new best friend Ryan Weller should be arriving at any minute."

Phoenix huffed in disgust. His operational territory was getting more crowded by the minute, but he supposed having help from two seasoned veterans might be good. With Blake Babcock back in Guyana, Phoenix knew the action was about to heat up.

CHAPTER SIXTEEN

Cheddi Jagan International Airport
Timehri, Guyana

Leaning against the side of the SUV from SKY Security Services was Kendra Diaz, a woman from Ryan's past who he had never expected to see again. Her appearance had startled him so much that he'd dropped his duffel bag on the ground.

Ryan bent to pick up his bag, using the moment to regain his composure, then introduced his wife to Kendra. They shook hands as the two women sized one another up. Ryan had never told Emily about his romantic interlude with the former cartel sicario, but she must have sensed it.

Kendra Diaz's real name was Catalina Tinoco, but when she became a sicario for the Aztlán Cartel, she'd changed it to Kendra Diaz to protect herself and her family. She was a beautiful Mexican woman with silky black hair and soulful brown eyes—good with a gun but even deadlier with a knife.

Not that long ago, Kendra had been sent by the Aztlán Cartel to kill him, attacking Ryan aboard his sailboat as he was trying to leave the island of Trinidad. Ryan had thrown her overboard during the mad scramble and thought she had drowned when he was unable to locate her body. Soon after, the Venezuelan secret police had imprisoned Ryan on Margarita Island. Kendra had come to his rescue, helping Ryan escape from prison in exchange for assisting Kendra to free her sister from the clutches of the murderous leader of the cartel, Jose Luis Orozco. After an extended gun battle that destroyed the cartel's leadership, Ryan had given Kendra an old fishing trawler they had used to smuggle drugs into Mexico to draw Orozco out of hiding. Kendra and her sister had disappeared over the horizon, and Ryan had hoped to never see them again.

But there Kendra stood, squaring off with Emily like two women about to catfight in the backwater country of Guyana. Ryan didn't know exactly how to feel about working with Kendra again or introducing his wife to a woman he had slept with in the past. Kendra had been a thorn in his side from day one, even when they'd worked together to save Yasmine, and the sex had been more of a weaponized courtesy than the joining of two lovers. It troubled Ryan that Larry Grove had sent him to Kendra's company, and he wondered how much Iceman knew about his prior dealings with the former sicario.

If this is your idea of a joke, Larry, it ain't funny.

To break up the standoff between the two women, Ryan said, "*You're* SKY Security?"

"The 'K' is for Kendra," she said proudly, with a smile of satisfaction. "Yasmine fell for a guy named Slater after we arrived in Guyana. We needed a way to make money, so we started a security business that became quite lucrative. If you hadn't guessed already, the word 'SKY' is a combination of our initials."

"Yeah, I figured that one out," Ryan said.

After Ryan placed the bags in the storage compartment of the SUV and he and Emily were seated inside, he asked, "How is Yasmine?"

"She's good. You'll see her and the kid in a few minutes."

It didn't take them long to reach a small compound along the Demerara River in a little settlement called Land of Canaan. Kendra pressed a remote she kept on the sun visor, and the gate rolled back. Once through, the gate closed automatically behind them.

The grounds were well-kept, with small flower beds and several rows of fruit trees bearing everything from avocados to apples. Two modest houses were set back from the river on stilts, one on each side of a man-made canal where the old trawler, F/V *Kaytlyn*, rested against a small dock alongside a smaller wooden boat with a high-horsepower outboard strapped to the stern. Another building housed the security office, with a spacious garage for vehicles, gear, and weapons lockers.

Kendra parked by a small house on the west side of the canal. "This is my place. You'll bunk here, and I'll stay with Slater and Yasmine."

Upstairs, she showed them around the simple one-bedroom layout with an attached bathroom and kitchen.

"Don't worry," Kendra said. "I washed the sheets, and there are fresh towels in the bathroom. Coffee is in the cabinet above the maker, and the fridge is stocked. Let me know if you need anything else, and I'll get it for you. Once you're settled in, we'll talk operational strategy."

Emily watched out the window as Kendra walked across the compound toward the office building. "She doesn't seem to like you very much."

"We had our share of difficulties," Ryan replied.

"Did you love her and leave her?" Emily asked pointedly.

"She tried to kill me on several occasions."

"Was that before or after you slept with her?"

"Look," Ryan said, straightening from where he unpacked his bag. "I asked you to come along so you could help, not give me grief about a woman from my past. Whatever happened back then doesn't matter now. It's water under the bridge, and we have work to do."

"Did you ask for her help?"

"Em, I had no idea she was even here. The last time I saw her, she and her sister were sailing away on that boat out there, and I went on to marry you. If you want to bitch someone out, call Larry Grove and talk to him. He told me we'd be working with SKY, but he left out the part about who owned the company."

"And if you would have known?" Emily asked, crossing her arms.

"I'd still be here. Megan Babcock needs our help, no matter who's on the team."

"Okay. I'll give you that."

"Now, can we put the cattiness behind us and get started on this op?" Ryan asked.

"What if Megan doesn't call?" Emily asked.

"We still need to stop the sale of MCG to the Iranians, but I don't know how we're going to do that. I'm a hammer, not a diplomat."

Emily glanced out the window again as they both heard the sound of a truck driving through the gate into the compound. Moments later, she said, "Looks like you don't have to be in charge. Iceman is here, and so is some other guy."

Ryan peered out the window and groaned.

"What?" she asked.

"The other dude is the spook I met on Saint Kitts. I call him Jim-John Bowie." He had to explain the name and the significance of it to Emily, who just nodded, then he added, "I guess we better go see what the spook wants."

"Does that mean Kendra is a spook?" Emily asked.

Ryan shrugged. "Not as far as I know. I bet she's a contractor like me."

"Was she a spook when you worked together in Mexico?"

"She was a desperate woman willing to do whatever it took to save her sister, including breaking me out of prison, so maybe you should thank her for that. Otherwise, I might still be rotting away on Margarita Island instead of being your boy toy."

Emily put her arms around her husband's neck and kissed him. "Well, I do like my boy toy. Maybe I will thank her." She pecked him on the lips again and released him.

Ryan had the sudden urge to spirit Emily back to Fort Lauderdale so they could sail away together. He didn't owe Megan Babcock anything. He'd never met her until a few days ago and wasn't beholden to anyone to save her. For a long moment, Ryan considered leaving her to flap in the wind, but his subconscious wouldn't let him sleep at night, knowing he hadn't done everything possible to save her from dying a miserable death at her husband's hand. And for what—treason, money, love?

What does Blake Babcock desire so much that he's willing to kill an innocent woman?

No, Ryan decided. He couldn't just walk away.

The couple strolled hand in hand across the grass to the security office. Inside, they found the place crowded. Not only were Kendra, Larry Grove, and Spooky John in attendance, but Slater and Yasmine Harden had also joined them.

"How's the kid?" Ryan asked after hugging Yasmine.

"He's growing up." She patted her smooth belly. "We have another one on the way. I'm two months along."

"Congrats," Ryan said.

After dispensing with the pleasantries and introducing everyone, the group settled down to business.

"Have you heard from Megan?" John asked Ryan.

Ryan picked up the desk phone and dialed his answering service for the third time that day. Hanging up, he said, "Nothing yet."

"Can we take her against her will?" Larry asked. "If her husband is trying to kill her, shouldn't we do something about it?"

"It's a terrible situation," John said. "I agree we should move. If we can isolate her from Blake and get her off the pills, she'll have a shot at a decent life."

"But we still have to deal with Blake," Ryan said.

"I say we shoot the bastard when we scoop up his wife," John said, changing his stance from the last time he and Ryan had talked on the plane on Saint Kitts.

"I know the CIA has a long history of operating like that in Latin America," Larry said, "but the rest of us have to operate by a different playbook."

"While that's true, I just don't have a problem putting a treasonous bastard in the grave," John replied.

"We work here," Yasmine cut in. "SKY Security Services has a reputation to protect. We don't go around indiscriminately killing people."

"I want to recon the Babcocks' place and devise a rescue plan," Ryan said.

"The house is part of the MCG shipyard," John said. "So, there are plenty of guards and roving patrols."

"It's a three-hour drive to New Amsterdam," Kendra said. "When I heard we were helping on this op, I pulled some preliminary research. There's not much on open source, but you can get an idea of the compound layout from Google Maps. It sits on the confluence of the Canje and Berbice Rivers."

"The drive should give us plenty of time to look at the photos. How soon do we leave?" Ryan asked.

Slater spoke up for the first time. "We can run a two-truck convoy down there this evening and be ready to recon at first light tomorrow. I've got trucks and gear ready to go."

"What are your qualifications?" Ryan asked. Slater was over six feet tall and looked more like a California surf bum than an operator, but Ryan knew they came in all shapes and sizes.

"I was in the Air Force," Slater replied but didn't elaborate.

Ryan grunted.

Slater shrugged and pulled his blond hair into a man bun.

Yasmine saw the conflict brewing between Ryan and her husband and intervened by saying, "Slater was a PJ. He knows what he's doing."

"Cool," Ryan said. He had a new glimmer of respect for the man now that he knew he hadn't been a mechanic. While there was absolutely nothing wrong with just being a mechanic in the military, it was a far cry from the hard work and determination it took to become a pararescue specialist. Like Ryan and all the other men who had been part of special operations, Slater had been through the grinder and come out the other side with a skill set second to none when it came to waging war.

In the workshop, they inspected the gear packages Slater had prepared. There were chest rigs with armor plating and plenty of pockets for spare mags, medical kits, and personal items. Glock 17 pistols and B&T APC9-SD pistol caliber carbines, or PCC, with integrated suppressors rounded out the weapons loadout. Ryan had never shot one of the PCCs, but he knew the B&Ts were reliable and, according to Kendra, they could operate using B&T, Glock, or SIG Sauer P320 magazines, doubling the usefulness of the mags they would be carrying. The SKY team had loaded all the seventeen- and forty-round Glock magazines with hollow points.

Kendra had also put aside a Springfield M1A Loaded sniper rifle and a couple of SVDM Dragunov rifles. While SKY Security typically carried AK-74s while on patrol, they had opted for suppressed weapons that everyone was familiar with.

The first item Ryan picked was a Gerber folding knife. He felt naked without a weapon of some kind, and the knife was the easiest option for concealed carry.

"All right, let's saddle up and get moving," Ryan urged once everyone had their kit. He wanted to get to New Amsterdam so he could lay eyes on the house and grounds around MCG Marine Defense before dark.

The six-person team didn't take long to load up and head across the country. The Amazonian rainforest basin dominated the interior of Guyana. With over eighty-seven percent of the country covered by heavy forest, experts considered the country one of the wildest places on earth. Most of the roads were still simple dirt tracks, nearly impassable after rainfall, but paved roads ran between the major cities. Ryan and his team took full advantage of them, driving northeast to Georgetown and then arcing along the eastern curve of the Atlantic coast before crossing the Berbice River Bridge.

Yasmine had made reservations at a rental house near the MCG compound, and the group checked in before doing anything else. After unloading their gear and clothing duffels, the team dispersed to settle housekeeping chores and survey their surroundings. Emily and Kendra seemed to have buried the hatchet as they went to buy groceries while Ryan and Spooky John took a walk.

"So, what do your friends call you?" Ryan asked as they headed up the street toward the MCG compound.

"I told you. People call me John."

Ryan chuckled.

"What's so funny?"

"You didn't say you had friends," Ryan replied. "Most people would say, 'My friends call me John.'"

"In my business, friends are hard to come by, and I have trust issues."

"In your line of work, I suppose you do."

"And you don't have trust issues?" John asked.

"I'm married. My wife has enough trust issues for the both of us."

John laughed. "I bet she likes that joke."

"Probably not. So, what's your last name, John?"

Without missing a beat, John said, "In the agency, we like to use first names. Supposedly, it makes us harder to identify." He pointed toward the gated entrance to the MCG facility. "I see two guards armed with AKs. Probably have a sidearm, too."

The gatehouse was more of an open-air building with a central station for the guard booth. On the far side of the entry and exit gates, concrete pillars stretched up to a metal roof that covered the whole affair. Each gate was a sturdy wrought-iron barricade that had to be rolled out of the way to allow a vehicle to pass.

Ryan saw no way to easily ram the gate and knew it would have to be destroyed by explosives for the team to gain entry, but doing so would negate the stealthy nature of their mission and needlessly destroy the property of an industry that was obviously helping the people of Guyana struggle out of poverty by providing jobs and assisting with educational opportunities for the less fortunate.

Unless the Iranians got their hands on the company, and then they'd fold tent and head for the desert.

Ryan wondered if purchasing MCG was part of the Iranian's plan to ratchet up tension between themselves and the rest of the free world. They were already harassing U.S. Navy warships in the Persian Gulf and trying to seize oil tankers in the Straits of Hormuz. In response, the Navy had sent a squadron of their newest F-35 joint strike fighters and a destroyer to deter further incidents. Ryan knew the U.S.'s attempts weren't likely to dissuade the determined aggressors. All the attention was probably emboldening Reza Soroush to continue his efforts, which was also probably one of the reasons Iran wanted to get their hands on MCG's tech. But whatever the Iranians' ambitions were, they weren't good for the rest of the world.

"Mangrove swamps surround the compound except for the entrance here, the big shipping quay on the Berbice River, and a smaller dock on the Canje," John said. "Tomorrow, we can send teams to scout the various entrances, but however we get in, the front gate will probably be the easiest way out."

"If we're driving, yes," Ryan said. "But we could always escape by boat from the docks."

John nodded. "We'll need a fast boat."

"A third option would be to dust off in a helicopter," Ryan concluded.

John rubbed his chin thoughtfully. "Not a bad idea. You could land in the compound near the action."

Ryan pointed toward a nearby bridge over the Canje River. "Maybe we can get a look at the docks from there."

The two men headed for the bridge, taking a side street past a home goods store and through a residential neighborhood. Fishermen had beached their brightly painted wooden boats beneath the bridge beside the thick abutments that jutted up from the water. Most had outboards tilted up to protect the props from the mud and rocks, while others were powered with a simple set of oars.

A river channel ran under the bridge, carefully marked by

directional buoys placed by MCG and a local sugar plantation farther upriver, who had dredged it in a joint operation to expand the functionality of the waterway.

Tall trees and bushes grew along the Canje except under the bridge at the boat landing. Small grassy islands divided the river on either side of the deeper channel. A breeze carried the tang of salt air along with rotting fish and the stench of mud flats uncovered at low tide. Ryan breathed deeply, inhaling the bouquet as if it was life-giving.

"What the hell is the matter with you?" John asked. "This place stinks."

"Smells like home," Ryan replied.

"Where did you grow up? A garbage dump?"

Ryan chuckled. "Coastal North Carolina. What about you?"

"Texas," John let slip. Realizing his mistake, he gritted his teeth. "You got a way of twisting things around, Weller. I'm not sure I like hanging out with you."

"Afraid you might give up all your secrets, Jim-John Bowie?"

John laughed. "I've been called a lot of things, but never Jim-John."

"If I were to shake your hand, you would introduce yourself as Mister ...?"

"Bowie. Jim-John Bowie."

"Let's forget the bridge," Ryan said. "Maybe one of those fishermen will take us for a ride."

Ryan negotiated a ride in a bright blue boat in exchange for a U.S. twenty-dollar bill. He and John helped push the little vessel into the water as the boat's owner, a bearded teenager named Orin, who wore nothing but surf shorts to showcase his washboard abs, jerked the rope on the motor's pull start. The engine chugged to life, and they were soon puttering up the river.

Orin steered toward the west bank.

"Can you take us to the other side?" Ryan asked. He wanted a better look at MCG's dockyards and defenses.

The driver shook his head. "They don't like us to get close. They'll send a security patrol out to harass us if we do."

Ryan tried not to stare as they passed the MCG docks, but his eyes were drawn to the large boathouse at the water's edge with a steel roll-up door that blocked their view of the inside. Beside another dock was a 6.5-meter rigid hull inflatable center console boat, and behind it was a full cabin SAFE Boats International Defender with triple Yamaha outboards. Ryan had driven a boat similar to it many times, as DWR used one as a runabout when conducting port construction surveys or maritime salvage operations. He didn't see any machine guns on the boats, but he was willing to bet another twenty-dollar bill that there were firearms on board or close at hand to keep away intruders.

Orin kept the throttle steady as they passed out of the mouth of the Canje and turned east to follow the mangrove coastline. The river water looked like chocolate milk, and giant freighters swung at anchor both up- and downstream. Unlike modern container ports, these mighty ships were still loaded and unloaded by hand, with gangs of laborers swarming the decks and holds.

Once around the bend, they continued east along the Berbice River, swinging wide to avoid MCG's massive concrete shipping quay equipped with tower cranes and large warehouses. Gaspar had built an impressive compound, with railroad tracks leading out of the largest warehouse to the edge of the quay.

"Take us up to the CGX terminal," John instructed after they'd slowly motored past the sprawling facility.

The young Guyanese increased power to the motor and

shot them upriver. "Not much there," Orin called over the wind. "The laydown yard is just a dirt lot."

Ryan figured John would report back to his handler on whatever they saw. It seemed the CIA kept tabs on just about everything.

Once they had passed under the Berbice Bridge, Orin slowed so they could get a good look at the new construction. A crew was building a large dock that extended from the riprap shoreline. It was hard to envision, but eventually, this would be a deep-water port capable of handling millions of barrels of oil and tons of agricultural products. Guyana was about to join the cargo container era.

John circled his finger above his head, telling Orin to take them back to shore. The teenager turned the little boat in a wide circle, and they zipped through the muddy water back toward their starting point.

As they passed the MCG docks again, Ryan remembered that he needed to call Chuck Newland to ask if he'd found them a plane and a pilot.

Ryan smiled to himself as a plan started to form in his mind.

CHAPTER SEVENTEEN

Back at the Airbnb, Ryan used his satphone to call Chuck Newland. "Did you find me a plane?"

"Turns out I know a lot of guys down there. Most of them are contractors for our government in some shape or form," Chuck replied. "So, whatever you want, we can get."

"A helicopter?" Ryan asked.

"No problem."

"What about a float plane?" Ryan asked.

"Shouldn't be a problem, either. As a matter of fact, there are a lot of those in Guyana because of all the rivers."

"Line me up one of each for a flight out of New Amsterdam," Ryan said. "My timeline is flexible right now. We're still working out the details."

"Keep me posted," Chuck replied.

After a few more pleasantries, Ryan ended the call and then dialed another number.

Greg Olsen answered after three rings. "What's up, my wayward brother?"

"You guys still working that salvage job near Dominica?"

"Just wrapping things up. Why? Are you going to get off your lazy ass and join us?"

"No. I need Scott and TJ for a quick op. And I was hoping I could get you to bring *Dark Ocean* down to Guyana. Things are moving quickly, and we might need some of your assets."

"You're in luck. I just happened to be headed that way to check out a job. Big things are brewing down there. Guyana's the new offshore oil frontier."

"Cool," Ryan said. "How soon can you get my guys down here?"

"*Your* guys?" Greg clarified.

"You know—the team. I've got five good shooters already, but I could use their expertise."

"I'll check flights. Who's paying for this excursion of yours?"

"People with very deep pockets," Ryan replied. While no one had talked about who would foot the bill for Megan Babcock's rescue, Ryan figured the CIA had contracted with SKY Security, so he ought to be able to submit the bill to them. If not, he could arrange something with Megan if she agreed to be rescued.

"I like the sound of that," Greg said. "I'll get my secretary on it and call you later."

Ryan knew Greg meant his wife, Shelly, and he figured she'd whack Greg in the back of the head for calling her his secretary. After chuckling, Ryan said, "Next day or two would be good. They can bring their own kit if they come in on a private flight."

"Roger that. Want to give me a heads-up about what's going on?"

"Wish I could, boss, but Big Brother has *big* ears."

"I understand," Greg said. "I'll talk to you later."

Ryan ended the call and headed back into the house,

happy he had team members on the way that he could trust with his life. The current team consisted of both known and unknown elements when it came to their reactions under fire. If he was going into a dangerous situation, Ryan wanted men who had his back, no matter what.

Larry Grove had Ryan's back and had since they'd worked together in the Navy. Kendra had proven untrustworthy in the past. He didn't know if she was working with him or still wanted to kill him. Jim-John Bowie was a spook. Nothing he said could be taken as gospel. Ryan had never worked with Slater, so he was an unknown quantity despite his military training. And Emily was a private investigator, more at home shooting photographs with a camera than shooting people with a gun.

Ryan told the group gathered in the Airbnb's kitchen about the availability of aviation assets and the pending arrival of two more team members.

"Do we even know where Megan Babcock is?" Emily asked.

"That's what we'll find out tomorrow," Ryan replied.

"What if she's not at the house in the compound?" Emily pressed.

"Then we wait for her to call," Ryan replied.

"And if she doesn't?" John asked.

"Then we go ahead with whatever plan you've cooked up to stop the sale of MCG," Ryan stated.

John seemed to ponder that for a moment as he rubbed his chin.

"You do have a plan to stop the sale, right?" Larry Grove asked.

"Well, I was hoping the State Department would have put pressure on Gaspar Industries, and things would have stalled by now, but ..." John trailed off, leaving the others to wonder what he was about to say next.

"I'd like to know what the Iranians have on Babcock to force him to sell. If State can't sway him, they must be blackmailing him somehow," Larry said.

"Or he decided just to take the money and run," Ryan added. "He owns seventy percent of Gaspar Industries. Maybe he's just liquidating assets."

"But why?" Larry persisted. "Babcock could just sit back and let the money roll in. Gaspar is a billion-dollar-a-year corporation, and the U.S. military would pay him handsomely for MCG's tech."

"The only one who can answer those questions is Babcock himself," Ryan stated.

"I wonder if Megan had a prenup," Emily pondered aloud. "Maybe her husband is in violation of it by selling out."

"A prenuptial agreement wouldn't mean anything since she signed over a majority stake," John countered.

Ryan's phone beeped, indicating he had a message. He checked the screen to see a text message from Greg informing him that Scott and TJ were en route aboard a private plane. The two DWR assets would land at New Amsterdam Airport in two hours.

After glancing at his watch, Ryan texted back that he would be there to pick them up.

"Is that Megan?" John asked.

"No. I need to go to the airport and pick up our additional shooters. Kendra, can we get your sister to bring us two more sets of kit if they can't bring their own?"

"I guess, but we're running low. This mission is taxing our resources."

"I thought you were tied in with the CIA? Aren't they funding your venture?" Ryan asked, thinking SKY should have unlimited resources courtesy of the Company's backing.

"We're a private company," Kendra replied. "We only have

what we've been able to purchase for ourselves as our business grows."

"You should get your people to loosen the purse strings a little, John," Ryan admonished.

The CIA officer shrugged. "Not my call."

"Can we get the gear or not?" Ryan asked Kendra point-blank.

"I'll see what Yasmine can come up with."

Kendra stepped away to make the call.

Ryan consulted his phone to see how far the airport was from their makeshift headquarters. According to Google Maps, the only route to the airfield ran through town along Canje Road, and then he'd have to turn onto a dirt road at Rose Hall Estate, a large sugar plantation. Except for Gaspar Industries, the sugar industry was the largest employer in the region, with plantations lining both sides of the Berbice River.

When Kendra returned to the room, Ryan asked her for the keys to the SUV. She glanced at Emily, then volunteered to drive Ryan to the airport. Emily nodded her approval, allowing her husband to travel alone with his former lover.

Ryan could read the signals flashing across the room and figured everyone else could, too. The two women were still standoffish but seemed to have come to an understanding during their time shopping, which Ryan knew was always a therapeutic bonding experience for women.

On the way to the airfield, Kendra glanced over at Ryan. "I like your wife. She's nice."

"Thanks. Kinda of why I married her. That, and she's hot."

Kendra smiled. "I never got a chance to thank you for helping Yasmine and me after everything that happened in Mexico. I'm glad we got out safely."

Ryan nodded.

"I know we didn't always see eye to eye in the past. I used you as bait to draw out Orozco, and I'm sorry. I was desperate."

"No worries," Ryan replied, preferring not to think about how Kendra had knocked him out and strapped him to a pallet of cocaine laced with claymore mines.

"I know you never thought you'd see me again, but I'm glad we crossed paths."

"What do you want, Kendra?" Ryan asked. "You want to stop the truck right here and go at it for old times' sake, or just shut the hell up and drive? Working with you is not my idea of a good time, but we've got a job to do."

Kendra gripped the wheel with both hands, knuckles white, her mouth set in a tight, angry pucker.

"I'm sorry," she said.

"I'm not," Ryan replied. "I gave you that boat so you'd go away."

"I said I was sorry."

Ryan crossed his arms and stared out the window at the passing buildings and houses. Eventually, the town gave way to sugarcane fields and the Rose Hall Estate. The smell of burning vegetation filled the air, and columns of black smoke rose into the sky. Ryan knew it was standard operating procedure to burn off the dead leaves before harvesting the sugarcane, leaving only the bare stalks behind. In the Everglades, they called the ash that fell from the sky "Black Snow," which caused all manner of health problems for the people living nearby.

They crossed over a canal lined with small barges used to bring sugarcane in from the fields to the factory on the edge of the river. Kendra turned onto a narrow dirt road that ran on a levy between two canals and eventually ended at the airstrip, a three-thousand-foot scar of cracked and faded concrete in the otherwise green earth. Kendra had to drive onto the runway to get to the small hangar near the middle of the strip. Ryan saw the approaching plane bearing in on them, wheels down, landing lights on, and ordered her to haul ass.

Kendra arrived at the hangar just as the Dornier 228 touched down. The pilot only needed a short stretch of the runway to bring his aircraft to a stop. He taxied over to the hangar and throttled the engines down to idle. The side door opened, and the airstairs fell into place.

Ryan got out of the SUV and leaned against the vehicle's hood, crossing his arms as his two friends stepped onto the tarmac. They carried two large black backpacks on their shoulders and a black Pelican case between them. Scott Gregory was six feet, three inches of muscle, and tattoos. He had thick blond hair and a burgeoning beard to accompany his shaggy mustache. TJ Cab was shorter at five eight, with spiky black hair and hard blue eyes. Both men had become hardened warriors in the Navy, Scott as a SEAL and TJ in the Maritime Expeditionary Security Force.

As the two men approached, Kendra shifted the vehicle into Reverse and let her foot off the brake. Ryan's leaning post drifted backward, and he suddenly lost his balance, scrambling to catch himself before he toppled over. Both his friends laughed so hard they dropped the Pelican case.

"Get in the damned truck," Ryan growled, not enjoying Kendra making a fool of him. Although, he could understand her reasons for screwing with him since he'd been such an asshole to her on the ride over. He owed her an apology, which he never gave.

Scott and TJ picked up the Pelican case, tossed it into the back of the SUV with their backpacks, and climbed into the back seat. Ryan took his place in the passenger seat as the Dornier started its takeoff roll. Kendra had to wait until the plane was back in the air before driving away from the hangar.

By the time they arrived back at the rental house, Ryan could see that TJ had lust in his eyes for Kendra. He pulled the man aside.

"She's a cobra, dude," Ryan warned. "You can't let your guard down around her."

"How do you know her? It seems like there's some history there," TJ said.

Ryan gave his friend an abbreviated version of his tumultuous relationship with the former sicario, ending with, "She tried to kill me before we ended up working together to rescue her sister. You can't trust her."

TJ nodded thoughtfully. "I'll take it under advisement."

"You do what you want, but don't say I didn't warn you," Ryan said. "And don't mix business with pleasure until we're done here."

"Yes, sir!" TJ snapped off a mock salute.

Back in the Airbnb's living room, the team gathered for a dinner of fish, rice, and vegetables that Emily and Slater had cooked while Ryan and Kendra had been at the airport. TJ immediately started nosing around Kendra, and Ryan knew his feelings on the subject had been ignored. He doubted TJ would want anything to do with Kendra after he got a taste of her hot-and-cold personality, but to Ryan's surprise, the two of them hit it off and talked freely. It was the most relaxed Ryan had ever seen Kendra.

Ryan couldn't decide if he was jealous of TJ for being the object of Kendra's attention or angry at his friend for not heeding his advice. In the end, he decided to do what he did best with his feelings: stuff them deep down inside, and Charlie Mike—continue mission.

There were bigger stakes at play than his bruised ego.

CHAPTER EIGHTEEN

Ocean Trakker
Atlantic Ocean

Megan Babcock felt like she was swimming through a sea of black as she rose to consciousness.

Whatever drug she'd been given had kept her severely disoriented, and she didn't know how long she'd been comatose. Despite all the rest her body had gotten while under sedation, her mind was groggy, and her limbs lethargic.

As her eyes fluttered, Megan became aware of a loud beeping sound that seemed to pierce her eardrums. She wanted nothing more than to relax back into sleep, but the beeping persisted, and Megan quickly became annoyed with it.

"Karen," she mumbled. "Turn off the alarm clock."

Her assistant never responded, and as the beeping continued, Megan lifted her arm to cover her eyes from the harsh light blazing from overhead. The movement of her arm brought with it a sudden stabbing pain in the crook of her elbow. Wincing from the intensity of the sharp prick, Megan held her arm straight up and examined the intravenous needle that had been inserted into her vein and taped in place against her skin. Her eyes traced the tubing from the IV needle to the machine dangling from a hook on the wall above her head.

Examining the machine more closely, Megan saw it emitted the sharp beeping sound that was assaulting her senses and warning the fluid in the IV bag had run dry. She counted four empty bags hanging from the hooks on the machine and wondered why she'd been kept under sedation.

What's happening? Why am I here?

The last thing Megan clearly remembered was her husband, Blake, shoving her backward after she'd confronted him about the sale of MCG Marine Defense in their villa on Saint Kitts. After falling to the floor, Megan had screamed hysterically at Blake, and he'd slapped her hard enough across the face to bloody her mouth. Then, a stranger had rushed into the room, and he'd shoved a hypodermic needle into her arm.

Involuntarily, Megan reached to rub her shoulder where he'd pricked her skin. Her fingertips traced a tiny bump on her arm, and she contorted her body so she could see the red welt left by the puncture of the needle. The more she touched it, the more the spot itched.

Above her, the IV machine continued to beep incessantly with a shrillness that hurt her brain. Megan blinked her eyes to adjust to the light flooding the room from the single light bulb trapped in a metal cage overhead. She could smell diesel fuel and feel the throb of an engine reverberating through the steel hull plates. The tiny bunk she rested upon was nothing more than a thin mattress pad covered with a sheet and a scratchy wool blanket thrown over her body.

Sitting up, Megan found she still wore the plum-colored yoga pants, white sports bra, and tank top she'd put on after returning to the villa. And there was a new smell of sweat and fear emanating from her body. Lifting her right arm, she sniffed her armpit and recoiled in horror.

Glancing around the tiny steel room, Megan realized it wasn't the luxurious cabin of her yacht or the balconied stateroom of a cruise ship. However, she knew she was on an ocean-going vessel of some kind and that her room lacked any sort of luxury. The only amenity other than the bunk was a combination stainless steel sink and toilet. She'd seen something similar to it in a popular streaming show about women in prison and wondered if she was now in prison. She stood on wobbly legs and started punching buttons on the IV machine, trying to get it to stop beeping.

Megan pressed all the buttons at least twice, but the machine kept wailing its displeasure at not being fed fluid from the bag. Completely enraged, Megan lifted the heavy machine off the wall hook and slammed it into the steel deck of her little cell. The IV machine chirped, and the beeping faded, but after a heavenly moment of silence, it began to wail again.

Drawing back her foot to kick the machine, Megan realized just in time that kicking it would only injure her bare toes. Her gaze fell on the black cord stretching from the machine to the wall socket, and Megan snatched it from the wall. Instantly, the beeping stopped, and the machine became an inert object once again.

Megan's next problem was that she was still attached to the IV machine via the clear, plastic tubing. Peeling back the tape, she winced as it ripped out the hairs on her arm. She pulled the needle from her vein and threw it on the floor beside the IV machine.

Free of her tail, Megan staggered to the only door in the tiny room. She grabbed the long lever to disengage the locking dogs on the hatch and gave it a mighty tug. At first, she thought the door lever was stuck, so she tugged on it with all her might, but no amount of effort would make the lever budge.

Megan turned her back to the thick metal bulkhead and slid down to the floor. She put her head in her hands and tried to reason out the purpose of her captivity. She was a billionaire and the owner of one of the most influential companies on the planet—at least, she had been before Blake had conned her into signing over seventy percent of Daddy's company. She wished her father was with her now to impart some wisdom. Megan had wasted precious years of her life not heeding her father's advice, but he had stood beside her through thick and thin, dutifully coughing up the money she demanded to live her ostentatious lifestyle.

As Megan thought about the events of the past few days, she realized she no longer had a headache throbbing just beneath her temples like she usually did. Her mind felt clearer than it had in years. She wondered if Ryan Weller had been right about the pills. He'd been right about a lot of the unpleasant things in her life.

A loud thud resounded through the ship, and Megan scrambled back to the bunk, terrified and paranoid that someone was coming for her. She pulled the blanket up over her trembling body and lay huddled beneath it, waiting for Blake or the stranger with the hypodermic needle to come through the door, but nothing happened.

Megan hid beneath the blanket for a long time and eventually drifted off to sleep. Terrifying visions of Blake and

Karen attacking her with knives and forcing her to sign over the rest of the company filled her dreams. Blake's head grew overly large as he laughed, almost like a cartoon.

Suddenly, Blake was above her in a puppet booth. Strings ran from his fingers down to each of her joints, and he made her dance and wave like a simple marionette. Megan even wore a court jester's hat while Blake told rude and uncouth jokes as he manipulated her mouth on the small stage. The audience roared with laughter with each joke, and when she saw they were tossing money onto the stage, Megan realized she was naked. Each time she tried to cover herself up, Blake would pull a string and jerk her hands away to expose her naked body to the audience, who now leered at her with gleaming wolf's teeth in their salivating mouths.

The crowd started to move in on Megan, but Blake held her in place with the strings, not caring that the men were attacking her, groping her, and forcing her to the ground.

As the hungry wolves climbed on top of her, Megan startled awake with a scream, her body bathed in a cold sweat.

She lay on the bunk, panting and crying, trying to erase the last vestiges of the dream from her mind. But the more she tried to force the memories away, the more vivid they became, even in her waking state.

Without warning, the blanket flew off her body, and the wolves came after her again. Except it wasn't the men from Megan's dream with gleaming teeth, but a hefty woman leaning over her and smacking her across the face.

Megan recoiled farther into the corner of the bunk, pressing her body against the cool steel of the bulkhead in an attempt to escape the villainous-looking woman in a pair of green scrubs. The woman had short blonde hair and a ruddy complexion that suggested to Megan that she was of German descent.

"You have been a naughty girl," the nurse said, her heavily accented English proving Megan's theory to be correct. "You have broken my machine." She grabbed Megan by the arm and tried to drag her across the bunk as she produced a hypodermic needle from her pocket. "It is time for you to go back to sleep."

"No!" Megan screamed and lashed out with her foot, striking the woman in the wrist. The needle flew from the nurse's hand and rolled across the deck.

Megan brought her foot back again and drove it toward the woman's head with every ounce of strength she could muster. At the last second, the nurse ducked, and Megan's foot whistled just past the woman's ear.

The nurse trapped her leg by wrapping a muscular arm around it, pinching it between her shoulder and neck, and began to pull Megan from the bunk.

With her free leg, Megan kicked the woman in the stomach, doubling her over and driving the air from the woman's lungs. However, the nurse retained her grip and dragged Megan off the bunk. Megan landed hard on the deck, banging the back of her head against the steel, and for a moment, she saw stars bursting before her eyes.

As the nurse tried to regain her breath, her grip loosened on Megan's leg, and Megan kicked herself free of the woman's grasp. The prisoner drew back both feet and thrust them forward in one powerful kick that knocked her German assailant off her feet. Scrambling forward, Megan tried to grab the hypodermic needle from where it had landed near the combination toilet and sink.

Before she could reach it, the nurse latched onto Megan's ankle and jerked her backward. Lashing out with everything she had left, Megan fought to free herself from the woman's tenuous hold. Her next kick caught the woman in the chin and snapped her head back.

Free again, Megan crawled toward the needle and grasped it in her right hand. She used her teeth to tear the cap free and then spun toward the woman who had been trying to put her back to sleep. Megan pounced, trying to shove the needle into the woman's arm, but the sturdy nurse fought back, and the two women struggled for control of the powerful sedative inside the hypodermic.

Mustering all her reserves, Megan shoved the woman's arm aside and buried the needle in her neck, pressing the plunger home. Wide-eyed, the woman's hand reached for the needle protruding from her skin and managed to pull it free, but it was too late. The drug had flooded her system, and her body fell limp with sleep.

Breathing hard, Megan sat back on her butt, propping herself up with her arms as she stared at her attacker. After a few moments, Megan reached out with her foot and gingerly nudged the woman in the side. When she didn't move, she gave the nurse a more vicious kick that sent a shudder through the woman's body.

"Take that, bitch!" Megan muttered. All those years of self-defense classes had finally paid off. *Thank you, Daddy*.

Megan centered her breathing, but the adrenaline was still coursing through her veins hard enough to make her hands shake as she checked the pockets on the nurse's scrubs for anything of value. She came up with a set of keys and a cellphone. The iPhone would only unlock via facial recognition, so Megan held it over the nurse's slumbering face, moving it around until the software recognized the owner and it unlocked with a chime. Megan then changed the passcode before slipping it into the pocket on the side of her yoga pants.

She stood and adjusted her clothing. The fight had torn her shirt and left her bra twisted on her slim frame. With everything back in place, Megan opened the cell door and glanced up and down the narrow passageway. There were doors on both sides of the passageway with stairs at the end. Quietly, she stepped into the passageway and closed the door behind her, seating the lever in place and locking it with the small length of looped rope attached to the bulkhead that had prevented her from opening the door.

At the stairs, she leaned over and looked up and down through the opening between the runs. Knowing help would most likely be topside, she headed that way. While she wanted to run up the stairs to seek help, she reminded herself that Blake and the stranger had engineered her manufactured sleep. Tempered with the thought of being thrust back into the cell, Megan proceeded with caution.

At the top of the stairs, Megan found herself at the helm of an automated bridge. Stretched out before her was the endless ocean horizon, with big blue waves glistening in the sunlight. Megan Babcock stood on the bridge of the freighter and gazed down at the vast expanse of the empty cargo deck.

"Where am I?" she whispered in wonderment.

Far below, she saw a crewman walking along the port rail, his hand gripping the railing for support. He wore an orange safety vest over a yellow survival suit and a blue hard hat. Her first thought was that someone needed some serious training in fashion because all the colors clashed inharmoniously.

Pulling the iPhone from her pocket, Megan tried to dial out. The screen immediately told her the call had failed, and she noticed there was no service available. It was useless to continue to try to use the cellular phone without a tower to connect to in the middle of the ocean.

Megan knew she needed to act quickly before someone discovered her on the bridge. She searched the console in front of her for any means of communication. When her gaze fell on the satellite phone, Megan hoped her luck had changed for the better. She picked up the handset and started to dial Blake's number, then suddenly stopped. He was the one who had put her in this position. She couldn't call him for help, and the two other man she had depended upon for advice were dead. A sob welled in her chest for her father and Denny McGuire.

With her finger hovering over the phone's keypad, Megan wondered who she could call. Then she remembered the business card Ryan Weller had given her. She checked her pockets and found them empty. Someone had taken the card from her person.

Megan searched her memory for the number on the card, having memorized it quickly since it was short and catchy. The jingle she had set the number to popped into her head, and she hummed it as she punched the numbers into the keypad.

"Maritime Recovery. May I take a message?" the woman on the other end of the line asked.

"Can I speak to Ryan?" Megan asked.

"There's no Ryan at this number."

"Bob!" Megan suddenly remembered. "Bob Parker."

"Oh, yes. What is your message?"

"This is Megan Babcock. Tell Bob I am being held hostage on a ship—some kind of freighter. The name is ..." Her voice trailed off as she visually searched the bridge for the vessel's name. "The name is *Ocean Trakker*." She repeated the name and then spelled it. "Tell Bob to get here as soon as possible. I need his help!"

"I will let him know," the woman said politely.

Megan didn't know if the woman had registered anything she'd just said, so she repeated the most crucial detail. "I'm being held hostage on the *Ocean Trakker*! Tell Bob to come right away."

"I understand, ma'am," the operator replied. "I will contact him immediately."

The call ended before Megan could say anything else. She set the phone back in its cradle and stared out at the rolling ocean. Her belly trembled with fright, and Megan thought she might vomit.

Megan wondered if anyone would ever be able to save her.

CHAPTER NINETEEN

New Amsterdam, Guyana

The ringing of Ryan's phone brought him to a halt as he and Spooky John walked near the entrance to MCG Marine Defense and plotted the best way to infiltrate the facility.

Jerking the phone from his pocket, he checked the caller ID to see it was from his answering service. His mind immediately jumped to Megan Babcock.

"Hello, this is Bob Parker, Maritime Recovery."

"Mister Parker, you have an urgent message from a woman named Megan Babcock."

"Go ahead," Ryan said, his body surging with epinephrine.

The operator relayed Megan's message in full, then spelled the name of the ship when Ryan asked.

"The *Ocean Trakker*," Ryan repeated. "Thanks for calling." He pressed the *End* button and turned to Spooky John. "Showtime, my not-always-so-friendly ghost. Megan is being held hostage on a ship. Let's gather the troops and plan an extraction."

The team of eight had splintered into three groups to scout the separate entrances to MCG Marine Defense, hoping to discover the best way to infiltrate and escape with Megan in tow. With one phone call, all their efforts had come to naught, as Megan wasn't even on the property.

After making phone calls to the team leaders and telling them to muster at the rental house as quickly as possible, Ryan made a fourth call to Greg Olsen.

"What's up?" Greg asked in greeting.

"I need some more help, Hot Wheels."

"When don't you need help?" Greg chided.

"I always need help," Ryan replied. "Just ask my wife."

"She would know. Now, tell me what your problem is today since you've already dragged away two of my best crewmen."

"I need you to find a ship for me. It's called *Ocean Trakker*." He spelled the last word, then added, "Our principal is on that vessel. The sooner we can find it, the sooner we can rescue her."

"I thought she was in Guyana?" Greg said.

"We did, too, but she just called my Maritime Recovery answering service to ask for a rescue at sea."

"I'll get right on it and call you as soon as I know something," the owner of Dark Water Research replied.

"Thanks," Ryan said, then ended the call.

Ryan and Spooky John headed for the house, getting there ahead of the others as they had the shortest distance to travel.

"What are you thinking?" John asked. "I can see the wheels turning."

"We have to wait until we know the location of the ship

and what type of vessel it is before we can plan our assault," Ryan replied.

"I agree," John said. "I guess we play the waiting game."

The wait wasn't long, as TJ, Kendra, and Slater arrived first, and then Larry Grove, Scott, and Emily entered the house. With everyone gathered in one spot, all they needed were the coordinates of their target.

Ryan's phone rang thirty minutes later with a chirp that told him the call came from the U.S. He recognized the number as the main switchboard at Dark Water Research. He answered with a cheery, "Hello, this is Ryan."

"I know who it is, dumbass," Ashlee Williams replied. "How many times do I have to tell you that you can do all this research with an app on your phone?"

"Time is of the essence, Ash. A woman's life is at stake. Give me the details and spare the sarcasm."

"You know you're fun to tease?" DWR's petite, redheaded computer specialist replied.

Ryan glanced around the room at the expectant faces. He didn't need any ribbing today. The urgency of their operation was too great. "Do you have the coordinates or not?"

"The *Ocean Trakker* is registered in Panama. She's currently in the Atlantic Ocean, northeast of Barbados. She's traveling south at eight knots." Ashlee read off the exact coordinates she had for the vessel, using the proprietary software she'd helped develop with a company called MarineSat AI that located and tracked vessels of all shapes and sizes by analyzing satellite views of the vessels.

"Thanks, Ash. You might have just saved a life. Keep texting me updated coordinates." Ryan ended the call without waiting for her next quip and turned to his people. "We have a target, and we know where the ship is. Now, how do we get there?"

"According to the map, the ship is about four hundred

miles away," Spooky John said. "If we had a helicopter, we could refuel in Barbados, then fast-rope to the deck of the *Ocean Trakker*."

"How do we get off?" Ryan asked. "A helicopter won't be able to land on the freighter."

"We'll have to climb a ladder or have a winch with a bucket," Scott suggested.

"Let's assume Mrs. Babcock is incapacitated," Larry Grove advised. "She might have been able to make a distress call, but between that time and when we get there, her captors might discover she's on the loose and do something drastic."

"Agreed," Ryan said.

"We should just take the ship and bring it to port ourselves," TJ said.

"We'll have to clear the boat of hostiles no matter what," Ryan said. "We won't know how many shooters are onboard until we get there."

"I'm glad we have all this gear with us," John said, "but flying in and out of Barbados without clearing customs will be tough, and they'll want to check the passenger manifest and our cargo load."

Speaking to John and Larry, Ryan said, "Can you guys work with the State Department to get us clearance to refuel in Barbados?"

"We can try," Larry said.

John shrugged.

"The rest of you, get the gear together and get ready to travel," Ryan instructed. "I need to make a call about a helicopter."

Stepping outside onto the back deck, Ryan pulled out his phone to call Chuck Newland. Spooky John joined him and moved in close for a quiet conversation before Ryan could dial the pilot's number. "What you're doing for Megan is noble and noteworthy, but it's not my job. I need to stay here, close to MCG. Those are my orders."

Ryan snorted. "You better skedaddle back to whatever hole you climbed out of John. You've got your orders."

"Don't get smart with me, Ryan. I'll knock your block off."

"I'm the one who should get the first swing after all the bullshit you and your *friends* have put me through."

Before John could say anything else, Emily stepped out onto the deck. "Let's play nice, boys. We're all on the same team."

"Are we, John?" Ryan asked. "Are we on the same team?"

"Yes, we're on the same team," John said. "We play ball for America."

"Or the next highest bidder," Ryan said.

"Enough!" Emily cried. "Stop poking the bear, Ryan."

John smirked. "You've been given your orders."

"You stop, too, John," Emily reprimanded. "I don't know why you guys can't get along. You're like a couple of schoolkids harassing each other on the playground. Now, we have work to do. If you're not joining us, John, then please leave. I think you want to help us, but only you can decide what your next move will be."

Ryan nodded. "She's right, John. We could use your help to get in and out of Barbados, and every gun counts on this trip."

The case officer sighed. "I'll call my handler."

"Thank you," Emily said to the case officer. "And thanks for keeping my husband safe on Saint Kitts. I always appreciate it when someone has his back."

"You're welcome," John said, then headed down the steps to the street below.

"Have you made your call yet?" Emily asked her husband.

"I'm doing it now," Ryan replied, punching in a speed dial

contact and holding the phone to his ear. When Chuck Newland came on the line, Ryan asked, "Who has a helicopter down here? We need to make a fast trip."

"I know a couple of guys," Chuck said. "How soon do you need it?"

"ASAP, with room for seven passengers."

"Roger that," Chuck said. "Where are you?"

"New Amsterdam. There's a strip outside of town."

Larry Grove stepped out onto the porch. "You got a bird?"

"Yeah. We got one, right, Chuck?" Ryan asked.

"We sure do," the pilot replied. "How about a Sikorsky S-92 outfitted for search and rescue?"

"Perfect. How soon can it get here?" Ryan asked.

"I'm in Georgetown right now. We can take off as soon as we run the preflight checks. I figure we can be there within an hour," Chuck said.

"We'll see you in New Amsterdam," Ryan said. "And Chuck? Bring some fast-rope gear if you can find it."

"We have clearance to refuel in Barbados," Larry said.

Ryan relayed the message to Chuck and then ended the call.

Kendra stepped onto the deck and said, "We're all set. The gear is in the SUVs."

"Then let's roll," Ryan said.

AN HOUR after speaking to Chuck on the phone, a Sikorsky S-92 painted in a two-tone gray camouflage pattern flew in low over the New Amsterdam strip and landed near the white SUV that contained the members of Ryan's team.

Before the rotors could slow, the side door of the helo popped open, and a helmeted crewman motioned for everyone to board. Each team member grabbed a duffel bag or backpack and lugged it onto the aircraft while Ryan and Scott manhandled the Pelican case. Ryan patted the co-pilot, Chuck Newland, affectionately on the shoulder before taking his seat.

Once they had everything loaded and were seated in the sling seats along the helicopter's outer walls with seatbelts fastened, the crewman signaled to the pilot, and the craft quickly rose into the air, nosing slightly down to gather speed.

It took two and a half hours to fly to Grantley Adams International Airport on the southern coast of Barbados, sweeping in off the sparkling sea and crossing the rocky coastline. The pilot set the helicopter down on the tarmac outside the general aviation building and called for a fuel truck to top off the bird.

While they waited for the fuel truck to arrive, Ryan checked his phone. Despite her sarcastic rapport with Ryan, Ashlee Williams had been texting him updates on the *Ocean Trakker*'s location every fifteen minutes.

Chuck and the helicopter's pilot, who introduced himself as Craig Meyer, stepped into the cabin and sat down with Ryan and the team.

"What's the plan?" Meyer asked. "I've been hearing so much about you from old Chuck Wagon that I was starting to believe you could walk on water."

"'Chuck Wagon?'" Ryan said with a grin as he glanced over at his friend.

The chief pilot for Dark Water Research shrugged. "Shit happens."

"You ever notice the dude has a huge appetite?" Meyer asked, slapping Chuck good-naturedly on the back. "We used to go into the chow hall, and old Wagon here would wipe 'em clean."

"You guys served together?" Scott asked. "I didn't think anyone liked Chuck that much."

"We were in the Air Force together," Chuck replied, giving Scott the middle finger. "Me and Fort flew MH-53M Pave Lows for the 20th Expeditionary Special Operations Squadron."

"So, you know all about this bird," Ryan said, turning to Craig Meyer. While the body of the Sikorsky S-92 reminded Ryan of the old Air Force Pave Lows and the MH-53E Sea Dragons the Navy flew, the cockpit and nose section of the S-92 appeared to have more in common with a H-60 Black Hawk.

"Kinda, my baby," Meyer responded. "I've got a lot of hours in both. You want it flown? I'm your guy."

"Wait, back up a sec," Scott cut in. "Your call sign is *Fort?*"

Craig Meyer smiled. "Ironically, I'm from Fort Myers. I guess it was the best name these cheese dicks could come up with."

After a momentary laugh from everyone gathered in the cargo compartment, Ryan said, "Okay. Let's get back on track here. We have about an hour of flight time between here and the current position of the *Ocean Trakker*. The ship is a 475-foot-long general cargo vessel with two cranes amidships with towers on the port side. We can fast-rope onto the bridge roof and make our way down from there. A ship like this probably has a crew of twenty to thirty people, not counting any hostiles they may have aboard to guard Megan."

"Any idea who you're going up against?" Fort Meyer asked.

"Not a clue," Ryan replied. "If we need to get out in a hurry, can you rig a sling for us?"

"I've got the basket, but the winch takes time to raise and lower," Meyer replied. "We brought a fast-rope, and I hope you brought gloves."

"We've got them. Double pairs for everyone," Ryan replied.

The team had stopped at a hardware store on the way out of New Amsterdam and purchased gloves for everyone in the group. The friction from the rope sliding through their hands would build up enough heat to necessitate two pairs of gloves to keep their hands from blistering.

Emily, Kendra, and TJ were the only members of the team who had never fast-roped before, so Ryan had asked the three of them to sit the mission out if that proved to be the only method to ingress the ship.

Fast-roping could be a dangerous insertion method, and it took a lot of training to do it properly. Ryan had seen plenty of guys break bones from coming down the rope too fast or letting go too early. While Emily carried a private investigator's license, she wasn't a trained shooter, and he didn't want to endanger his three teammates unnecessarily by knowingly placing them in a hazardous situation.

"I guess we'll know the score when we arrive on station," Meyer stated.

"Fuel truck is here," the crewman reported.

Meyer went to the cockpit to aid in the refueling process, and the rest of the team sat back to relax and enjoy a moment of solitude before going into battle.

"What will we do while you're on the ship?" Emily asked her husband.

"Be ready for anything," Ryan replied.

"I don't suppose this bird has a gun I can use to provide overwatch, does it?" Emily asked.

Like Ryan, she remembered the last time he'd fast-roped onto a freighter with Scott Gregory. On that mission, they had tracked down a vessel loaded with diesel fuel and ammonium nitrate that was headed for Fort Lauderdale, and Emily had used a machine gun mounted on their support helicopter to kill the lead terrorist who had Ryan and his team pinned down on the ship.

"You could leave the Springfield M1A or one of the Dragunovs," Kendra suggested.

"We can do that," Ryan replied.

Emily had been lucky to have an M60 mounted in the previous helicopter that could throw a ton of lead downrange, but the two sniper rifles Kendra had requested be left behind required optics to shoot effectively. Between the movement of the helicopter and the undulation of the ship, it would be damned near impossible to hit anything unless they'd trained profusely in that type of environment.

But still, Ryan was glad his wife and Kendra were going to remain behind, out of harm's way, with TJ there to protect them.

Once the refueling operation ended and the tanker truck pulled away from the landing pad, Fort Meyer and Chuck Wagon spooled up the twin GE turboshaft engines. Sikorsky had designed the S-92 to transport oil executives and workers to offshore fields, and the manufacturer had incorporated many noise reduction features, making the cabin one of the quietest Ryan had ever ridden in. He could at least hear himself think as the helicopter lifted off the pad and hover-taxied along the runway before it rose higher and turned northeast toward the last known position of the *Ocean Trakker*.

CHAPTER TWENTY

"Coming up on the *Ocean Trakker* now," the crewman called out to Ryan and his team after twenty minutes of flying northeast from Barbados over nothing but open ocean.

Everyone turned to look out the windows built into the flanks of the Sikorsky S-92 helicopter.

Ryan got up and went forward to the cockpit. "Any signs of life?"

"Not a one," Chuck replied.

"Keep going at this elevation, then swing us around to come in from the stern," Ryan instructed.

"Lots of antennas on that bridge," Meyer commented. "Might be easier to come in amidships between those two cranes."

"Do you have enough clearance for the main rotor?" Ryan asked.

"Looks like enough," Meyer responded. "If not, I can always back off and drop you right there as I hover over the cranes. It will be a cleaner drop, and we won't have to worry about the rope getting tangled in one of the antennas."

"Roger that," Ryan said, then turned to the team. They were already geared up for battle, having donned their plate-carrying chest rigs, checked their weapons and comms units, and pulled on both pairs of gloves. The crewman opened the side door and attached the fast-rope to the winch frame above the door, ready to kick it out if Meyer failed to land on the ship on the first pass.

Ryan stood in the doorway, gripping the frame and intently watching as Meyer maneuvered the aircraft into position, coming alongside the ship to match its speed before turning to nose the Sikorsky into position between the cranes. Below them, the *Ocean Trakker* was still quiet as a mouse. No guards ran into position. No one shot at them, and no blaring alert sirens warned of an impending attack.

With a rotor span of fifty-six feet four inches, Meyer easily set the Sikorsky down on the flat deck of the cargo vessel. As the team disgorged from the cabin, the crewman shouted to Ryan, "We'll wait here. If something goes wrong, we'll take off and come back for you when the coast is clear."

Ryan flashed a thumbs-up.

Before landing on the ship, the group had formed into teams. Ryan, Scott, and Larry Grove were Alpha Team, while John, Slater, and TJ composed Bravo Team. Emily and Kendra remained behind as rear security with the helicopter on the deck.

While the Alpha Team took the port side of the ship, the Bravo Team headed down the starboard rail, both angling for the rear superstructure that rose six stories into the air at the aft end of the cargo vessel, hoping to make this a quick operation.

Reaching the superstructure, Ryan and his team started sweeping through the berthing, galley, dining, and mechanical spaces while John and his men raced straight up the ladder-well toward the bridge.

As the Red Team cleared the spaces, they secured the *Trakker*'s crewmen in their quarters, telling them to remain inside. Most didn't argue, knowing it was best to allow pirates to have the run of the ship, but a few became belligerent. One ran straight at Ryan, and he butt-stroked him with the stock of his B&T carbine, knocking the man off his feet and leaving him with a bloody and broken nose.

Scott stepped over the crewman's writhing body and secured his hands behind his back with flex cuffs.

Over the radio comms socketed into each of their ears, the men of Alpha Team heard Spooky John report, "Bridge is secure."

"Roger that," Ryan replied. "We're still on the move."

"Happy hunting," the CIA officer replied.

The team next encountered a man wearing coveralls with a name tag that said he was the chief mate. Scott slammed the chief mate against the bulkhead and leveraged his height and weight advantage as he pressed his left forearm against the man's throat and shoved his gun barrel into the man's stomach. "Tell me where Megan Babcock is!"

"Two decks up," the chief replied in a hoarse whisper.

Scott released his death grip on the mate's throat, grabbed him by the shoulder, and shoved him roughly forward. "Show me."

The chief mate led the way up two flights of stairs to the deck just below the bridge. He pointed to a door and said, "She's in there."

"Open the door," Scott demanded, pushing the reluctant mate forward again.

As they approached the hatch, Ryan signaled for Scott and Larry to form into a gun stack, with Scott in the lead. Larry moved ahead of Ryan and took the number two position. Ryan let the two SEALs lead the way without complaint.

The chief mate opened the door and was immediately shot dead by an unseen assailant in the room.

Scott stepped over the man's inert form and entered the room low and left, with Larry right on his tail, swinging to the right. Silenced shots echoed off the steel bulkheads as Ryan hung back, seeing there wasn't room for all of them to operate inside the tiny compartment.

"Clear," Scott called over his shoulder.

"Clear," Larry echoed.

Ryan then entered the compartment, stepping over the dead nurse to where Megan Babcock lay on a bunk with an IV attached to her arm. She had a bloody nose and two black eyes.

He keyed his comms unit. "Dark Angel is secure. I repeat, Dark Angel is secure. She is incapacitated, and we are preparing her to move."

"Standing by," John replied.

"They have her on ketamine," Scott said after studying the label on the bag hanging from the IV machine.

"Let's get her unhooked," Ryan said.

"How are we going to move her?" Larry asked.

"We need a stretcher," Ryan replied. "I think I saw one on the wall outside."

Larry disappeared into the passageway and returned moments later with an orange plastic backboard with black straps to secure a patient in place. The three men rolled Megan Babcock onto her side and slid the backboard under her. Quickly, they strapped her arms, legs, and head into place, and then Ryan and Scott hefted the backboard with Larry leading the way. The DIA agent keyed his mic and said, "Alpha Team on the move. We're headed for the helicopter."

"Roger that," came the reply from above. "We're heading out. Which stairwell are you going down? We'll link up."

"Port side," Larry replied into the comms.

"Copy that," John said. "See you in a few."

The three-man Alpha Team was moving quickly down the ladderwell when the Bravo Team caught up with them, taking the lead and tail positions as they maneuvered the stretcher through the turns of the stair landings. Ryan wondered where all the hostiles were. Their absence didn't sit well with him. So far, the only person who had defended Megan was a woman wearing nursing scrubs in the compartment where Megan had been incapacitated. She had been the one to shoot the first mate dead when he'd opened the hatch, and Scott had drilled her in the head with a three-shot burst from his MP5.

A hatch slammed open below as they approached the final landing, and two shooters stepped out. Larry and John instantly responded, killing them before the shooters could raise their AK-74s to their shoulders. It paid to have the best, and it paid to be a winner. While the hostiles had been holding their firearms loosely by their hips, Ryan's men had the stocks of their carbines welded to their shoulders, eyes scanning ahead for potential targets.

Peeling off the gun stack, John and Slater edged down the passageway toward the open hatch that swung lazily back and forth on its hinges as the ship rolled with the waves. Ryan instructed the rest of the team to head for the helicopter.

They ran straight into a trap.

As Larry opened the hatch to exit the superstructure, TJ stepped up to swing through with his gun up and ready for action. He was immediately struck in the chest by a barrage of bullets and knocked off his feet.

At the same time, gunfire echoed farther down the passageway that John and Slater had peeled off to defend.

"Shooters above us!" Scott cried. "I'm putting the stretcher down."

While Scott had kept Megan's head elevated, Ryan had

been leading the way down the steps with her feet toward him. Now, she was head down as Ryan continued to grip the end of the stretcher. He didn't want to leave her exposed at the base of the stairs.

Ahead of him, Larry kept leaning out of the hatch and firing off controlled bursts at the enemy.

"RPG! RPG!" someone screamed over the comms net, but Ryan didn't immediately recognize the voice, and the rocket-propelled grenade exploded in a thunderous roar.

"Sorry, Dark Horse, we're out of here," Craig Meyer called over the radio. "That RPG just struck the base of the aft crane and barely missed my bird."

The sound of the rotors grew louder and momentarily drowned out the gunfire.

Ryan gulped. They were in one helluva jam.

John and Slater used the open hatch as cover while Scott tried to return fire at the men above. Larry kept popping out to cover TJ, but a hail of lead kept driving him backward before he could drag TJ to safety. The kid had taken multiple rounds to the chest, but the ceramic plate had stopped them from penetrating his body. He was bruised but not bloodied.

At least Emily is safe on the helicopter, Ryan thought.

"Frag out!" John shouted and sent a grenade bouncing down the passageway.

It detonated with a shattering crack that made their ears ring and seemed to shake the entire superstructure. Tiny metal fragments pinged off the steel bulkheads and sizzled through the air.

Outside the superstructure, a new weapon sounded. Ryan recognized it as the deep boom of a single hypersonic round spat from the barrel of a long gun. He wondered if one of the hostiles had a sniper rifle. Three more loud reports echoed off the steel, and the gunfire outside the superstructure died as abruptly as it had begun.

"Exterior is clear," Kendra said over the comms.

Ryan turned to Scott. "Grab the stretcher, and let's go. Larry, you get TJ. John and Slater, hold the fort."

There was no need to reply as everyone began working together. Scott hefted his end of the stretcher, and the two men ran out of the superstructure and down the port-side rail, headed for the steps up onto the flat cargo deck so they could signal for the Sikorsky to return.

Ryan glanced over his shoulder once to see Emily and Larry Grove had TJ supported between them, and Kendra, John, and Slater brought up the rear, dispatching any hostiles who tried to prevent their extraction.

While Ryan was thankful the two women had come to their rescue, he was pissed that Emily had put herself in danger. He didn't know what he would do if something happened to her. His heart ached just thinking about losing her.

"We're clear! We're clear!" John called over the radio.

"Coming in hot!" Chuck said.

Ryan and the rest of the team assembled on the cargo deck, ready to board as soon as Fort Meyer landed the Sikorsky.

Seconds later, the big bird swooped in from the sky and alighted on its wheels.

"Get to the chopper!" someone yelled in a terrible impersonation of Arnold Schwarzenegger.

No one had to be told twice. Ryan and Scott hefted the backboard and ran for the open rear cargo door, followed by everyone else.

Once they were safely aboard, Meyer threw power to the turboshaft engines, and the Sikorsky lifted into the sky, backing away from the *Ocean Trakker*. The rotors barely cleared the crane arm listing to the starboard side and the tangle of cables dangling from it.

Once the bird was clear, Meyer heaved back on the collective, and the helicopter quickly left the ship in its wake.

"Where to?" Chuck asked over the tactical comms unit.

Ryan glanced at Spooky John.

The CIA officer shrugged. "Georgetown."

"Georgetown," Ryan repeated to Chuck, then turned to check on Megan Babcock. She was still unconscious. Slater knelt over her, attaching a bag of saline from his med pack to the IV infusion needle still embedded in the woman's arm.

They had accomplished one task in rescuing Megan Babcock, but now, they had to stop the sale of MCG Marine Defense, and Ryan had no idea how to do that.

CHAPTER TWENTY-ONE

SKY Security Services
Land of Canaan, Guyana

Ryan Weller stepped gingerly through the living room of Kendra Diaz's stilt house, careful not to make the floorboards squeak underfoot. He leaned against the bedroom doorframe and peered in at his wife, who sat beside the still form of Megan Babcock.

"How's she doing?" he whispered.

"She's sleeping again." Emily stood and stepped over to Ryan, wrapping her arms around herself. "I got her to eat a bowl of soup and drink a glass of water. She's been through the wringer judging by all the bruises on her body."

Ryan nodded thoughtfully, glad Megan was safe for now. Even if they didn't stop the sale of MCG Marine Defense, he might personally visit Blake Babcock and deliver some good old-fashioned Southern justice. A man who laid his hands on a woman deserved to have his ass kicked or be dragged through a briar patch behind a pickup truck.

But plotting revenge would have to wait for another day. *Ocean Trakker* now sat dockside at MCG, and work had commenced to repair the crane that had been damaged by an RPG during the rescue of Megan Babcock.

After departing the *Ocean Trakker* aboard the Sikorsky S-92, their pilot, Fort Meyer, had made a beeline for Eugene F. Correia International Airport in Georgetown, arriving on fumes but landing safely, nonetheless. Yasmine Harden had arranged for two SKY employees to bring the team's SUVs back from New Amsterdam. The SKY men had met the team outside the CIA's hangar at Correia with two vehicles and a local doctor. After loading Megan into the back of a transport, the doctor examined her and declared she didn't need urgent medical attention but rather rest and fluids.

Now, the billionaire business owner slept fitfully inside the rustic cabin Kendra called home inside the SKY Security Services compound. It was the best place for Ryan to keep his principal, with a gated entrance from the street to the south, the Demerara River to the north, and a six-foot-high chain-link fence topped with razor wire surrounding the entire property. The trees along the eastern and western sides of the compound hid most of the fence. It gave the illusion of security but wouldn't hold back an enemy force for long, and the trees also gave combatants a place to hide. Still, it was better than shacking up in the Marriott, with too many entrances to control.

"I'm going back outside," Ryan told his wife. "Thanks for watching her."

"It's the least I can do," Emily replied. "She looks like a lost soul."

"She will be for a while. Probably need a lot of therapy after all this is over."

"How long are we going to stay here?" Emily asked.

"I don't know," Ryan replied. "I guess we're waiting for John to get a signal or for Babcock to make a move."

A moan from the patient caused them both to turn back toward the bed and then Megan said weakly, "Ryan?"

Stepping over to the bed, Ryan knelt beside it. "Yeah, Meg. It's me. How are you feeling?"

"Terrible. Do you have some more water?"

Emily handed Ryan a glass of water, and he held it so Megan could drink from the straw.

When she stopped drinking, Megan released the straw from her pale lips and laid her head back on the pillow. "Thank you."

Ryan set the glass down and stood.

"Don't go," Megan said sleepily, her eyes closed. "Stay with me."

"I'm right here," Ryan whispered. "You're safe."

Megan reached out her hand, and Ryan took it gently in his. She lightly squeezed his fingers. Then her hand slipped from his as she drifted off to sleep.

"Just rescuing her, huh?" Emily asked suspiciously. "Looks a lot chummier than that."

"Seriously, Em?" Ryan asked, turning to face her. "The woman has been through a tragedy. What am I supposed to do? Pat her on the shoulder like she's one of my buddies and tell her to buck up? Nothing happened between us, and nothing ever will. Get it through your thick skull, woman."

Ryan pushed past his wife, knowing his biting words had probably cut her deeply, but her suspicion that he and Megan had shared a more intimate relationship spoke to her lack of trust in him. He thought they'd moved past all that nonsense, but women were like archaeologists—they could easily dig up the past and present it like a modern fact.

At the bottom of the stairs, Ryan drew in a deep breath

and exhaled his anger. He turned to find Emily at the top of the steps, staring down at him.

"I'm sorry," Ryan said. "I had no right to say that to you, but you gotta trust me. Nothing happened between me and Megan."

"I know," she replied, arms crossed. "What I said came out wrong."

Ryan walked back up the steps and put his hands on his wife's shoulders. The wind teased her golden hair, and he pushed a strand out of her face, taking in her searching cobalt-blue eyes. "I love you, Em. I always have, and I always will."

"Damn you, Ryan. I can't stay mad at you."

He grinned wickedly. "Too bad we're not alone. We could have makeup sex."

Emily laughed and playfully pushed him away. "You're incorrigible. Get out of here before I do something wild."

Ryan pulled her close. "I'm wild." He growled, trying to imitate a bear but sounding more like a playful mutt.

Emily rolled her eyes. "Nope. You ruined it."

Ryan kissed her on the forehead. "I love you."

Emily rested her forehead against his, then kissed him tenderly. "Go get this job done so we can get out of here, okay? Remember the other night when I got back from Tampa? That was just a warm-up."

Ryan kissed her again. "Oh, I remember, and I'm ready to go again." He turned serious. "I did my part here. I got Megan back in one piece. If I had my way, I'd like to put her on a jet and take her Stateside, but I think Spooky John is counting on having help for whatever he's planning next."

"Whatever it is, we'll face it together," Emily promised.

Ryan walked down the steps and headed toward the security office. He took his time walking through the property, enjoying the warm, tropical sun, the smell of the fruit trees, and the laughter of Yasmine's son as he and Slater tossed a baseball back and forth.

Ryan stopped to watch, suddenly overcome with the memory of a boy he'd rescued in Haiti. He and James had played catch whenever they could, and Ryan wondered how the kid was doing now. The last time he'd seen James had been during an operation to rescue missionaries from Port-au-Prince. Overcome with sadness at being unable to watch James grow up and see the kind of man he would become, Ryan turned away from the security office and walked down to the river's edge.

While Ryan had never felt the need to be a father, he did think about it occasionally, wondering if he would have been any good at the job. Maybe he had been selfish in pursuing a career fraught with danger, but he didn't see himself becoming a parent at this point in his life.

With a deep sigh, Ryan thrust his hands into the pockets of his shorts and then headed for the office to learn their next course of action.

Stepping through the door, Ryan could hear a buzz of conversation. Kendra and Yasmine were on the phone with clients in their respective offices while TJ had stretched out on Kendra's couch, nursing his bruised ribs. Meanwhile, Slater was prepping gear and a two-man team to escort an Exxon oil VIP from Cheddi Jagan International to the parliament building in downtown Georgetown.

Ryan wandered past the offices and into the garage area, where he found Scott Gregory and Larry Grove bullshitting about their days in the SEALs.

"Where's John?" Ryan asked.

"He went out. Not sure where," Scott replied. "You know how those spooks are."

Ryan nodded. He knew all about John's tendency to disappear. He wondered what the CIA officer was up to and who he was meeting with.

Despite whatever Spooky John was working on, Ryan knew he had to find another way into MCG to get to Blake Babcock. The man deserved one helluva beatdown for what he'd done to his wife, and if he was capable of doing such dastardly things to her, then he was definitely capable of greater evil. Ryan could feel it in his bones.

He had met wicked men before who had just needed to be put down. The evil burning within them had caused pain and suffering to those who crossed their paths. While Ryan knew he should never consider himself to be judge, jury, and executioner for men like them, he did believe they should be removed from polite society.

An old refrain popped into Ryan's head as he looked over the surveillance photos and a map of MCG's compound collected before rescuing Megan Babcock from *Ocean Trakker*: "Kill them all and let God sort them out." The words had become something of an ethos for military commands and had even been printed on shirts Ryan had seen his high school wrestling team wearing, with a slight amendment of: "Pin them all and let God sort them out."

Ryan had once looked up the origin of the phrase and had found it was supposedly uttered by Arnaud Amalric, an official representative of Pope Innocent III, just before he helped murder hundreds of Christian Cathars in France. Amalric's words had been more to the effect of, "Kill them all. God will recognize his own." Ryan reasoned God would know his own and judge the good and the evil alike. How they got to their judgment day was another story.

"What are you thinking about?" Scott asked, joining his partner at the table where they had gathered their intelligence.

"Just trying to figure out how to stop the sale of MCG and plant Blake Babcock six feet under," Ryan replied.

"Last I heard, the sale is being held up," Larry said. "Someone finally forwarded the information to the Committee on Foreign Investments, and they learned Subsurface Kinetics is a front for the Iranians."

"We have such a thing?" Scott asked.

"The committee is supposed to approve or disapprove all purchases of U.S. companies by foreign countries," Larry stated.

"They must be in the pocket of the Chinese," Scott muttered. "Those bastards are buying everything."

"What happens if the committee redlights the sale of MCG?" Ryan asked.

"The committee can disapprove it, but their recommendation goes to the president, and he has the final say," Larry replied.

"He'll approve it for sure," Scott stated. "Uncle Joe Brandon has a hard-on for the Iranians. I bet two dollars that he's getting a kickback on the six billion he released to them towelheads for those five American hostages."

"After the Hamas paraglider attack on Israel, your favorite uncle froze the funds again," Larry replied. "The attack coming on the heels of the hostage exchange wasn't a good look for the administration, and Congressional pressure forced him to backpedal."

"But he could still approve the sale of MCG to Subsurface Kinetics," Ryan said.

Larry shrugged. "No one knows what goes on in the president's mind."

"What's the DIA's take?" Ryan asked. "I mean, you're still here, so either your superiors want the deal stopped, or you're here on a sightseeing junket."

"The DIA feels it would be best to stop the sale," Larry

said. “However, they aren’t in a hurry to get into a shooting war with Iranian MOIS agents.”

“Too late. We probably already did that on the *Ocean Trakker*,” Ryan replied.

“I agree,” Larry replied, “but my orders are not to engage the Iranians further.”

“What about Babcock?” Scott asked.

“He’s fair game,” Larry said. “The DIA has no interest in him other than to stop the sale of MCG.”

“That’s strange,” Ryan said. “I would think they would want to keep Babcock on a leash given how much military research Gaspar Industries does and all the government contracts they have.”

“Babcock isn’t the owner. His wife is,” Larry stated.

“*Au contraire*, my friend,” Ryan said. “Blake tricked his wife into signing over seventy percent of Gaspar Industries to him. He owns the controlling stake, and he’s the one pushing the MCG sale through.”

“How did you learn this?” Larry asked.

“Our not-so-friendly ghost told me,” Ryan said. “I spoke to Megan about it, and she had no idea how he manipulated her into signing over the company. In fact, Blake had her taking arsphenamine pills that contain arsenic.”

“He was killing her with poison?” Scott asked incredulously.

“Or using it to control her,” Larry said.

Ryan stared at the surveillance data gathered on the table, trying to formulate angles and plans. Killing Blake Babcock was a start, but he couldn’t just walk into the compound and execute the man. And if the president approved the sale of MCG Marine Defense, the whole operation would be dead in the water.

“What if we quit focusing on Babcock and went after Subsurface Kinetics instead?” Scott asked as if reading Ryan’s thoughts. "If it's a known front for a hostile regime, should we allow it to continue to do business on American soil? Why don't we just raid the place?"

"We can't do it," Ryan said. "We might kill a few guys and break some furniture, but the company will still exist. We have to find a way to shut it down completely and lock out its funding."

"Easy," Scott said. "We call your FBI buddy in Miami. What's his name again?"

"Tim Dupont," Ryan replied.

"Get Tim to go to a judge and get a warrant to raid the place and seize all the company's assets," Scott said.

"That's an excellent idea," Larry concurred. "But it'll take time to organize a warrant, and we have to provide proof of wrongdoing to the FBI so the judge will sign off on it."

"How do we get the proof?" Ryan asked.

"Proof of what?" Spooky John asked, suddenly appearing at the table.

Ryan explained their conversation and the new twist on getting the FBI to raid Subsurface Kinetics.

"I like it," John said. "Unfortunately, I've been asked to stand down from this investigation. I've been given a new assignment."

"Dare I ask what?" Ryan said.

John shrugged. "You can ask, but I can't tell you."

"Or you'd have to kill us," Scott said, repeating the old saw.

"Exactly," John answered with a wink. He extended his hand to Ryan, who shook it firmly. "Dark Horse, great to work with you again, and I'm glad we secured Dark Angel. At least we accomplished something together."

"But you were tasked with stopping the sale," Ryan said. "Why stand down now?"

"Because I work for an agency that is as fickle as the weather."

"What are we supposed to do? Stand down with you?" Ryan asked.

John shrugged. "Personally, I would forget about MCG and take Megan back to the States. If you did anything, I would suggest figuring out how to untangle her from Blake and retaining her corporation."

With that, Spooky Jim-John Bowie disappeared out the door, leaving Ryan and his team to ponder their best course of action.

CHAPTER TWENTY-TWO

As Ryan stood on the porch of Kendra's house, sipping coffee, the sun started to peek over the horizon. He was still contemplating their next move against Blake Babcock when his phone rang.

"This is Ryan," he said, not recognizing the number on the screen.

"Bad news," Jim-John Bowie said. "The president approved the sale of MCG to the Iranians."

"Is he stupid or just trying to undermine the United States?" Ryan asked, pissed that the president could be so dumb. Annoyingly, though, it also seemed to be on par with the man's previous actions when it came to securing the nation's defense. Uncle Joe Brandon might have gotten more votes than any other president in history, but his term in office had been marred by scandal and corruption.

"You'll have to be the judge of that," Spooky John said. "But that's not the reason for my call."

"What is?"

"I spoke to my handler, and we quietly kicked this up the

chain of command. I'm not saying it comes from the Seventh Floor, but I'm sending you some intel. What you choose to do with it, or who you give it to, is up to you."

"Intel about what?" Ryan asked.

"A certain company in Miami that we recently discussed," John replied cryptically.

"Interesting," Ryan said. "And what are you getting out of this?"

"Don't be a horse's ass, Dark Horse. We're protecting vital national security interests."

"Okay. Send the information," Ryan said.

"Should be in your email inbox. You're still using Proton-Mail, correct?"

Ryan's phone chimed, and he glanced at the screen to see he had a new message. He wasn't surprised the CIA had his email address. "It just came through."

"Hope it works out for you, Dark Horse."

With that, John was gone, and the phone went dead in Ryan's hand.

He clicked on the email icon on his phone and found large attachments he would need to download to open. Tucking the phone away, Ryan tried to enjoy the rest of his coffee as the sun continued to rise on another hot, steamy day in Guyana. But the coffee had turned cold, and he felt too amped to just stand quietly on the porch.

Dumping the rest of his mug over the rail, he went inside to tell Emily he was headed for the security office. He found her in the bedroom with Megan. The patient seemed to be recovering well. Propped up on pillows, Megan sipped coffee from a blue mug. The skin around her black eyes had turned a jaundiced yellow, but the swelling had gone down.

"I'm headed out," Ryan said.

"Megan and I are going for a walk later," Emily said. "We're both getting restless."

"Sounds like an excellent plan," Ryan agreed. "Some fresh air will do you both good."

"Thank you, again," Megan said.

"I told you that it's my job. I volunteered for it when I gave my card to you. You don't have to keep thanking me," Ryan replied.

"I know, but it seems like you went out of your way to rescue me when you didn't have to."

"Ryan will chase a purse snatcher if he sees one," Emily stated. "Rescuing you was probably more fun."

"Purse snatchers don't normally shoot at you. Dodging bullets kinda sucks. I'll be in the office if you need me." Ryan left before the women could start in again about his bravery and compassion. It was more like feeding an addiction.

And his pulse quickened at the thought of what the email the CIA case officer had sent him might contain.

In the security office, Ryan asked Slater if he could borrow his computer. The taller Air Force veteran motioned to his vacant office and said, "Have at it."

Ryan sat at the desk, opened an Internet browser on the computer screen, and then put in his email and password for his ProtonMail account. Once he opened his Inbox, Ryan clicked on the new message he knew was from John. The first attachment contained photos of a Persian-looking man exiting the offices of Subsurface Kinetics, with the name "Xerxes Adi" typed beneath it. Included in the attachment was a biography of the MOIS operative.

While seeing Adi outside the business wasn't a smoking gun connection between Subsurface Kinetics and Iran, the next attachment changed everything. The first PDF file was a flowchart with the Central Bank of Iran at the top. Muhammad Farhad, the governor of the CBI, had been appointed by the president of Iran. They were both party hardliners, refusing to back the call for privatization of the bank, claiming the bank's independence would offer a toehold for the Zionists to control their monetary system.

The money tree in the PDF followed millions of dollars from the CBI to multiple banks in Switzerland and Panama as it flowed through several offshore shell companies until it landed in Subsurface Kinetics' bank account, appearing as a transaction for the fictious sale of hydrographic survey equipment to Syria for oil exploration.

"Interesting," Ryan muttered.

The final PDF file contained a hierarchy of Subsurface Kinetics owners and board members, including several prominent Iranian-American businessmen and a known member of the Majd, the internal security apparatus of the Palestinian terror group Hamas.

"How in the hell is this company doing business on U.S. soil?" Ryan wondered aloud.

While he didn't know the best way to use the evidence to shut down Subsurface Kinetics, he knew a guy who might be able to put it to good use.

Reaching for his phone, Ryan hoped Special Agent Tim Dupont was in his office at the FBI's Miami Field Office. He hit the speed dial button and leaned back in the swiveling office chair as he listened to the phone ring in his ear.

"Special Agent Dupont. How may I help you?"

"Wanna bust some Iranians in South Florida?" Ryan asked.

"Uh ... who is this?" Dupont asked.

"Let's see," Ryan said. "You scored a big win in Haiti and then arrested a cold case killer on St. Thomas, all thanks to yours truly."

"I like it when you do the legwork, and I get the glory," Dupont replied, now knowing exactly who was on the other end of the line.

Ryan studied the photo of Xerxes Adi as he spoke. "Unfortunately, you'll have to do some legwork on this case."

"You mentioned Iranians. What are you into?"

"How does a presidentially approved deal to sell top-secret submarine technology to an Iranian front company in Miami sound?"

"Damn, bro! What did you stumble into?"

"Let's say I was coerced more than stumbled. I'll forward you some information from one of my contacts. I want to see if you can use it to get a warrant and seize Sub K's assets to shut down this deal."

"I can try." Dupont gave Ryan his work email.

Ryan leaned over the keyboard and forwarded the message he'd received from Spooky John to his FBI buddy. "Great. I just sent it over to you."

A moment later, Dupont whistled. "This is some interesting stuff, Ryan. How did you get your hands on it?"

"You know that agency that isn't supposed to operate on U.S. soil but frequently does?"

Dupont pondered the question momentarily, then said, "The one with that farm in Virginia."

"You nailed it."

Dupont sighed. "It's a long shot, Ryan. I can't make you any guarantees that a judge will sign off on a warrant if I can't tell him how I obtained this information."

"That's your department, Tim. All I can say is the sooner you get it done, the better. If this sub tech falls into Iranian hands, you and I both know it will be forwarded to China within hours."

Dupont sighed again. "I'll see what I can do."

"That's all I'm asking, buddy."

"I'll call you when I know something."

"Thanks, Tim."

Ryan ended the call and leaned back in his seat again. With any luck, Subsurface Kinetics would soon be out of business.

Now, all Ryan needed to do was take care of Blake Babcock.

CHAPTER TWENTY-THREE

Ryan joined his wife and Megan Babcock as they walked among the fruit trees planted in the SKY Security Services compound. Megan was moving well despite her ordeal, and the bruising on her face looked less severe in the sunlight. The simple jean shorts and V-neck T-shirt she'd borrowed from Emily were a far cry from the lavish attire she'd been wearing on Timothy Hill Overlook when Ryan had first met her.

"How long ago did you sign the company over to Blake?" Ryan asked to get the conversation rolling and not skirt around the issue.

"Ryan!" Emily admonished with a glare. "Megan doesn't need to think about that right now."

"It's okay," Megan said, touching her new friend's arm. "It's all I've been thinking about since you rescued me. I want to get Daddy's company back, but I don't have the slightest idea how I'll do it."

The trio walked in silence a bit farther, stopping to enjoy the shade of the spreading avocado and mango trees.

"I believe it was about two years ago," Megan stated. "I

started having headaches, and soon after, Blake came back with the pills and a pile of paperwork for me to sign. I guess one of those papers gave him a majority share." She rubbed her temples as if to relieve a headache building there.

"Are you okay?" a concerned Emily asked.

"I'm fine. I guess it's a reflex now. My head has been clearer than it has been in years. Getting off those pills was the best thing for me. I guess I should thank you, Ryan, for telling me about them."

"I wish I hadn't had to," he replied. "Your husband should have been protecting you instead of trying to kill you and destroy your company."

"That's water under the bridge, now, isn't it?" Megan said. "I want to focus on moving forward and getting the company back."

"Where do you think Blake is now?" Ryan asked.

Megan shrugged. "I don't know, but if he's selling MCG, I think he would want to stay in New Amsterdam."

"At your house inside the compound?" Ryan confirmed.

"Yes."

"Can you draw me a layout of the compound and the interior of the house?" Ryan asked.

"What are you thinking?" Emily demanded.

"I've put some legal action in the works to try to hinder the sale by getting Subsurface Kinetics shut down, but if that fails, I want to go after Blake. Maybe we can turn him, persuade him not to sell."

"Can you just stick a knife in his cold heart for me?" Megan asked.

"I'm not an assassin," Ryan clarified.

"I've seen you in action," Megan said. "You can handle yourself. And I'll gladly pay you to kill him."

Ryan plugged his ears with his index fingers. "We're not having this conversation."

"So, you're doing all of this out of the goodness of your heart?" Megan asked.

"Not quite. We do need to talk about payment at some point," Ryan replied. "We incurred quite a bit of expense in rescuing you, and by you calling me, we have a verbal contract for that service."

"I understand," Megan answered. "It's what I expected. No one does anything for free, especially when they know I'm rich as shit and can pay whatever they ask for their services."

"Whoa," Emily said. "We're all friends here."

"Are we?" Megan asked. "I appreciate all of your help, but when it comes down to it, if I have to pay, that makes all of you employees, not friends. And when I pay, I expect my people to do what I ask."

"Fine. We're just some random people you hired to rescue you. But that means I can put you on a plane back to the States and be done with this business," Ryan said flatly. "I don't need to go after Blake. You can let your pack of lawyers deal with him."

"That might be the best way," Megan mused. "But I still like the thought of you killing him. We are in a destitute Third World country, and no one will care if he goes missing. He'll just be another casualty of the restless natives."

"You're a heartless woman," Ryan said.

"After what I've been through, I have to be," the businesswoman said.

"I get that," Emily interjected. "Blake has duped you, poisoned you, and held you against your will. I'd have difficulty forgiving someone if they did that to me."

A chime from Ryan's phone interrupted their conversation. As he pulled it from his pocket and opened the text message, he pondered Megan's situation and her use of the term "employee." While Ryan had a duty of care to his clients, they were never more than his principals, and there were bigger things at stake than Megan's feelings. A hostile nation was trying to steal advanced military technology from under their noses, and if Ryan could stop that from happening, then it was his duty to try.

He read the text message from Spooky John twice before he put the phone away. His face must have betrayed his feelings because Emily asked, "What's wrong?"

"The crane on the *Ocean Trakker* has been repaired. They're loading cargo onto the ship at the MCG docks," Ryan said.

"They're loading *my* equipment," Megan Babcock stated mirthlessly. "I want you to stop them."

"Are we signing a new contract?" Ryan asked.

"Yes. We are," Megan said resolutely.

"Good. Let's go to the office, and we'll draw something up. I'll also give you the payment details for the rescue operation. After that's paid, I want you to draw a map of the compound and your house."

They walked quickly across the SKY Security Services grounds and entered the office. Ryan again commandeered Slater Harden's office and sat in front of the former pararescue specialist's computer. He pulled up his banking information and gave Megan the routing and account numbers. She then used the computer to access her bank account.

"Blake locked me out," she said, staring at the computer screen in disbelief. "That son of a bitch!"

"He must have planned for you to never leave that ship," Ryan said.

"That asshole!" Megan shouted. A flash of white-hot anger burned through her so brightly that she picked up the stapler from Slater's desk and hurled it across the room, scoring a direct hit on a photo of Slater and his Air Force team in combat fatigues beside a Black Hawk helicopter. The stapler flew apart and scattered staples across the room as the picture frame fell off the wall and its glass shattered.

Slater ran into the room. “What the hell is going on in here?” His narrowed gaze fell on the broken photo, and his cheeks bulged as he clenched his teeth together. He turned to the group. “I want you all out of here. You’ve disrupted our lives enough, and I won’t stand for this foolishness.”

“I’m sorry,” Ryan hastily apologized, once again coming to the heiress’ rescue. “Megan just learned her husband locked her out of her bank account. The strain has been a bit much for her.”

Emily busied herself with picking up the broken stapler and whatever loose staples she could find.

Slater picked up the photo and shook the broken glass into the trash can. He set the photo on the desk, placed both hands on the desktop, and leaned down to look Megan in the eye. “I appreciate the severity of your situation, Mrs. Babcock,” he said, his voice hard and low, “but I don’t tolerate such behavior from my son, and I won’t tolerate it from you, either. Please refrain from sudden violent outbursts while you are a guest at my establishment.”

“Do I deserve a good spanking?” Megan asked, her lips twitching in a smile.

“If you ask me, your father should have taken you over his knee a long time ago,” Slater replied sternly. He straightened to his full height and added, “I expect you to pay for the frame and the stapler.”

Megan threw him a mock salute. As she’d regained her health after being drugged, she’d also regained her rich girl entitlement and sass. And it was finally dawning on her just how much her husband had screwed her over. Unfortunately, she had chosen to take it out on the people who had helped her the most.

"Do you have a bill for Megan?" Ryan asked Slater. "You should settle with her for your services."

"As a matter of fact, I do," Slater said with a bemused smile.

"I can't access my bank account, remember?" Megan said, angry at the two men for ganging up on her.

"I'm sure a pretty little rich thing like you has more than one bank account, Mrs. Babcock," Slater stated. "One you've hidden from your husband. So, pay up because I have lawyers, too."

Ryan liked Slater's style. He wasn't scraping and bowing to a pretty girl with a boatload of money. Slater had his own pretty girl and was making his own money. And, to Ryan, the look on Megan's face said that Slater had struck a nerve.

Sitting back down at the computer, Megan Babcock accessed her secret account, wired Ryan's fee to him, and then wired money to Slater to cover the security company's expenses.

"Satisfied?" she asked.

"I'm happier," Slater replied as he checked to see the money had moved successfully into the SKY Security Services account. Ryan checked his balance, too, to confirm Megan's payment had arrived.

"Now, Megan, do you want to draw up a fresh contract for me to go to New Amsterdam?" Ryan asked.

"Yes." The billionaire businesswoman brushed her blonde hair out of her eyes and stood. "I want you to prevent Blake from loading MCG equipment and resources onto that freighter."

"You in on this, Slater?" Ryan asked.

The security man held his hands up, palms out. "I'm out. I've got my own work to do."

"TJ! Scott!" Ryan thundered.

The two men entered the room. TJ clutched his right arm to his ribs.

"I know you two turkeys were eavesdropping," Ryan said. "Who's on board?"

"I'm out. My ribs hurt too much," TJ said.

"More like you're trying to get laid," Scott shot back. "I'm good to go, Ryan."

Ryan looked his tattooed friend in the eye and nodded.

"All right, Megan, here's the standard contract," the troubleshooter said after taking his place behind the computer and pulling up the documents he used when working as a troubleshooter. "It basically says you agree to pay for all services and expenses incurred while recovering your equipment. The service fee is nonnegotiable, but I won't charge you expenses if we only make a partial recovery or don't recover your property at all. You're welcome to read it and e-sign at the bottom."

Megan sat behind the computer again as Ryan vacated the seat. "You'd better get it," she replied, scrolling to the bottom to sign her name.

"We'll do our best, but as this sale is legitimate and your husband has negotiated in good faith with Sub K, we'll be stealing the cargo."

"Piracy seems to be a way of life for you, based on this fee," Megan replied.

"You're lucky he isn't charging you a fifty percent finder's fee," Scott said.

Megan e-signed the contract with a flourish and said, "I can assure you, my husband did *not* negotiate the sale in good faith."

Ryan stood. "Since Slater has asked you to leave, would you like us to escort you to the Marriott Hotel in Georgetown?"

"Is that an extra fee?" Megan asked sarcastically.

"Free of charge if it gets you out of our hair," Slater said.

Megan turned to Emily. "Will you join me, or will you charge me for your friendship?"

"I'm happy to join you as long as my husband doesn't need me."

Ryan shook his head.

"Then it's settled," Megan said. "Emily and I will get a suite at the Marriott."

Ryan called the hotel and made a reservation in Megan Babcock's name. The hotel manager fawned all over the phone at the prospect of such a wealthy client visiting his fine establishment.

Slater volunteered to drive and organized one of his men to act as an armed escort, while Ryan called Chuck Newland to see if the pilot was still in Guyana. As Megan turned toward the door, Ryan snapped his fingers, pointed at the blank sheet of paper on the desk, and mimed drawing on it. Megan happily sat down and began to draw.

When Chuck answered Ryan's call, he said, "I figured you'd be calling me again, so I hung around to see what shook out."

"We need a smaller bird. It will be just me and Scott flying to New Amsterdam."

"We've got a Robinson R44. Will that work?"

"Sure will," Ryan confirmed, knowing the helicopter had four seats.

"How soon do you want to be airborne?" Chuck asked.

"As soon as possible," Ryan replied, watching Megan's sketch take shape. "I'll see you when you get here."

He ended the call and stared down at the two drawings Megan had hastily done, showing the layout of the house and the compound. They looked like something a two-year-old had scrawled without the Crayola colors, but at least he had something to orient himself with. Ryan questioned Megan about each building and added labels to the warehouses, workspaces, and rooms in the house.

By the time Megan answered all of Ryan's questions, Slater had the SUV fueled and ready to roll, and Emily had packed her bag for the trip. Ryan met the women at the vehicle. He hugged and kissed his wife goodbye, and she cautioned him to be careful. Megan Babcock shook her rescuer's hand.

"Thank you," she said. "I really am grateful for everything you've done. Please be safe."

"Be good company for my wife. She knows how to handle herself if you get out of line," Ryan replied.

"That's only how I keep you in line," Emily retorted good-naturedly.

"Let's go!" Slater called through the open window.

The women climbed in, and Slater headed out of the compound.

Ryan watched the white SUV until it had disappeared behind the trees on East Bank Public Road. He wished he was in that SUV, headed for the airport so he and Emily could fix their boat and get underway on their Pacific voyage. He was sick of fixing other people's problems instead of concentrating on his relationship.

And now he was going into battle once again.

CHAPTER TWENTY-FOUR

Instead of going after Emily and demanding they forget all about the mission and run away together, Ryan thrust his hands in his pockets. He had a contract to honor and a rich woman who would pay them handsomely for it—if they made it out alive and the Iranians didn't put a price on his head for meddling in their business.

With a weary sigh, Ryan headed back into the office to find Scott.

The former SEAL stood in the garage with Larry Grove, who was in no hurry to return to his job in Washington, D.C. He grinned as Ryan approached. "Got room for one more?"

"For you, Iceman, we always have room, but you might have to sit on Scott's lap in the helicopter. Just don't talk about the first thing that pops up."

"You're a twisted man, Weller," Larry said.

Ryan shrugged. "Scott hasn't had a lady friend in a while, so be careful."

"I think he should sit on your lap," Scott shot back with a grin.

"How about the loadouts?" Ryan asked, changing the subject. "What do we have?"

"When TJ and I flew over from *Dark Ocean*, we brought MP5s. Nice squirters, but we only have two. One is mine. You and Larry will have to flip a coin for the other one," Scott said.

"I'll take the B&T from here," Ryan said. "It's not a bad alternative, and I'm familiar with it."

"You and Iceman will have to grab Glocks from SKY's armory, too," Scott said.

"Roger that," Ryan said. "What about kit?"

"The same, brother. TJ and I only came with what the two of us needed."

Ryan located what he and Larry needed in SKY's weapon locker, then came back fully outfitted for battle. He wished he had a few grenades at his disposal, but he did find some thermite cord for cutting steel and added it to his pack.

As the three men wrapped up their kit, they heard a helicopter hovering overhead. They quickly went outside to find Chuck had arrived in a bright red Airbus EC120 Colibri helicopter instead of the smaller Robinson R44. As he came in for a landing in the small clearing near the river, Ryan was thankful for the upgrade in aircraft. The EC120 carried more passengers and had a larger fuel tank, giving it an extended range.

Walking past Kendra's house with his gear in a backpack, Ryan glanced up at the porch, where Kendra and TJ had watched the helicopter's arrival while holding hands.

Ryan shook his head and muttered, "What in the world is happening? The sicario and the fishing guide. It makes no sense."

While it had been years since Ryan had last seen Kendra, he couldn't escape the fact that they still shared a physical bond from their time together. Ryan had thought that when she'd sailed out of sight all those years ago, it was the last he would ever see of her, and he'd hoped never to cross paths with her again, but there they were, in the heart of Guyana—except this time, Kendra had hooked up with Ryan's friend. Or it appeared that way. TJ was smitten as a kitten.

Ryan tried not to wonder what Kendra's game was now. During their last op together, she had lured Ryan into being the sacrificial lamb to lure out the elusive cartel leader. He prayed Kendra wasn't using TJ in a similar fashion. The kid deserved better.

"Let's go!" Scott shouted over the roar of the helicopter's rotors.

Ryan picked up the pace and jogged the last bit to the EC120. After stowing his bag between Scott and Larry in the cabin, he climbed into the front left seat. Sitting in the co-pilot's seat, Ryan had an incredible view through the bubble nose of the helicopter. He reached for the headphones hanging from an overhead hook and placed them over his ears before adjusting the boom mike.

"What's up, Chuck Wagon?" Ryan asked.

The pilot held up his middle finger and grinned at Ryan, who could see his reflection in the mirrored aviator sunglasses Chuck wore beneath his white Stetson cowboy hat.

"This is the nicest Robinson R44 that I've ever been in," Ryan commented as he twisted in his seat to check out the cabin.

"Knowing you, I figured you could use the extra room for pax and payload, and I was right."

Chuck pulled up on the collective and hauled back on the cyclic, and the EC120 rose off the ground, scattering dust and leaves and whipping the nearby tree branches around like they were caught in a hurricane.

"I appreciate you taking the initiative," Ryan said.

"I'd rather you bring me back a souvenir," Chuck said. "Or an envelope full of cash."

"Here, I thought excitement and adventure carried you through."

"That only goes so far. Flying DWR's King Air in straight lines gets a little boring," Chuck replied candidly. "I'd love a free gun or a good party like we had on that first wild ride in Key West."

"I'll see what I can do," Ryan said, grinning at the memory. "But I make no promises."

Chuck shrugged. "Either way, I'm getting paid, and this has already been a helluva ride."

He vectored the helicopter toward New Amsterdam, flying at ten thousand feet following the flight path the control tower at Cheddi Jagan had given him.

It didn't take long to cover the fifty-three miles to their destination over lush, jungle-covered land dotted with little farms carved from the undergrowth. About fifteen miles from the Berbice River, the landscape changed to massive sugarcane fields for as far as the eye could see.

"Can you take us down so we can get a closer look at the MCG docks and facilities?" Ryan asked.

"Sure thing, boss."

Chuck turned and flew south, then banked around to fly upriver, keeping the helicopter about fifty feet above the stained water. Fishermen in little boats ducked as they zoomed overhead. Chuck slowed as they approached the MCG Marine Defense facility and came to a near hover as they passed by, turning the bird slightly and crab-walking it through the air so Ryan had the best view possible.

Ocean Trakker sat moored to the concrete shipping quay. Its once clear deck, where they had landed the Sikorsky S-92 during the rescue of Megan Babcock, was now cluttered with shipping containers and a long, cylindrical object covered in tarps. It looked to Ryan like the MCG employees had packed up the entire facility ahead of the move overseas.

"Circle around the compound, then drop us at the heliport outside the Berbice Hospital," Ryan instructed.

"Roger that," Chuck replied.

They flew around the eastern and southern sides of the MCG compound, observing the heavy mangroves and river swamp backed right up to the razor wire fence that surrounded the entire property. The doors of several buildings had been left wide open, and workers stopped what they were doing to stare up at the red helicopter as it buzzed overhead. Ryan saw forklifts packing crates into shipping containers but no actual submarines, and he commented on this to his friends.

"They're supposed to be in that big warehouse by the dock," Larry advised. "They roll them out on railroad tracks and load them onto ships to take them out to the ocean for testing. Could be what's under that tarp on the *Ocean Trakker*."

Ryan didn't need to ask how Larry knew the information. The DIA had its own intelligence network outside of the normal FBI and CIA channels, and since MCG worked extensively with DARPA, their military minders had probably been to the facility numerous times to check on their technological investment.

Chuck straightened the helicopter and climbed over the trees lining the Canje River. Below, one of the SAFE Boats International Defenders used by MCG as a picket and patrol boat came racing in from the Berbice River and slowed near the Canje docks as the helicopter crossed the river and descended toward the grass landing zone outside the nearby hospital.

Dark Water Research's chief pilot settled the bird on the grass and slowed the rotor speed.

Before Ryan removed his headphones, he asked, "Chuck, can you find us a seaplane? It might come in handy."

"I know exactly where to find one," Chuck replied. "In fact, Fort Meyer would be happy to co-pilot."

Ryan grinned. "I bet he would."

He hung the headset on its hook and climbed out of the helicopter, finding Scott and Larry outside the rotor arc with all their gear in a pile at their feet. The three men hurried away from the landing pad as Chuck added power to take off.

The three men hustled toward the gate out of the hospital grounds before anyone could stop them. Once on the street, they hailed a passing microbus used as a local taxi and rode a mile to a hotel in downtown New Amsterdam. Ryan rented two rooms. Then they played the children's game Rock, Paper, Scissors to determine who would get to sleep alone. Scott was the winner after a best two out of three, meaning Ryan and Larry would have to share a room.

"At least we won't have to listen to him snore," Ryan said to Larry.

"I don't snore!" Scott replied indignantly.

"That's not what the ladies say," Larry replied with a grin.

"They wouldn't know," Scott said with a grin. "I keep them up all night."

"That went off the rails in a hurry," Ryan said. "Let's stow our gear and get something to eat. I'm ready for lunch."

The restaurant was on the top floor of the five-story hotel. It had a full bar and open-air seating, giving the patrons sweeping views of houses and buildings painted in bright colors and roofed with corrugated tin sheets. The three operators ordered sandwiches and cold beers and sat in the shade of big umbrellas. The oil money hadn't flowed much past the Guyanese government offices, and Ryan doubted if it ever would. Many countries that relied on petrodollars never dispersed them to the general public. Instead, the rulers of the kingdom or the brutal dictators who ran the countries kept the riches for themselves. If there was a shining example of that, it was Guyana's neighbor, Venezuela.

"What now?" Scott asked as they finished their lunch. "We already have the place scouted, and Megan drew you a map. My guess is there won't be much stuff left in the warehouses by the time we get there."

"Fewer places for the enemy to hide," Larry countered.

"Our main focus will be the house," Ryan stated. "Our target will either be there or on the ship."

"What's your thought process here?" Larry asked. "I know you have a plan."

"I think we go in late tonight or early in the morning and catch them all napping," Ryan said. "We can scoop up Babcock and then figure out how to steal a ship. If Babcock isn't around to sign the paperwork, then maybe the sale won't go through."

"Seems legit," Scott said. "He'll probably start crying as soon as we black-bag him."

"From the background I read, he was an Army Ranger—and I think he and Spooky John served together as John said the target knew him," Ryan said.

"Or they met while they were in D.C.," Larry suggested.

"Either way, Babcock's had some training," Ryan said.

"Good training, too," Scott commented. "Not as good as us SEALs, but you know, not everyone can make the cut."

Ryan didn't know if Scott was taking a swipe at him personally, at Blake Babcock, or the rest of humanity in general, and he didn't bother to ask. He was used to the frogman's overbearing ego.

He glanced down at his phone to see he had a new text message from Emily. She and Megan had made it safely to the Marriott, and after checking in, Megan had ordered room service and then passed out after three stiff drinks. Emily's message said she felt more like her personal assistant than a friend.

That didn't surprise Ryan as Megan had a personal assistant in Saint Kitts, and someone had probably been coddling her since she'd been born. In fact, Ryan felt like he was coddling Megan, too. She had hired Ryan as her fixer to repair the damage her husband had done to her business. Remembering her earlier words in the orchard, Ryan wondered if she hoped he would take care of Blake permanently.

Since they weren't planning to infiltrate Blake Babcock's home until much later, Ryan signaled the waitress for another round of beers. After she'd brought them from the bar, the three men discussed tactics and how best to crash Babcock's party.

With security on high alert around the MCG compound, slipping past the patrols and capturing Blake Babcock would be tricky. Ryan had no doubt that a law attributed to Edward A. Murphy, U.S. Air Force captain and aeronautical engineer, would come into play: "Anything that can go wrong will go wrong." The follow-up to that refrain was generally: "Left to themselves, things will generally go from bad to worse."

The situation they faced was bad enough, and Ryan prayed Murphy wouldn't turn up to make it worse.

CHAPTER TWENTY-FIVE

MCG Marine Defense
New Amsterdam, Guyana

Things had gone from bad to worse for Xerxes Adi as he slammed the receiver into the phone cradle on Blake Babcock's desk and fumed over the news he'd just received.

He leaned back in the leather office chair and rested his chin on his hand as he contemplated the recent events.

The FBI had raided the offices of Subsurface Kinetics and seized all the assets associated with the business, including the money he planned to use to pay Blake Babcock for the purchase of MCG Marine Defense.

Reaching for his secure satellite phone, Adi stood and left the room, walking up the stairs to the rooftop patio. He dialed his superior at MOIS and waited for the phone to sync with the orbiting satellites and connect to the home office in Tehran. When the call finally connected, Adi breathed a sigh of relief. He hated calling his superior to have this conversation, but placing the onus on his boss took the pressure off his shoulders.

Kamran Farrokh answered with his usual courteous greeting. Adi pictured the elderly cleric in his opulent office, surrounded by colorful Persian rugs, gold lamps, and a desk and bookshelves constructed of locally grown walnut. Farrokh often wore the more traditional *qabaa*, a V-neck robe with one side crossing the other at the waist and falling to the slippers Farrokh favored. Coupled with a white crown-style turban and a long beard streaked with gray and white, the cleric portrayed himself as an orderly and knowledgeable man.

Adi imagined his boss stroking his beard as he listened to his agent recount the horror of the FBI's raid on Subsurface Kinetics. When he finished, Adi waited for Farrokh to give him further instructions, but he heard only silence. He pulled the phone from his ear to check that the call was still connected.

Finally, the cleric said, "It is a shame the FBI has raided our company. We worked hard to set up this deal."

"Yes. We did," Adi concurred. "Do we have other money we could use to pay Babcock?"

"Of course. Is everything loaded aboard the ship?" Farrokh asked.

"It is," Adi confirmed.

"The deal is already done. We shall not need the money. You are to take the equipment without paying Babcock. You will bring him with you to Bandar Abbas as a defector. He is still our puppet and will continue to run Gaspar Industries as we suggest."

"Yes, my *mufti*."

"You have your orders," Farrokh said. "Start immediately."

The head of the MOIS severed the connection, and Adi stood rooted to the rooftop, listening to the silence that darkness had brought on. Other than the hum of insects, Adi could hear no other sounds. Lights from the various surrounding buildings cast long shadows over the tree-shrouded house. Adi's skin had grown damp with sweat from the warm night air and the anxiety he felt in the pit of his stomach. He inhaled deeply, steeling himself for the confrontation with Babcock, smelling the brackish water and the decay in the mangrove swamps.

Babcock would not go willingly to Iran. The man treasured the pleasures of the infidel with all his heart, and in the austerity of the ultra-religious Iran, Babcock would balk at not being able to partake as he would in a freer country.

But that was not Adi's concern. Farrokh had issued his orders, and Adi was to see them through to completion. He guessed the MOIS had only allocated the funds they needed to this operation and would not part with any more money to satisfy Babcock, especially as they already had the man on the hook over his despicable vices.

Using the satphone again, Adi dialed the captain of the *Ocean Trakker*. When Captain Aziz came on the line, Adi ordered him to prepare the freighter to get underway. They would be leaving as soon as possible.

Adi went downstairs to the bedroom he had occupied since their arrival from Saint Kitts. He found the black syringe kit he had used when doping Megan Babcock, took out a syringe, and filled it with ketamine from the vial he also removed from the bag. After ensuring the needle was ready to plunge into Babcock's arm, Adi headed for the master bedroom.

Pushing through the door into Babcock's palatial suite, Adi prepared to shove the needle into the man's arm and drag his inert body onto the *Ocean Trakker*. He had forgotten about the young girl, a gift to Babcock for his cooperation. Adi's men had snatched the twelve-year-old from her home in

Tehran and smuggled her to Guyana for Babcock's pleasure. The prepubescent girl was naked under Babcock, who was thrusting away, white buttocks flashing in the dim light.

Apparently, Babcock hadn't heard the door open, but the girl stared at Adi with vacant eyes. He ignored her and jammed the needle deep into Babcock's right buttock.

The instant the needle pierced the man's flesh, he locked up, quivering with shock. Adi used that moment of paralysis to inject the ketamine into Babcock's bloodstream.

Seconds later, Babcock went limp and passed out on top of the girl. Adi tossed away the syringe and grabbed Babcock by the arms. He rolled the man off the girl, who immediately scrambled back against the headboard and pulled her knees to her chest, wrapping her arms around them for protection.

Adi stepped into the hallway and called for his bodyguard to join him. Darya was a beast of a human, standing well over six feet and pushing a scale's needle past two-hundred-fifty pounds with his thick muscles.

"Hurry, Darya! We must get him to the ship," Adi said, stripping the balled-up top sheet off the bed to wrap around the naked and sedated Babcock. He tossed it to Darya, who spread it on the floor, then unceremoniously dumped Babcock onto the hard tile and wrapped him with the sheet.

"What about her?" Darya asked, motioning to the girl, who watched their every move with coal-black eyes under a thick, dark unibrow. Tears glistened on her cheeks, but she hadn't made a sound since Adi had entered the room.

"Leave her. She's of no use to us."

Darya hefted Blake Babcock onto his shoulder. "I will take him to the ship."

Adi found a rolling suitcase and quickly threw clothing into it, so Babcock had something to wear when he awoke. If truth be told, Adi wasn't looking forward to that conversation.

"I stay?" the girl asked in Farsi, her voice low and full of fright.

Adi paused and looked down at her frail form. The girl remained tucked into a ball at the headboard. He just nodded and left the room, towing the half-empty suitcase behind him. Babcock could find a new suit of clothes in Qom, where the finest tailors in all of Iran made rich robes for the clerics, and he'd have more girls to feed his addiction by plucking them off the streets as Adi had done with the girl in the bedroom.

Leaving the house, Adi turned on laser tripwires that would alert him to any movement in the building. If the girl left, so be it, but if someone came for Babcock, he wanted to know.

Babcock had shuttered the MCG facility and dismissed the workers, save for several engineers who had agreed to work for Subsurface Kinetics. They hadn't volunteered to go to Iran, but that wasn't Adi's problem, either, since Darya had already herded them onto *Ocean Trakker* under the guise of moving to Miami. As he strode through the empty compound, Adi prayed the captain was ready to get underway as instructed.

Ironically, Darya dumped Blake Babcock onto the same bunk his wife had occupied before her rescue. The deck still had a red stain from where the nurse had bled onto the steel. Adi tossed the suitcase inside the small cabin, and then he and Darya stepped into the passageway. Darya dogged the hatch behind them, but he didn't secure the lock as they had with Megan. If Blake got out of hand, Adi still had a healthy dose of ketamine left. Babcock could sleep all the way to Iran.

Adi strode up to the bridge, where he found the captain sipping coffee. The MOIS agent poured a mugful for himself from the pot and then asked how soon they could get underway.

"The engine is warming up now. However, we can only leave once the Berbice River Bridge opens at five a.m. It opens once per day for an hour and a half."

Adi swore and clenched his teeth before taking a sip of coffee. There was nothing they could do but wait.

CHAPTER TWENTY-SIX

MCG Marine Defense
New Amsterdam, Guyana

"You see anybody?" Ryan Weller asked into his comms unit.

"Negative," Scott Gregory and Larry Grove both replied.

The three men had just walked past an unmanned gatehouse and spread out in the MCG Marine Defense compound, each taking a different path toward the house set off to the eastern side of the manufacturing facility.

Ryan had an uneasy feeling about the entire situation. The last time they'd observed the place, there had been roving patrols made by the Defender boats along the Berbice and Canje Rivers and armed guards standing at the gate, checking the identification of everyone who entered. He figured they would at least encounter resistance inside the fence, but they hadn't seen anyone so far.

"Converge on the house," Ryan instructed his team.

Moments later, the three men arrived at their prearranged rendezvous point at the rear of the house. They knelt in a cluster of trees in the middle of an ornately tended garden bearing fruit trees and a wide variety of flowers. Ryan imagined that in the daytime, the garden looked spectacular. As it was, it smelled fantastic, the scents of the flower blossoms drifting on the breeze.

Ryan wished he had a night vision monocular so he could better study the exterior of the home or even a thermal scope to see if anyone was moving inside. As houses went, it wasn't overly large or ostentatious for a billionaire, but it was a helluva upgrade compared to the shacks just down the road. He wondered if all the workers had split once they'd found out they were out of a job, and then he wondered how long it would be before the locals started stripping the place for spare parts. With no one standing guard, the Guyanese would have free reign of the place.

"Screw it," Scott said impatiently. "Let's just go in. There's no one here, anyhow."

"We'll stack up on you, Romeo," Ryan said, and he moved into the middle position while Iceman took up the rear.

"'Romeo?'" Scott asked as they moved toward the house, guns shouldered and ready for action.

"We're still working out a code name for you," Ryan replied. "Romeo seems appropriate for all the women you've dated."

"I think maybe we should call *you* that," Scott said. "Everywhere we go, we run into some woman you've been with."

"Fine. I'll go back to calling you 'Cowboy,'" Ryan said.

"Clam it up," Larry snapped. "Just because the troops have left the compound doesn't mean we can let operational discipline go to hell."

"Roger that, Iceman," Scott replied.

"Stay cool, Playboy," Larry said with a chuckle.

The French doors at the back entrance led into a spacious living room. The doors were unlocked, and the three men quickly entered and swept their sectors before moving through the rest of the lower level, clearing the kitchen, dining room, office, and a second parlor.

"Let's check out the second floor," Ryan said as they regrouped at the bottom of the stairs.

They walked silently up the marble steps onto a broad landing, then started down the hallway, stopping to clear each room. The only person they found in the house was a young, naked girl, huddled on the bed in terror at the sight of the armed paramilitary contractors.

"What do we do with her?" Scott asked.

"Nothing. We don't have time to deal with her," Larry said.

But Ryan knew he was wrong. They couldn't leave her. He moved forward, lowering his weapon to show he wasn't going to hurt her, but the girl still pulled away. He spoke gently to the her, but she didn't seem to comprehend his words. Ryan switched to Spanish, kneeling beside the bed.

"I found her clothes," Larry said, bringing them over and placing them on the bed. "Get her dressed and let's go. Babcock is probably on the ship."

"Yeah. I know," Ryan shot back. He couldn't leave this young girl to fend for herself, but she didn't seem in a hurry to comply. It appeared that she'd been through a traumatic experience, and neither his English nor his Spanish was getting through to her. He stood and gestured to the clothes, then turned to go. If there were time, they would come back for her.

Still exercising a great deal of caution, the three men exited the house and began moving toward the shipping quay.

Up ahead, they could see lights glowing aboard the *Ocean Trakker*.

Every building they stepped into was empty, devoid of MCG employees and most of the equipment. Some machinery, either too heavy to move or embedded in the concrete, had been left behind.

By the time Ryan, Scott, and Larry arrived at the quay, they could hear and feel the heavy vibration of the ship's engine. Crewmen milled about on deck while a supervisor shouted orders.

"What are they waiting for?" Scott asked.

"Probably the bridge opening," Ryan replied. "I never understood why old man Gaspar built on this side of it since it only opens once a day."

"Tactical error on his part," Larry replied. "What's the plan now?"

Ryan had been pondering this exact question as they'd moved through the compound. He'd hoped to find Babcock in the house and be able to drag him out without having to go back aboard the freighter, but as predicted, Murphy had come out to play. Things had gone wrong and would continue to degrade the longer the mission dragged on. That was the nature of their business.

"You still think the sub is under that trap?" Scott asked, pointing toward the ship.

Crowding the deck where they had landed the Sikorsky a couple of days prior were cargo containers and a long dark hull barely visible under a canopy of tarps secured with ropes and bungee cords to the freighter's deck. As they watched, crewmen began peeling off its covering.

This flurry of activity concerned Ryan as he studied the submarine. He estimated it to be one-hundred-fifty feet long and perhaps forty feet wide. It was not the typical round shape of most modern submarines with a bulbous nose, but more oval in shape, with a short sail located just forward of amidships. He wished he could get a closer look at the underwater vehicle for curiosity's sake but decided it could wait.

"They only have one working prototype," Larry commented. "MCG was in the process of building another, but I don't see it."

"How did America let this happen?" Scott asked as the crane arm swung overtop of the submarine. It appeared as if the crewmen were about to move the submersible.

"A weak administration who's sold their soul to the highest bidder," Larry remarked dryly.

Ryan consulted his phone, finding the next bridge opening was at five a.m. "We have an hour before the ship gets underway," he told the others. "I don't have a plan for any of this. I expected Babcock to be in the house."

"I guess we'll just have to rescue him from the ship. We can't let the Iranians hold him hostage for pallets of cash and economic concessions like they do with other American detainees," Larry said. "And I doubt Babcock would defect willingly to Iran. His tastes are too lavish."

"We have an hour, and the clock's ticking," Ryan said.

"Then we'd better get a move on because it looks like he might escape in that submarine," Scott said. "And there's two ways onto the ship—up the gangplank or climb the mooring lines."

"Gangplank it is," Ryan said.

"Rules of engagement?" Larry asked.

"Weapons free," Ryan replied. "Consider everyone as a hostile."

With that, the men started toward the ship, leaving the shadows of the building behind and running through the ring of light cast by the shipboard lights. Scott was the first onto the gangplank, raising his MP5 and shooting the crewman standing guard at the top with a suppressed three-round burst.

The gangplank swayed under their feet, and the loose boards rattled with each running step. Fortunately, the sound of the ship's engine drowned out their progress and prevented the crew on deck from alerting their shipmates to the three men invading the freighter.

Unbeknownst to Ryan and his two teammates, the alarm had already sounded aboard the *Ocean Trakker*.

CHAPTER TWENTY-SEVEN

Aboard *Ocean Trakker*

Xerxes Adi's phone had alerted him to the intruders entering the Babcock home inside the MCG compound. He wished he'd planted some cameras around the facility so he could see the forces amassed against him, but he'd figured the ship would be long gone by the time someone came for Blake Babcock.

He cursed the delay of having to wait for the bridge to open. Turning to Darya, who had joined him on the bridge, Adi said, "Load Babcock into the submarine." Then, to the captain, he instructed, "We have armed intruders on the way to the ship. Lower the submarine into the water. I will take it, and you can follow when the bridge is open."

"Yes, sir," Captain Aziz replied. He lifted his radio to his lips and gave the order to strip the submarine of its covering and to use the aft crane to lift it over the side of the freighter.

As Aziz and Darya carried out their orders, Adi headed

for the main deck. He carried the syringe kit in his left hand and his Glock pistol in his right. Should someone dare to get in his way or not follow his instructions, he would shoot them. There was no time for niceties. The future of Iran was at stake. With this new submarine technology and their nuclear missile capability, Iran would control not only the Strait of Hormuz but the entire Middle East. Finally, they could erase the Zionist state of Israel off the map.

The MOIS agent waited impatiently as the crew began to strip the submarine of its covering, and the crane swung into place over the sleek black hull.

Darya appeared with Blake Babcock cradled in his arms. He'd dressed the unconscious man in shorts and a T-shirt. The big enforcer was "farm strong," as Adi had heard Americans say. It was a strength born of intense labor in his youth on his family's farmstead near the Caspian Sea. He moved with ease with the sleeping billionaire defector in his arms.

"Get him inside quickly," Adi instructed.

While Darya carried Babcock up the sub's boarding ladder, Adi headed into the bowels of the ship to find one of the technicians. He needed someone who could drive the submarine if he failed to wake Babcock from his ketamine-induced slumber.

Adi found MCG's chief engineer, Dave Sharpe, in the bunk room where Darya had locked him and the three other engineers who had agreed to work for Subsurface Kinetics. Adi summoned Sharpe outside at gunpoint and threatened to shoot the others if they made a move.

The Iranian prodded the American engineer through the ship with the barrel of his pistol. Just as they reached the main deck, red lights started to flash, and a low siren blared throughout the ship.

Intruders had come aboard, and Adi didn't have a moment to spare.

"Get into the submarine!" Adi yelled at the engineer. "Do it if you want to live."

Sharpe scrambled up the boarding ladder and entered the sub through the open hatch in the sail with Adi right behind him. Pausing at the hatch, Adi glanced fore and aft, seeing the crewmen from the freighter attaching the sling hooks to the submarine. With the ship under attack, he felt a keen sense of urgency to get underway.

Inside the submarine, Adi glanced around at the controls. While there were plenty of old-fashioned handwheels and valve levers, the submarine primarily operated via touch-screen computers.

"Get this thing started," Adi ordered Sharpe, and the engineer sat behind the control panel, pressing buttons to bring the computers to life.

Adi bent over the unconscious form of Blake Babcock and unzipped his syringe bag. He prepped an injection of flumazenil, a drug used to wake surgical patients from sedation, then administered it to the unwitting billionaire and waited for Babcock to come out of his stupor. Leaving his kit on the deck, Adi stood and went topside again, summoning Darya out of the submarine.

"Make sure no one gets to the bridge," Adi ordered. "Kill all the infidels."

Darya grinned as he climbed down the boarding ladder. He pulled it away from the hull and motioned for the crane to lift the submarine off the deck. Adi kept one hand on the ladder rung welded to the outer pressure hull and watched as the crane swung the submarine over the side of the ship. Two of the freighter's crew held ropes, one attached to the bow and the other to the stern, to keep the sub from swinging around like a top under the crane hook. Slowly, the crane began to lower the sub toward the water.

Gunfire echoed off the ship's steel hull. Adi remained

confident that the infidels would meet their destruction at the hands of the surviving members of his security team.

Moments later, the submarine rode low in the Berbice River, dark water lapping against the gleaming black hull. Adi ran to the stern, cast off the guide rope, and then unhooked the aft crane sling. Moving quickly to the front, he did the same for the bow line and sling. Once the submarine was free, he climbed into the sail and secured the first hatch, dogging it tight against the outside world, and then continued down through the second and latching it closed, too.

At the bottom of the ladder, he found Babcock starting to stir and the engineer jockeying the controls, doing a two-man job by himself. Adi snatched up the epinephrine injection from the syringe kit and jammed the injector into Babcock's bare thigh. Babcock's eyes snapped open, and he inhaled a deep, ragged breath as the artificial adrenaline surged through his body.

"Get up, fool!" Adi screamed. "We are under attack, and I need you to help drive the submarine."

BLAKE BABCOCK GLANCED AROUND, trying to get a grasp on his surroundings. The last thing he remembered was being on top of the young girl, satisfying his carnal lust. Now, he was inside the MCG Marine Defense prototype submarine.

His body felt both lethargic and incredibly powerful all at once. His skin crawled from the adrenaline rippling through his veins, and his heart hammered so hard he was afraid it might burst from his chest.

Xerxes Adi shoved the barrel of a black pistol into his face and screamed again, "Get up!"

Babcock shook his head, trying to make sense of the situation. "What's going on?"

"The freighter is under attack. If only you get up and help the engineer, we will escape in the submarine."

Rising to shaky feet, Babcock staggered forward and sank into the seat beside Dave Sharpe, who began to issue rapid-fire orders. Sharpe already had the submarine online and the electromagnets energized.

Babcock reached out and grasped the throttle dial used to control the flow of electricity through the ceramic-coated superconductor magnets along the port and starboard sides of the propulsion tube. Before energizing the circuit, he ensured the helium-filled pulse tube refrigerator was actively cycling to keep the magnets cryogenically cooled. Down the center of the propulsion tube was a smaller resistive magnet that consumed part of the electromagnet's power. This allowed the submarine to generate a stable magnetic field and prevent the superconductor magnetic field from breaking down at extreme temperatures and becoming a bad electrical conductor, which would hamper the efficiency of the submarine.

Just bumping the throttle caused the submarine to surge forward. Babcock grabbed the joystick to control the waterjet nozzle that steered the submarine like an oversized personal watercraft, similar to a Yamaha WaveRunner or a Kawasaki Jet Ski.

The submarine raced through the dark water, cutting a long, shimmering wake behind it. Since the dredged channel was only twelve feet deep, the sub had to run on the surface until it reached the open ocean.

Babcock concentrated on manning the controls while Sharpe monitored the temperature gauges and the performance of the magnets and cryocoolers.

"The batteries are low," Adi said, pointing toward the screen that monitored the battery levels.

"They'll charge up as we run," Sharpe explained. "As the

seawater passes through the propulsion tube, it generates a low electrical charge, which we siphon off to run our custom batteries. They use a combination of aluminum, sulfur, and chloroaluminate salt instead of the standard heavy metals in other batteries."

"I don't care about the technical specs," Adi crabbed. "Just get us out of here!"

Babcock concentrated on the computer screen in front of him. A camera embedded at the top of the sail showed the channel ahead, lit with bright red and green lights on the buoys. Farther out, he could see the lights on the Berbice River Bridge. A glance at the performance screen showed the submarine was traveling at a sedate eight knots. Flicking another switch, Babcock turned on two powerful spotlights to illuminate the water ahead.

The submarine immediately responded as Babcock increased their speed, shooting forward like an arrow from a bow. Babcock backed off the throttle dial as the waves grew, and their speed slowed to twenty-seven knots. At that speed, it would take them just under an hour to clear the shipping channel and move into water deep enough to submerge.

The Potosi Bank at the mouth of the Berbice River sloped gradually into deeper water before reaching the continental shelf. The dredged channel ended in about twelve feet of water, sufficient for most cargo vessels, but the submarine had a submerged draft of thirty-two feet, and Babcock didn't want to submerge in anything less than forty for fear of running aground or striking an uncharted sunken wreck.

"Can't this thing go faster?" Adi demanded.

"We're limited by the hydrodynamic properties of the submarine on the surface," Babcock responded. "If the magnetic tunnel isn't full of water, it will cause cavitation. I may have to reduce speed even further to have more effective control."

Adi swore and rested his hand forebodingly on Babcock's shoulder.

The American businessman didn't fail to notice the gun still in the Iranian's hand. Babcock concentrated on the view ahead using the camera feed on the screen. While he had piloted the submarine several times before, Babcock had never done so under the pressure or urgency that Xerxes Adi exerted. The adrenaline from the epinephrine injection was wearing off, and his eyelids fluttered. Suddenly, Babcock's energy was depleted, and he wanted to lie down and sleep, but he was in no position to do so.

In that moment, Blake Babcock realized with perfect clarity that his life had spiraled out of control. A hostile actor had hijacked his submarine, and he knew he had to do something to straighten out his mess.

Babcock had to act, and he had to do it soon.

CHAPTER TWENTY-EIGHT

Bullets slammed into the steel just above Ryan's head as he ducked behind a corner of the passageway aboard the *Ocean Trakker*.

The opposing force had Ryan, Larry, and Scott pinned down, and they were leapfrogging down the passageway and maintaining a constant stream of fire.

"Cover me!" Ryan shouted.

Larry And Scott poked their suppressed gun barrels out and skipped bullets down the metal bulkheads to try to hit the enemy with ricochets.

Ryan raced across the passageway, opened a hatch, and jumped inside the compartment. It was a dimly lit bunkroom that he remembered backed up to a ladderwell from the last time he'd been on the ship.

There was no other exit to the berthing compartment, so Ryan decided he would create one. They needed to gain an advantage in the gunfight, and he only saw that happening by flanking the enemy force.

Slinging his backpack to the ground, Ryan removed the roll of flexible linear thermite cord and started sticking the

V-shaped charge on the bulkhead adjoining the ladderwell. He had one shot at getting this right. If he screwed up, he wouldn't get a second chance. There were a host of ways things could go wrong, from the stairs blocking his exit to Ryan having guessed wrong, and there was nothing on the other side of the bulkhead but another compartment in which to be trapped. In all of those cases, Ryan and his team would be overrun and killed.

"Come on, Murphy, don't screw me now," Ryan muttered as he finished making a large circle with the thermite. He inserted the detonator into the charge, then turned his back to the bulkhead. Once ignited, the thermite would burn as bright as a thousand suns and blind a person if they looked directly at it. Ryan was inherently familiar with shaped charges, having used them extensively in his explosive ordnance disposal career and then to cut metal underwater as a commercial diver and salvage expert.

Clicking the detonator, he instantly heard the metal sizzle and burn. Seconds later, a massive chunk of the bulkhead clattered onto the deck behind him. Ryan turned, and a wave of relief washed over him at having guessed right. Despite the edges of the hole still glowing red-hot, Ryan ducked through into the ladderwell, careful not to burn himself. With his flanking position secure, Ryan began shooting bad guys.

It didn't take long for the opposing force to zero in on his position, but Ryan's quick thinking had taken the pressure off Larry and Scott, freeing them to step out and return fire.

Ryan shot two more tangos, then called out that his sector was clear. Moments later, Iceman and Cowboy joined up on his six as they headed out of the superstructure onto the cargo deck.

The submarine had disappeared.

A sinking feeling opened in the pit of Ryan's stomach. Babcock had escaped.

And once the submarine was out in the open ocean, it would be next to impossible to find.

The team had no time to dwell on Babcock's escape. They were still responsible for restoring the *Ocean Trakker*'s cargo to its rightful owner.

"Secure the rest of the ship," Ryan directed his men. "Get that engine shut down first so this tub can't leave."

"Roger that, boss," Scott replied.

"Hold one," Ryan said, having a sudden thought. "Larry, get on the horn and see if the Navy has any assets in the area that can track that submarine. I know we've got listening devices in the water around the world. Can you have them key in on the Berbice River?"

"I can check," Larry replied.

"Do it. Scott, you're with me. We're going to the bridge."

"Fresh mag. Ready to tag and bag," the former SEAL rhymed.

Ryan headed for the nearest hatch into the superstructure as Larry dug out his satphone and started making calls to Washington, D.C.

Moving quickly up the stairs to the bridge, weapons tight to their shoulders, the two contractors found the ship's captain standing by for orders.

"I knew you were coming," Aziz said calmly, making no attempt to resist. "The spy, Adi, has left me to take the blame."

"Shut down the engine," Ryan ordered.

The captain called the engine room, and the engineers began their shutdown procedures.

"Gather the crew and have everyone leave the ship," Ryan instructed.

"I would rather they gather in the crew mess," the captain replied. "The sun will be out soon, and I don't want them standing around in the heat. I assure you we are hardworking people. We are not part of the armed force that came with Adi. We are simple seamen who work hard to provide for our families."

"I understand, Captain," Ryan replied.

Captain Aziz smiled. "Besides, we could all use a good breakfast."

Ryan's stomach growled at the thought of eating. He, too, was hungry.

"I could use some bacon and eggs right about now," Scott whispered.

"Gather them in the mess, Captain," Ryan instructed.

Again, Captain Aziz used the ship's intercom to hail the crew and requested they gather in the crew mess immediately. Although they seemed to have things under control for now, Ryan wished he had more shooters or at least some assistance from his friendly ghost, Spooky John. The man had been there every step of the way, but now, the CIA officer had seemingly abandoned the project at this critical juncture. Ryan knew he had to follow orders, too, but some follow-through from Headquarters would have been excellent.

Scott slipped out to check the rest of the ship while Ryan remained on the bridge with Aziz until the engineer had shut down the engine, and the diesel generators were online to provide power throughout the ship's spaces.

"All right, captain," Ryan said, "let's take a head count and see if anyone is missing."

In the crew mess, Captain Aziz ordered everyone to sit, then counted the heads of the men and women gathered there. "I am missing two of my crew," he said.

"How many men were in the security detail?" Scott asked.

"Seven," the captain replied.

"Nine dead," Scott said to Ryan. "Two of those must be the missing crew. We also found three guys locked in a berthing compartment. They say a man took away their chief engineer at gunpoint but don't know what happened to him."

"That must have been the other man Adi forced into the sub along with Blake Babcock," Captain Aziz said.

"What's Adi's full name?" Ryan asked, feeling a tickle in the back of his mind at the second mention of the man's name.

"Xerxes Adi," Aziz replied.

Ryan remembered the Iranian now. Spooky John's intel packet had included a photo of him in front of Sub K's office building. Ryan snorted in derision. They had just missed him.

"All right, Captain," Ryan said, shifting gears, "get a couple of your crew to move the dead bodies off the ship. We'll put them in the closest warehouse for now."

"It would be wiser to store them in the cooler," the captain replied. "The next time we are at sea, we can bury them there."

"You're a step ahead of me, Captain," Ryan said, impressed with the sailor's intuition. "We'll follow your suggestions."

Aziz hailed three fit-looking young men to do the dirty work. Ryan ordered Scott to keep them covered, then said to his partner, "I'm going to find Larry."

Scott nodded, keeping a tight grip on his MP5, ready for action if the crewmen tried anything underhanded as he escorted them to the location of the dead bodies.

Ryan stepped onto the cargo deck and walked toward where he'd last seen Larry Grove using his satphone. After he circled the massive deck, peering between the cargo containers, Ryan came upon an Iranian-looking giant with black hair and a prominently hooked nose. He had Iceman in a chokehold.

With the element of surprise on his side, Ryan raised his B&T carbine and peered through the holographic sight at the two struggling men. As Ryan tried to line the Iranian up in his sights, he couldn't help but wonder how the highly trained SEAL had gotten into such a predicament. But he also didn't want to injure his friend. Ryan couldn't shoot Iceman's attacker as he had no clear shot. Grabbing his Gerber folding knife, Ryan charged in and slashed at the bigger man, cutting a deep gash in the Iranian's arm.

The man screamed, but Ryan didn't know if it was in anger or from the pain. Blood flowed freely from the deep wound on the man's forearm, but somehow, the giant's grip seemed to have tightened on Larry's throat.

"Shoot the son of a bitch!" Larry rasped.

Before Ryan could raise his PCC, the Iranian threw Larry aside and charged at Ryan. The troubleshooter stumbled backward, trying to bring his gun into play.

A shot rang out, and the Iranian pitched forward. Two more shots thundered off the cargo containers, and the Iranian went down on one knee, breathing hard and bleeding from three bullet wounds to his chest. Blood frothed at the corners of his mouth as he tried to stand.

Larry walked calmly over to him and delivered a fourth shot to the side of the big enforcer's head. He holstered his pistol and wiped his mouth with the back of his hand.

"Friend of yours?" Ryan asked.

"Iranian intelligence," Larry replied. "He was trying to call Xerxes Adi when I came across him."

"He's the asshat that took the sub," Ryan replied. "He kidnapped Babcock and an MCG engineer to help him drive it."

"Figures," Larry muttered.

"Did you get through to the Navy?" Ryan asked.

"There's only one ship nearby—the USS *Cooperstown*, a littoral combat ship."

"She got a LAMPS bird on board?" Ryan asked.

The Light Airborne Multipurpose System was the Navy's airborne anti-submarine warfare unit fitted to an SH-60 Seahawk capable of dropping sonar buoys to listen for submarines. Once the helicopter found an enemy sub, they could launch AGM-119 Penguin anti-ship missiles or Mark 46 torpedoes as countermeasures.

"Probably. The *Cooperstown* already has the sonar active and is searching for the MCG craft."

"Get them to launch the helo," Ryan said, then pulled out his own satphone to dial Greg Olsen's number.

The sleepy-sounding owner of Dark Water Research answered on the fourth ring, just when Ryan was about to hang up.

"Where are you?" Ryan asked.

"In bed."

"No. Where's *Dark Ocean*?"

"We're off the island of Trinidad."

"Get over to the Berbice River area. We need help searching for a submarine."

"We won't be of much use," Greg said. "Our sonar isn't geared for that kind of operation."

"Doesn't matter. Get here now," Ryan said, then ended the call. He hit the speed dial button for Chuck Newland. As the phone rang, Ryan instructed Larry, "Get us permission to land on that LCS. We need to be in the hunt."

Chuck answered before Larry could respond, but Ryan saw the DIA agent dialing a number on his phone.

"Seaplane is gassed up and ready," Chuck said.

"Scrap that. Come to us in that EC120 helicopter. We need to fly out to a Navy ship. I've got three souls to fly."

"Copy that, Ryan. I'll call you back in a few minutes."

With the call ended, Ryan turned back to Larry, who was doing some fast-talking, trying to obtain permission to land on the *Cooperstown*.

Ryan walked to the freighter's rail and looked down at the quay. His next call was to his wife, who answered with a quiet, "Hey, babe."

"We've secured the freighter with all the MCG equipment on board. Bring Megan and have her unload this junk. The guys and I are about to go after the submarine that Blake escaped in."

"Okay," Emily said. "I'll wake Megan up. We'll get there as soon as we can."

"Chuck is arranging a helicopter right now. If you can get to Eugene Correia International, he'll give you a ride," Ryan said.

"How soon?" Emily asked.

"ASAP, babe. We need you guys here. Otherwise, the *Ocean Trakker* might try to leave with all the gear."

"I understand," she said. "I'll see you shortly. Love you."

"Love you, too," Ryan said and ended the call.

Ryan paced as he waited, the hunger in his belly turning to impatience. He wanted to get moving and search for the submarine. Even if they received permission to land on the *Cooperstown*, he didn't know what he and his team could do other than wait and hope the Navy could locate MCG's experimental vessel and somehow force it to the surface.

Larry ended his call and walked over to Ryan. "We can land on the *Cooperstown*, but that's only because the commodore of Surface Division 21 is aboard, and she likes you."

"Great," Ryan said, not catching the meaning of Larry's statement. "Now, all we have to do is wait for Chuck to get here."

"Let's find some chow. I can smell the eggs cooking from here," Larry said, steering his pal toward the galley. "We've got a few minutes before Chuck arrives."

They walked down to the mess and found Scott eating

eggs and drinking coffee. "All the crew is accounted for, and the dead are in the meat locker," he reported.

Ryan and Larry joined the queue for food and found eggs, toast, and oatmeal. Ryan passed on the latter, having never liked the stuff. He heaped eggs and toast onto a plate and sat at a table with Captain Aziz.

As Ryan ate, he explained that Megan Babcock was on her way to take charge of the ship's cargo and why they would unload it.

Once he finished eating, Ryan headed topside again to wait for Chuck's call. The captain joined Ryan at the rail and lit a cigarette. Without hesitation, Ryan bummed one and sparked it to life with the lighter the captain held out for him. He inhaled deeply and closed his eyes, not caring that he'd broken his fast or that his wife might yell at him for doing so. The rush of nicotine into his system seemed to calm his nerves.

Ryan checked his watch. The flight from Georgetown to New Amsterdam was only a distance of sixty miles. In a fast bird like the EC120, it wouldn't take long for the helicopter to arrive.

His phone rang, startling him out of his thoughts. A quick check of the caller ID told him it was Emily.

She barely allowed him to answer the call before saying, "We're leaving Georgetown now."

CHAPTER TWENTY-NINE

Thirty minutes later, the bright red Airbus EC120 Colibri that Chuck had flown to New Amsterdam yesterday set down on the concrete quay not far from the freighter *Ocean Trakker*.

Ryan, Larry, and Scott ran over to the helo, followed by the ship's captain. Ryan introduced Megan Babcock to Aziz, then hugged and kissed his wife. The three submarine hunters boarded the helicopter as Emily and Megan walked with Captain Aziz toward the ship.

Larry handed Chuck a set of GPS coordinates, and Craig "Fort" Meyer lifted them off the deck as Chuck entered the coordinates into the dash-mounted GPS.

Ryan watched as a white line appeared on the screen, giving them course direction and time of arrival to the USS *Cooperstown* (LCS-23), named for a town in New York. The ship's commissioning had taken place at the Baseball Hall of Fame during an induction of former military members who had gone on to play professional ball.

The *Cooperstown* was a sister ship to the USS *Little Rock*, which had assisted Ryan in two other missions. He hoped the captain of the *Cooperstown* would be as accommodating as Captain Michelle Spearing had been during those two operations.

Within moments, the EC120 had left land behind and was skimming over the bright blue ocean. The sun was still low on the horizon, blinding the men in the backseat but not the two pilots, who had their blackout visors down on their helmets. Ryan listened in on the provided headset as they approached the Navy combat vessel.

Fort Meyer hailed the USS *Cooperstown* when they were ten minutes out. He gave their flight designation and asked to be cleared for landing on the ship's flight deck, generally reserved for the SH-60 Seahawk quartered in the *Cooperstown*'s flight hangar.

"Copy that, Airbus 120. We have you on the radar, and your flight path is clear. Maintain five thousand angels and approach on heading two-three-two."

"Roger, *Cooperstown*," Meyer replied. He adjusted their course heading and moved to five thousand feet above the ocean's surface.

Ryan saw a Seahawk hovering about a half mile east of LCS-23 and assumed the bird was conducting sub-hunting operations.

Moments later, Meyer brought them smoothly in for a landing on the stern of the *Cooperstown*, and Ryan and his team quickly hopped out and ran toward the superstructure when the landing signalman waved them forward. Just as rapidly as it had arrived, the EC120 was back in the air on a return trip to Georgetown.

The ship's executive officer met the three-man team at the hangar hatch. The XO instructed them to turn their weapons and combat gear over to the master-at-arms, who checked to ensure they were unloaded and secure before allowing the XO to lead the men up to the bridge.

Stepping onto the bridge brought back a flood of memories for Ryan, and when he saw the dark-haired woman standing near the helm, he felt like he was having *déjà vu*.

"Captain Spearing," Larry said, coming to attention.

"At ease, Captain," Spearing replied. She rested her hand on the seatback of the captain's chair, where another man sat. "Welcome aboard, gentlemen. This is Commander Paulson, captain of the *Cooperstown*."

"Thank you, ma'am," Ryan replied. "And good to meet you, sir. Thank you for having us aboard." Paulson twisted in his seat, nodded to the three newcomers, and then turned his attention back to running the ship. "What happened to the *Little Rock*, ma'am?"

"She's being decommissioned," Spearing replied. "Rumor has it that the Navy is selling her to Guyana."

Ryan wondered why the Navy was selling the ship but didn't ask.

"Captain Spearing is the new commodore of Surface Division 21, in charge of all the LCS ships in Mayport," Larry stated.

"Congratulations, Captain," Ryan said.

Spearing nodded her thanks, then said, "Now, what's the story with this prototype submarine? Fleet command tasked us with helping you find it."

"It's a highly experimental submarine developed in conjunction with DARPA," Larry explained. "She's been commandeered by men trying to steal the technology and take it to Iran."

"Fleet command sent me the spec sheet," Spearing said. "It seems your prototype is built for stealth and speed, making it difficult for us to find her."

"We have to do our best, ma'am," Ryan said. "The submarine contains an Iranian spy and two civilians being held hostage to pilot it."

"I understand, Mister Weller," Spearing replied. "I'm quite aware of the time-sensitive nature of this mission. We're doing our best. The sonar techs are pinging the ocean floor from our combat information center, and the Seahawk has deployed sonar buoys along the most likely path of the vessel."

Ryan stared out over the expanse of water beyond the bridge. Somewhere out there was a rogue submarine with Blake Babcock aboard. A large part of Ryan didn't care about recovering the submarine, but he wanted to bring Babcock to justice for what he'd done to Megan and what he believed Babcock had done to the terrified little girl he had found in the master suite at the MCG compound. Remembering her caused Ryan to ask permission to step away to make a phone call.

"Granted," Spearing said. "It's not like you can go far unless you plan on swimming."

Ryan snorted at her joke and started for the door with Scott on his heels. As enlisted men who had spent more time on land than aboard ships during their Navy careers, they had always tried to avoid officer country whenever possible and being on the ship's bridge made them both uncomfortable.

Ryan found a place out of the wind and dialed Emily's number. He told her about the girl in Babcock's master suite and asked Emily to check on her. Once Emily had agreed, he ended the call and dialed Greg Olsen.

"We're aboard the USS *Cooperstown*," Ryan explained. "They're hunting for the submarine."

"I've got our sonar on as we head toward your location," Greg said, "but I don't think we'll find it. Our sonar is passive, meaning all we can see is what's on the bottom. We can't ping for the sub."

"I know," Ryan said, "but everything helps."

"I'll call you if I hear something."

"Thanks, Greg," Ryan said and terminated the connection.

He stood with his back to the aluminum hull of the ship and breathed in the sea air with deep, belly-swelling breaths, trying to calm his nerves and praying they would stumble upon a miracle.

CHAPTER THIRTY

Aboard the submarine

Blake Babcock listened intently to the echoing pings from the Navy vessel and the sonar buoys dropped from the circling Seahawk helicopter. He could easily flip a switch and send a distress signal to the Navy, but he didn't know how they would rescue him when they were traveling at forty knots almost one hundred feet beneath the surface of the ocean.

He needed to figure out a way to incapacitate Xerxes Adi. Once Babcock had done that, they could surface and return to New Amsterdam.

"I have to use the restroom," Babcock said.

Adi motioned with the pistol.

Dave Sharpe took over the controls as Babcock rose from his seat at the console and walked toward the head. He eyed the black syringe case Adi had left on the deck but kept going. There had to be a wrench or something he could get his hands on. One good blow to the head would put the MOIS agent out of everyone's misery.

Standing in the head, Babcock didn't find what he was looking for, but he did take the leak that had been his excuse for getting out of his seat. After washing and drying his hands, Babcock stepped into the passageway, carefully closing the door behind him, and quietly went to a tool room. Since the submarine was one giant electromagnet, everything inside the vessel had to be made of a nonmagnetic material or degaussed to prevent it from being attracted to the magnets or becoming magnetized.

Babcock found a two-foot-long spanner wrench and hefted it in his hand. The tool was constructed from titanium and felt much lighter than its steel brethren. Holding it down by his leg, Babcock walked quickly to the bridge.

As Adi turned to ask where he'd been, Babcock swung the wrench with all his might. He struck Adi in the side of the head, but the Iranian still managed to squeeze off a shot from his pistol before he collapsed.

The bullet ricocheted off the bulkhead behind Babcock, sizzled through Dave Sharpe's chest, and penetrated the control panel in front of the engineer. Babcock stared in horror at the destruction he'd caused as he felt the submarine slow.

Out of the corner of his eye, Babcock saw Adi start to rise. Desperate to escape the wounded submarine and his Iranian minder, Babcock swung the spanner wrench again, peeling back the MOIS agent's scalp and crushing his skull. As the man toppled forward, his body involuntarily spasmed, and he squeezed the trigger on his Glock again.

The bullet slammed into the gauge for reading the submarine's refrigerant pressure and shattered it into a thousand pieces. Immediately, the bulkhead turned white with ice as the cryogenically cooled gas blasted into the bridge space.

Babcock jumped to the controls, switching off the electromagnet before it had a chance to overheat or possibly explode, as some of the pulse magnets at the Los Alamos National Laboratory had done in the past. While the superconductor magnets in the submarine were not pulse magnets, Babcock didn't know the extent of the damage caused by the two bullets. If the electromagnets experienced a sudden surge of current, he and the submarine would be goners, vaporized into nothing by a burst of energy that would tear a hole in the sea.

Red lights winked on overhead as the batteries delivered emergency power. Babcock felt the submarine settle lower in the water column, tilting tail down from the weight of the waterjet nozzle. He tried to power on the control console in front of the dead engineer, but the screen remained black.

Panic welled in Babcock's chest at the realization that his emergency beacon no longer worked. He would be unable to signal anyone for help. No one was coming to rescue him.

Holding up his phone to use the flashlight app, Babcock tried to figure out what to do next. He bent toward the console to see if he could establish a workaround and didn't notice Adi had regained his feet. Focused on the repairs, Babcock felt something punch him in the side with a force so violent that it threw him off-balance. The bullet bit flesh milliseconds before his brain registered the clap of the gunshot.

Toppling over onto the console, Babcock dropped his phone as another shot rang out. Suddenly, the red emergency lights went out, and the submarine's interior fell into pitch blackness, save for the light from the cellphone under the console.

Babcock strained forward, feeling warm blood trickling down his torso. His legs were numb, and they didn't seem to want to cooperate. Then, in the silence, he heard a sound that chilled him to the bone.

A jet of water shot through the hull and splashed onto the deck. Babcock saw water puddling near his phone as he continued to struggle forward.

Adi laughed weakly and then coughed a raspy rattle from deep in his chest.

From out of the darkness, the Iranian whispered, "Now, we are both going to die."

CHAPTER THIRTY-ONE

Aboard the USS *Cooperstown*
Atlantic Ocean
Off the coast of Guyana

"Sonar has picked up what sounded like a gunshot," one of the techs shouted before giving a bearing to the location of the echo.

Ryan Weller stood in the dimly lit combat information center, or CIC, with Captain Michelle Spearing. Larry Grove remained on the bridge, and Scott Gregory sat in the enlisted mess drinking coffee.

The chief of the watch picked up the sound-powered phone and called Commander Paulson on the bridge with a report. Even in the bowels of the ship, the crew could feel the surge of the turbine engines as they ramped up to speed the USS *Cooperstown* toward the coordinates the tech had given.

"Another shot fired!" the sonarman relayed, then gave the chief an updated set of coordinates.

"Any other sounds?" Ryan asked, knowing a sub could break apart quickly if the hull had been breached.

Spearing elbowed him in the ribs, hissing, "Pipe down, civilian. Let them do their jobs."

Ryan had spent more time in a CIC as a civilian than he'd ever had as a sailor. Working as an active-duty EOD tech, he had done a six-month cruise aboard the USS *Bataan* (LHD-5) but had never set foot in the CIC, let alone officer country or the bridge. Standing in the *Cooperstown*'s CIC, Ryan should have known enough to allow the sailors to do their job and keep his mouth shut. There was a chain of command, and he was so far outside of it that he couldn't see the links.

"Minor echoes," the sonarman replied in answer to Ryan's question. "Wait. It sounds like the sub has hit bottom."

"What's the depth?" Ryan asked.

Spearing elbowed him in the ribs again.

"One-hundred-seventy feet, sir," someone replied.

"Now, *shut up* before I throw you out," Spearing warned.

Ryan's brain ran at a thousand miles per hour while they waited. The submarine was technically part of the contract he'd signed with Megan Babcock, and they would need to act fast if there were any survivors aboard. He was trying to remember the size and shape of the vehicle he'd seen on the deck of the *Ocean Trakker* to determine the best course for recovery when the sonarman sang out again. "Gunshot!"

A second later, he spun in his seat and yelled, "Two gunshots ... Hull breach!"

"Shit!" Ryan darted out of the room. He had his satphone in his hand as he charged up the ladderwell to the aft flight deck with Spearing hot on his heels.

The phone was dialing out as Ryan stepped outside.

"What's going on?" Spearing asked from behind him.

It was Ryan's turn to tell her to be quiet as the phone connected.

"We picked up four distinct sounds on sonar," Greg answered.

"The sub has a hull breach," Ryan said. "Where are you?"

"About twenty miles away," Greg replied.

"Vector in on the *Cooperstown*. We're over the sub. I need you here with the diving gear prepped. She's sitting on the bottom at one-seventy. We need rebreathers and a salvage kit."

"No. You'll go on surface supply. It'll be faster and give you a longer bottom time. I'll have the crew break out the kit."

Ryan ended the call and turned to head inside to find Scott.

"What's going on?" Spearing asked.

"If the hull has been breached, we need to get down there to rescue any survivors as quickly as possible," Ryan explained. "I've got a salvage vessel close by, and it's hauling ass over here to dive. I need an away boat to take me to the ship when it arrives."

"I'll speak to the captain," Spearing said.

"Thanks. Can you clear the salvage team in? They're aboard a ship called *Dark Ocean*. It's owned by Dark Water Research. They're an approved DOD contractor."

"Yes. I'll do that," Spearing said. She caught Ryan by the arm as he started past her. Gazing up at him, the captain said, "Be careful, Ryan."

"Yes, ma'am."

An hour later, *Dark Ocean* arrived on the scene and took up station over the coordinates flashed to it by the radioman aboard the USS *Cooperstown*.

After getting off the phone with Greg Olsen, Ryan had

called Megan Babcock, explained the situation, and asked her to email him technical drawings of the submarine so they could plan for the easiest and fastest recovery method. Once he had studied the schematics, Ryan, Scott, and Larry had crowded into the CIC to listen to the updates as the sonarman monitored the submarine beneath them. He'd reported when the sound of water striking metal changed to water splashing into water, meaning the submarine was filling up fast.

To look for survivors, Ryan had decided to dive using a rebreather since the surface supply hoses would prevent the hatches from closing, and he would need to lock in and out through the submarine's double hatch system in the sail to prevent further flooding. Knowing Greg was prepping the surface supply gear, Ryan had made a second call to him to ensure the crew aboard *Dark Ocean* had everything set for their arrival, including a rebreather for him to use to access the submarine.

Once *Dark Ocean* came to a stop over the top of the submarine and had switched on its GPS-guided dynamic positioning system to hold it in place, one of the *Cooperstown*'s boatswain's mates drove the Navy ship's rigid hull inflatable boat, or RIB, bearing Ryan, Larry, Scott, and Captain Spearing across to the DWR salvage vessel. Spearing had decided she wanted to observe the diving operation firsthand and had left the *Cooperstown* in the skilled hands of Commander Paulson.

Greg Olsen sat in his wheelchair on the aft deck when the RIB pulled alongside. Ryan jumped across to *Dark Ocean* and held the bow and stern lines for the RIB while Scott and Larry helped Spearing step across.

After casting off the lines, the RIB motored away, and Ryan turned to his friend. "What's up, Hot Wheels?" He bent and gave the man in a wheelchair a bro hug.

"You know—same shit, different day. Riding to the rescue of Ryan Weller, *as usual*."

"Not my rescue. There may be people trapped below. You got the rebreather ready?" Ryan said, understanding the crack at him for always calling for help when the situation got complicated but not taking it personally.

"Macintyre has it set up in the gear room. Check with him."

"Great! Thanks, bud."

Ryan clapped Greg on the shoulder, then ran to the gear locker. He had left his dive kit aboard *Dark Ocean* from the last time they had worked a salvage operation off Tortola in the British Virgin Islands.

Entering the gear room, Ryan found Macintyre, a member of the ship's company, already had Ryan's gear laid out on a worktable. Ryan immediately stripped to his underwear and started pulling on his wetsuit, followed by his dive boots. The taller Macintyre had combed his black hair into a thick braid. He was already dressed to dive and had his rebreather and spare gas bottles strapped into place.

"You've used a Choptima before, right?" Macintyre asked, laying his hand on a chest-mounted Dive Rite O2ptima CM rebreather.

Ryan nodded. "Yeah. I got checked out on it the last time I was on the boat."

"I thought you had. It's all set."

Ryan pulled on his dive harness and hooked the Choptima to the D-rings on his chest. Once Ryan had the rebreather fastened in place, Macintyre helped Ryan strap on two steel forty-cubic-foot bottles of gas, one to each side of his body. He attached a hose from one of the bottles to Ryan's rebreather. "You're all set, mate."

The two men shuffled onto the aft deck and donned their fins and masks.

"Descent line is rigged and ready," Paul Krause, another diver, advised, dressed in his own dive gear and ready to go down on surface supply, with a compressor on the boat pumping a gas blend into his hard helmet when he worked underwater. "Current is a bit strong. Use the tagline."

Ryan and Macintyre jumped into the water together and immediately descended through the pale blue water. They couldn't see the bottom, but as they dropped down with one hand on the descent line, the dark hull of the submarine quickly materialized out of the gloom.

The current moved at what Ryan estimated to be three knots, but once they reached the sand, the submarine's hull blocked most of it, allowing Ryan and his swim buddy to quickly cross the fifty feet between the descent line and the sunken vessel. Macintyre attached a rope to the descent line and uncoiled it behind him as he swam, intent on tying it to the submarine to better accommodate their swim back to the line.

With the rope secure, Ryan motioned that he was going to open the hatch. Macintyre gave him the "Okay" sign with his fingers. Ryan spun the wheel and then lifted the hatch, straining against the weight of the water bearing down on them.

He had to carefully negotiate the small hatch opening to keep from catching his dive gear, and once inside, Ryan motioned for Macintyre to close the hatch. The diver shut the hatch and spun the wheel to lock it in place as Ryan shone his dive light around the interior of the lockout chamber, searching for the button that would purge it of water using compressed air. The beam of light swept over it twice before Ryan realized what he was looking at, and then he pressed the button.

Slowly, the water drained from the lockout chamber, and once it was clear, Ryan opened the hatch at his feet. Typically, a sub's sail didn't act as a chamber, but MCG had specifically incorporated it into the experimental prototype's design to allow trapped sailors to escape if the sub suffered a catastrophic failure. Ryan was thankful MCG had built the vessel with this function in mind, as opening both hatches would have completely flooded the submarine's interior and ruined any chance of bringing someone out alive.

Ryan left all his dive gear in place as he slipped through the open hatch and into the submarine. Water had flooded the boat, and he had to swim forward to reach the bridge. He swept his light around as he hovered just off the deck.

A gruesome sight flickered in the beam. Two dead men floated in the water, face down, arms and legs dangling. One had a bullet wound through his upper spine, exiting out his chest, and Ryan recognized Xerxes Adi from the photo taken in front of the Subsurface Kinetics office. His scalp had been flayed open, the flap of skin floating up to expose the crushed white skull bone beneath. Blood oozed from both men, drifting in small clouds of black and red depending on how the light caught it.

Ryan took a deep breath to steady himself. He'd seen plenty of dead men, but it was always hard to come across a horrific scene like this. At least the Iranian MOIS agent was dead—or appeared to be. Ryan swam over and tugged on Adi's arm, careful to stay out of the man's reach in case he was playing possum, but Adi just bobbed up and down in the water, eyes wide open and mouth gaping as if he was trying to inhale one last breath of seawater.

Spinning in a slow circle, Ryan watched for any sign of Blake Babcock, although part of him hoped the missing billionaire was also dead. He immediately chastised himself. Ryan's duty was to find survivors and bring them out, not to pick and choose who lived and who died—at least not on this operation.

Moving past the bridge, Ryan tried to remember the layout he'd studied on the schematics Megan had sent. It really didn't matter since the boat had one central passageway. He swam through the final hatch into what appeared to be a torpedo room with empty racks and pressure tubes ready to be loaded.

Babcock's body was more vertical than the other two had been, and when he saw the beam from Ryan's light, he began to weakly kick his legs as if trying to get Ryan's attention.

The diver sank to the deck and angled his light upward to study the situation. Babcock had found a trapped air pocket and had his face pressed against the overhead to breathe what precious little air was left as he pushed himself up with his hands on the wheel of a torpedo tube.

If *Dark Ocean* had arrived an hour later, Blake Babcock would probably be dead, solving all of his wife's problems, but that wasn't the case, and Ryan couldn't leave the man to die.

The problem Ryan saw immediately was that Babcock was also bleeding. He had a bullet wound just above his hip on his right side. Red clouds of blood stained the water with each of his movements.

Slowly, Ryan rose to the overhead and eyed Babcock through his dive mask. When Babcock thrashed forward, trying to grab either Ryan's breathing loop or his mask, Ryan was ready for him, face-palming him and pushing Babcock under the water. As the man struggled to break free, Ryan shoved him backward, counting on Newton's third law of equal and opposite reaction to push them apart.

Luckily, he wasn't disappointed. The move gained him some freedom.

This guy is an idiot, Ryan thought as Babcock came at him again.

He pushed Babcock away again, forcing him to swim back to the air pocket to catch his breath.

Ryan approached a third time, holding up a regulator from the spare gas bottle he carried on his hip. Babcock shoved it into his mouth, greedily sucking on the air. With a fresh oxygen supply, Babcock seemed to calm himself. Ryan handed him a spare mask, and Babcock donned it with ease, expelling the excess water inside.

The next issue to tackle was the wound. It had to hurt like hell. Ryan moved closer and lifted the man's shirt to get a better look. The bullet had left a neat little pucker hole in his torso, but there was no exit wound. Ryan needed to triage the injury and get Babcock to the surface as quickly as possible. That meant a direct ascent and a ride in the "Iron Cadillac," as the divers liked to call the recompression chamber aboard *Dark Ocean*.

Using hand signals, Ryan explained the procedure for exiting the submarine. Babcock nodded in understanding. The two men ducked beneath the surface, and Ryan placed Babcock's right hand on his left hip so the man wouldn't strain the regulator hose coming from the tank attached there. Together, they swam through the torpedo room hatch and down the passageway to the bridge. Ryan kept the light focused on their destination and away from the two dead bodies.

There, he wrote on his wrist slate, asking the location of the submarine's emergency first aid kit. Babcock motioned toward another hatch, and Ryan swam over, pulled it open, and found what he was looking for. He opened the kit and was immediately enveloped in a cloud of Band-Aids and gauze pads as they floated away. Snatching a large abdominal pad and a roll of elastic bandage wrap from the kit, Ryan returned to his patient and started doctoring the wound, placing the ABD pad over the hole and then wrapping Babcock's torso with the elastic bandage to keep the pad in place.

With the triage as complete as Ryan could make it underwater, he unclipped the gas cylinder from his hip and handed it to Babcock. He first pushed Babcock into the lockout trunk before cramming himself into the tiny space. Once inside, Ryan closed the hatch and flooded the chamber. He kept a close eye on Babcock, watching the man's facial expressions for any sign of panic, but as the water rose, Babcock seemed content to let Ryan lead the way. As Ryan monitored him, he saw Babcock's eyes flutter. Ryan leaned forward to jam the regulator back into the man's mouth as he lost consciousness.

I'm not looking forward to a chamber ride, Ryan mused as he considered the best way to get Babcock to the surface. He closed his eyes and steeled himself for a straight shot to the surface.

Once the lockout chamber had filled, Ryan knocked on the upper hatch to let Macintyre know they were ready to come out. The wheel spun, and Macintyre pulled open the hatch as Ryan pushed up. With the hatch open, Ryan motioned to Macintyre that he needed help to secure the regulator in Babcock's slack mouth. Together, the two men tightened the reg necklace until it was so tight that Ryan figured it was cutting off the man's will to live, but the important part was that the regulator was secure, and Babcock was steadily breathing, as evidenced by the consistent trail of exhaust bubbles.

Leaving Babcock in the chamber, Ryan wiggled up through the hatch, carefully avoiding catching any of his gear. Outside the submarine, Ryan kept one hand on a ladder rung to keep from drifting away in the current, then stowed his dive light. When he looked up, he saw Macintyre beside him, and that Paul Krause had come down using the surface supply rig. Krause showed Ryan a slate, asking if Ryan wanted him to call for the diver launch and recovery system, or LARS basket.

Ryan nodded. Securing Babcock inside the basket would be far easier than clinging to the unconscious man on the ascent line in the ripping current. He took the slate from Krause and wrote instructions on it. They would need to take Babcock straight up and get him in the chamber with Doc Susan Everhart, *Dark Ocean*'s resident physician, as his attendant.

Moments later, Ryan saw the LARS basket arrive on the seabed, not far from the submarine. Krause swam over, untied the safety line from the descent line, and moved it over to the LARS basket.

With the line in place and Krause standing by the basket, Ryan and Macintyre lifted Babcock out of the submarine. Ryan fashioned a loop with the safety rope just under Babcock's armpits and, with Macintyre carrying the gas cylinder Babcock breathed from, the three divers dragged Babcock's limp body over to the LARS basket. Once there, Ryan flipped down one of the folding seats and shoved the injured man into it, then used the safety rope to lash him into place.

Ryan gave Krause a thumbs-up, indicating Babcock was ready to ascend. Krause spoke into his comms unit, and the basket ascended as rapidly as the winch could bring it up. Ryan knew that everyone topside would know what to do once the basket broke the surface.

He checked the computers attached to his rebreather. Everything was functioning normally.

They'd been underwater for an hour. Swimming over to the ascent line, Ryan mentally calculated his decompression time, even though the computers would automatically do it for him and give him the best gas blend at each safety stop.

He and Macintyre would have to spend several hours decompressing from this dive, but to save a life, it was worth it.

Gripping the line as he slowly made his way upward, Ryan thought over the last couple of days. Megan was safe. They had rescued Blake Babcock. And now, the only thing left to do was to raise the submarine.

Ryan knew refloating the submarine wouldn't be easy. If he'd learned anything during his time working for Dark Water Research, it was that what the sea taketh, she hated to give back.

CHAPTER THIRTY-TWO

Ryan scrambled aboard *Dark Ocean* almost three hours after going into the water to search the sunken submarine for survivors. He was tired and thirsty and wondered how Babcock was faring.

He and his dive partner, Andy Macintyre, sat on the dressing bench beside the cargo container that housed the surface supply gear and began shedding their dive equipment. Greg came over with bottles of water for each diver.

"How's Babcock?" Ryan asked between sips of water so cold it made his teeth ache. He set it aside to warm as he wormed out of his dive harness.

"Doc says he'll need a medivac. She's keeping him stable in the chamber," Greg replied.

"How long will he be in there?" Ryan asked. "I figured he'd be out by the time we exited the water."

"Shouldn't be long," Greg said. "In fact, we need to clear the deck so we can get him in the helicopter basket. You and Andy need to take your gear inside."

Both divers stood and headed for the gear locker, carrying their equipment. There was no sense in losing a precious piece of dive gear while the helicopter hovered overhead, lashing the deck with frothing spray.

The rescue bird was overhead by the time the two men finished stowing their gear, showering, and changing into clean clothes. Doc Everhart and a couple of crewmen moved Babcock from the chamber into the basket. With the injured man securely strapped down, they stepped back and watched the helicopter winch in the basket.

"Where's Iceman going?" Ryan asked Greg, seeing Larry Grove clinging to the basket beside the prostrate form of Blake Babcock.

"Babcock is a national security risk. Larry thought it best to keep him under observation."

"Makes sense," Ryan replied with a shrug. As long as he wasn't babysitting Babcock, he didn't care. He hoped the man received a life sentence for selling military secrets to the enemy.

After a moment, Ryan asked, "How's the salvage effort going?"

During his decompression stops, he had seen divers coming and going from *Dark Ocean*. Even Scott had taken a turn in the water, flipping Ryan the bird on his way up and down the line.

"The sub has sling points that make it easy to attach lift bags. Since it hasn't been on the bottom long enough to settle into the muck, we were able to lift it enough to get our web of slings under and around the hull," Greg explained. "The sling points are strong enough for when the submarine is being craned on and off a mothership, but we needed more support against the weight of the water."

Ryan did a quick calculation in his head. The sub was under 90.45 psi of pressure. That was like having the weight of a Mack truck sitting on top of the submarine.

"I've already spoken to Captain Aziz aboard *Ocean Trakker*.

I convinced him to bring his ship out so we can use his crane to lift the sub aboard after we bring it to the surface."

"I'm glad Megan Babcock is on the hook for all this," Ryan said. "Her bill is racking up fast."

"When the submarine is back on MCG's quay, we'll tally it all up. Should be a nice payday," Greg replied, smiling.

"What do you want me to do?" Ryan asked.

"I want you and Scott aboard that freighter, armed to the teeth. If the captain tries any shenanigans, you'll be right there to set him straight."

"Roger that, boss."

"I'll put the Yellowfin in the water and have someone drive you back to New Amsterdam," Greg said.

Ryan covered his mouth as he yawned. "How about tomorrow? I could rack out right now. I've been up since two a.m., been in a firefight, boarded a Navy vessel at sea, and rescued a shitbird from a sunken submarine. My day has been jam-packed."

"Grab some chow and get some rest," Greg agreed. "You can leave first thing in the morning. Besides, some *idiot* ordered the captain to shut down his engine, and it takes a long time to restart those cantankerous bastards."

"I didn't want Aziz scurrying out of port before Megan and Emily could get down there," Ryan reasoned.

"I probably would have done the same thing," Greg said. He held out his fist, and Ryan bumped it with his.

Ryan found Scott in the crew mess. He scooped heaping portions of food onto his tray before joining Scott at a table and explaining the plan.

"Good thing we got all of our gear back from the master-at-arms on the *Cooperstown*," Scott said. "I would have hated to leave Janelle behind."

"Who's Janelle?" Ryan asked.

"She's my MP5. Don't you name your firearms?"

"Can't say that I ever have," Ryan replied.

"Boring," Scott stated. "My favorite sniper rifle is named Karen. She'll drive a tack through your heart faster than my ex-wife."

"Good to know. I learn something new about you every day."

Scott grinned. "I call my pistol Shorty."

Ryan rolled his eyes and dug into his food. The chef aboard *Dark Ocean* always prepared a decent spread, and Ryan wasn't disappointed with this meal, either. He supposed his contract had paid for the beef roast, so he had seconds, followed by a couple of cold beers in the lounge as he talked to Emily on the phone.

She was eager for him to get back. She was tired of being Megan Babcock's assistant. While the heiress had needed a babysitter at the hotel, once Megan was on the ground at the MCG Marine Defense compound, she was all business, rehiring the workers and directing the unloading of the ship while cursing her husband up one side and down the other the entire time.

At least they were making progress, and Ryan was drinking beer instead of unloading a freighter. Yawning again, Ryan finished his beer and headed for his rack to sack out. Dawn would come early, and he had no idea what it would bring.

AFTER FILLING their stomachs with plenty of coffee and a hot breakfast, Ryan, Scott, and Captain Spearing boarded *Dark Ocean*'s runabout, a Yellowfin 32 Offshore center console.

The sun was burning the haze off the water as Ryan kept the throttles down on the Yellowfin's twin Mercury

Verado engines, heading for the mouth of the Berbice River.

At forty knots, the ride was just over two hours long, and Ryan was more than glad to step onto the dock and steady his sea legs.

Emily ran into his arms before he could sort himself out. He held her tight and breathed in and out, letting go of all the pent-up aggression and anger he'd accumulated over the past twenty-four hours, feeling his pulse slow and his blood pressure drop.

Megan Babcock sashayed down the quay in high heels, a skintight gold jumpsuit, and oversized sunglasses. Ryan guessed the entire outfit cost more than most Guyanese made in a year—and it made her look like a cheap hooker.

"Well?" Megan asked, noticing the look Ryan gave her.

"I see your personal assistant didn't lay out your clothes this morning," Ryan said.

Scott snickered.

"There is no reason to treat me rudely, Ryan. I am perfectly capable of dressing myself, and I think my outfit is lovely."

"It would look better on the bedroom floor," Scott muttered.

Megan slid her sunglasses down her nose and gave Scott an evil glare. "And who is this vile creature?"

Ryan made the introductions.

Megan continued to glare at Scott, who was grinning right back at her. She threw her head back to get the wisps of hair out of her face and said to Ryan, "Tell your *friend* that I'm unavailable at the moment. Perhaps he should check back around the time of *never*."

"Show me the hottest woman in the world ..." Scott started to say.

"Don't finish that sentence," Ryan said, holding up a

cautionary finger, knowing Scott would finish it by saying, "And I'll show you a guy tired of putting up with her shit."

Ryan introduced Captain Michelle Spearing to Megan and his wife. "She's our Navy rep for this ride and knows how to handle a ship if Captain Aziz gets squirrelly."

Ryan and Scott transferred their gear from the Yellowfin to the quay in a handy green duffel stenciled with "PROPERTY OF THE U.S. NAVY" that the master-at-arms had given them to carry everything in when they'd left the USS *Cooperstown*. They removed their grimy gear from the bag and started strapping on chest rigs and checking their weapons. Ryan hoped he didn't have to shoot any more people aboard the freighter. He didn't want to repeat the performance a third time, but he and Scott would be ready in case something happened.

Locked and loaded, Ryan, Scott, and Captain Spearing boarded the freighter, where Captain Aziz waited for them on the bridge with a fresh pot of coffee. He was also ready to get underway after having spent the previous night getting the ship's engine back online and scrubbing the *Ocean Trakker* clean of blood and debris from the various firefights.

"Sorry for the inconvenience, Captain," Ryan said. "I hope you understand."

"I am not an unreasonable man," Aziz replied. "My country is hostile to yours, and Xerxes Adi is not a man to be trifled with."

"You don't need to worry about him anymore," Scott said. "He's dead."

Aziz seemed unfazed by the news. "There are others more cunning and ruthless who will take his place."

"Let's hope they don't show up on this trip," Scott muttered.

"How soon can we get underway?" Ryan asked the captain

as Spearing observed the ship's controls and general condition.

"I was waiting for you to board," Aziz said. He lifted a mobile radio to his lips and gave orders in Farsi for the crew to cast off. "The bridge won't be open much longer."

As the crew cast off lines, Spearing asked Aziz, "Why are you helping us?"

"I am aware of the hostilities between our nations. I would be a fool not to be. We were once a peaceful nation, friendly to the U.S. until your CIA removed Mohammad Reza Shah in 1979. Since then, we have been a nation of unrest and hatred, just as they planned. One cannot go to war with a peaceful nation. I feel I must take a stand against the evilness of my government. This is the action I can take."

Ryan unslung his B&T APC9 and hung it from a hook on the bulkhead. "A show of good faith, Captain."

Aziz nodded and then returned to the business of getting his ship underway. Ryan asked if they could load the Yellowfin aboard, reasoning that carrying it on the freighter made logistical sense since the freighter would steam to *Dark Ocean*'s location.

The captain dispatched some crewmen to find some cribbage to rest the center console hull on, and then Aziz's men craned it aboard with ease.

It took another thirty minutes of work before the *Ocean Trakker* lumbered away from the MCG Marine Defense quay and headed for the Atlantic Ocean, passing under the open Berbice Bridge just before its scheduled closing time.

At just eight knots, the ship took a full nine hours to arrive at the submarine salvage site, during which time *Ocean Trakker*'s crew buried their dead at sea.

When the ship was an hour from the dive site, Ryan had hailed Greg Olsen on the radio and told him to start the lift. The crew of *Dark Ocean* had patched the bullet hole in the hull to prevent more water from entering the submarine and had only needed to inject air into the lift bags to raise the submarine to the surface.

Ryan kept watch through binoculars as the *Ocean Trakker* approached the dive site. *Dark Ocean* was the first thing to come into view, with the USS *Cooperstown* cruising north of their position. Greg ordered Captain Aziz to circle around and come in from the east so they could pinch the submarine between the two vessels.

The submarine rode just below the surface, with the sail hatches open and pumper hoses snaking over the side of *Dark Ocean* and into the submarine to clear the water from the interior. With each gallon of seawater weighing 8.34 pounds, they needed to remove as much as possible from the submarine, making her lighter for the crane to lift. While underwater, the danger came from the subsurface pressure, but trying to raise the submarine with all the water still inside would tax the crane to its breaking point and possibly crack the submarine in half.

"We have about sixty minutes before we can try to lift her," Greg radioed to the *Ocean Trakker*.

"Roger that," Aziz replied. "We're standing by."

"Let's get her hooked to the crane. Swing the aft one overboard," Greg ordered. "Drop the Yellowfin with it."

Aziz used his radio to give directions to the crane operator. Once the Yellowfin was free to roam the sea with Scott Gregory aboard, the crane operator swung the end of the boom over the submarine and lowered the cable to just above the sail. Since the *Ocean Trakker* hadn't left port after Adi and Babcock had escaped in the submarine, the crane still had the lifting sling attached, and DWR's divers quickly secured it to the submarine's lifting points and the web of lifting straps they had placed around the hull.

Time passed slowly as the water pumped from the submarine. Growing impatient, Greg ordered a third dewatering pump aboard to speed things up.

As he waited, Ryan scanned the ocean and the skies with binoculars, afraid Murphy would tip his hand in the form of more Iranians swooping in to disrupt their operation. With the USS *Cooperstown* lingering nearby, no one disturbed their salvage effort.

Andy Macintyre crawled into the submarine after an hour had passed, and the pumps had started to sputter from a lack of water. He declared the interior was empty, but the sump was still full of water. After moving the dewatering hoses under the grates, they again waited for the pumps to work their magic.

After another thirty minutes, Macintyre declared the sub was as free of water as they could make it. The crew pulled the water hoses out and laid them on the deck of *Dark Ocean* to be rolled up later for storage.

"Take her up," Greg called over the radio, and Aziz took over the lift operation.

Moments later, the submarine was back in its cradle on *Ocean Trakker*'s deck, and the crane swung back into its stow position. The USS *Cooperstown*'s RIB came alongside the freighter, and Captain Michelle Spearing departed with a wave.

Ryan breathed a sigh of relief as Captain Aziz headed for port. The mission was finally over. Megan had reclaimed possession of MCG Marine Defense and the prototype submarine, and the FBI had Blake Babcock under armed guard.

Ryan felt a certain satisfaction at completing this assignment after being abducted at gunpoint by CIA officers. He had done what the CIA couldn't—or had chosen not to do.

Forty-eight hours later, the *Ocean Trakker* was back at the MCG Marine Defense quay and had disgorged the submarine onto a railcar to transport the craft to a giant warehouse for repairs.

Despite the tragedy that had taken place aboard the submarine, Blake Babcock had demonstrated the stealthy nature of the submersible craft by eluding the Navy's shipboard sonar and their active sonar buoys, and the Navy had swiftly drawn up a contract with Megan Babcock to produce two more of the experimental boats for testing and evaluation.

Ryan packed away his borrowed combat gear and cleaned his gun on the kitchen island of Megan Babcock's house as Emily sat nearby.

"What happened to the girl?" Ryan asked.

Emily shrugged. "She wasn't here when we arrived. I'm not sure where she wandered off to."

Ryan shook his head sadly. His heart went out to her. She didn't speak the local language, and she had been deeply traumatized by whatever had happened in the master bedroom. Ryan could only guess who or what had caused the emotional scars the little girl would forever carry with her.

After his gear had been cleaned and stowed, Ryan went to see Megan Babcock in her office on the first floor. He leaned against the doorjamb. "Contract fulfilled. Are you happy?"

Megan leaned back in her chair and sighed. Ryan was glad to see she was wearing something other than the jumpsuit. Today, she wore white pants and a pink blouse with bedazzled flip-flops.

Where does she get these outfits?

"I'm satisfied that you fulfilled your end of the bargain, although Blake is still alive and refusing to meet with me or my attorneys," Megan said.

"How are things going here? Back up and running?" he asked.

"I lost one of my best engineers on that sub. Dave Sharpe was a genius when it came to electromagnetics."

"Sorry to hear that," Ryan said, remembering the dead man floating in the submarine with a bullet hole in his chest. He changed the subject to purge the memory. "Emily and I are going back to Florida."

"Too bad," Megan said. "I could use a guy like you to be the head of my corporate security."

"My recommendation would be Scott Gregory. The guy with all the tattoos that you met on the quay. We're going to chase the horizon," Ryan replied. "I've had enough of chasing bad guys."

Megan sighed. "I hope you're happy out there."

"I'll be happy when you pay the bill," Ryan said. "And just so you know, it won't be cheap."

"Just email it to me." She scribbled a private email address on a business card and handed it to Ryan. "I've got my hands full here, and I'll be tied up in court with Blake for the foreseeable future."

Ryan cocked his head and listened to the beat of an incoming helicopter rotor. "My ride is here. Good luck to you, Megan. You have the number to my answering service if you ever need to get in touch."

"I hope I'm never in that position again," she said.

Ryan turned to find Emily behind him. The two women hugged, and then he and Emily walked out to the helipad and tossed their gear into the bird. Chuck tipped his hat to Megan, who had come out to watch them depart and stood with her arms wrapped around her, looking frail and alone.

Once in the air, Chuck flew them to the SKY Security to drop off the gear before heading to Cheddi Jagan International Airport.

Ryan watched the scenery pass beneath them, the green jungle thick and beautiful from the air. He hoped he was never down in the midst of it again and prayed he and Emily would make it out of Fort Lauderdale before something else cropped up that demanded his attention.

Right then, the beautiful, tall blonde beside him would be more than enough to satisfy him.

LANDING on the grass inside the SKY Security Services compound, Chuck shut off the helicopter's engine, and the three of them climbed out. Ryan returned his weapons and gear to the locker in the garage and went to find TJ.

"We're leaving, bud," Ryan said, sitting on the couch beside TJ in Kendra's office. "You coming with us?"

"I'm staying," TJ replied. "Kendra and I want to figure out what's happening between us."

"Good luck with that," Ryan said, glancing at the former cartel sicario.

"I'm a very nice person, *Ryan*," she said.

Just not to me, he thought, replaying their time together. He plastered on a smile, trying to be happy for them. Turning back to TJ, he asked, "What about DWR and the crew?"

"That time in my life is over," TJ said. "I appreciate everything you guys have done for me. You got me over the hump when I was having a lot of mental issues, but I'm moving on now. Besides, you've had one foot out the door since I met you, and you've made it quite clear what your next move will be, and it's not leading a team of troubleshooters."

"Yeah. You're right," Ryan conceded. "What about your guide business in Florida?"

"I closed it, and I've already got a buyer for my boat," TJ replied.

"He already has clients lined up to come down here," Kendra added. "They want to do exploration trips to find big peacock bass."

TJ grinned. "She's helping me set up my new business."

"She's got killer instincts," Ryan joked. "But seriously, I hope it's a big success." Clapping TJ on the knee, he rose from his seat and stuck out his hand for TJ to shake. "Happy fishing, brother. Hope you catch the big one."

"Fair winds and following seas," TJ replied.

EPILOGUE

Two weeks later
Harbour Towne Marina
Dania Beach, Florida

Ryan rolled his eyes and sighed through puffed-up cheeks as he flipped the switch to check the running lights aboard *Huntress*.

Of course, they don't work!

Since coming back from Guyana, nothing seemed to have gone right. First, his sander had blown up, and the replacement had quit soon after. Since then, he'd made multiple trips to the hardware store and West Marine to purchase new tools and stainless-steel fittings, only to go back because he'd purchased the wrong item or needed more of what he'd already bought.

Walking into the cockpit, Ryan dropped down wearily beside his wife and laid his head on her shoulder. "I have to climb the freaking mast. The lights are out."

Emily stopped typing on her laptop as she worked to distribute the money Megan Babcock had paid them to recover her stolen assets and submarine. She patted the side of his face. "I know, baby. It sucks, but at least we're in the water and not on land anymore. The hard stuff is done."

Ryan sighed. "I know, but I just want to leave, and it seems like the universe is conspiring against us."

"What's the big hurry?" she asked.

Ryan took his head off her shoulder and slumped in the seat. "I just want to get going. I don't want to get tangled up in another job."

Emily smiled. "That seems to happen no matter where we go."

He sighed again. "I know." After drawing in another deep breath to calm his mounting frustration, Ryan exhaled and stood. "This shit isn't going to fix itself."

"Maybe instead of trying so hard, you should just relax. We'll leave soon enough."

"Not if everything keeps breaking and conspiring against me."

"I think you're suffering from a bout of resistentialism."

"What the heck is resistentialism?" Ryan asked, rolling the word off his tongue in a horrible mispronunciation.

"I read an article about it. The term was coined by humorist Paul Jennings in the late 1940s. He described it as a combination of resistance and existentialism to describe 'seemingly spiteful behavior manifested by inanimate objects' where it's said that these objects exhibit hostility toward humans."

"Well, something is screwing with me," Ryan said. "Whether it's this guy's made-up word or Murphy, they both suck."

All the months of sitting at anchor in North Lake at Hollywood Marina and on the hard at Harbour Towne hadn't done *Huntress* any favors. She was a sailing vessel built to take them around the world, and Ryan was more than eager to start the journey. This time, however, it wouldn't be a fast two-year trip around the world like he'd done when he was younger. He planned to take it slow and explore as much of the planet as possible—at least the tropical part of it. Ryan had no desire to see ice or snow ever again in his life, but if shit didn't stop breaking, they'd never leave port.

"All I'm saying is, take a breath," Emily said. "Remind yourself that you're on permanent vacation. Megan paid us, and after I disbursed all the funds, we still have enough to last a long time. Life is good. And besides, you have an extremely attractive wife who serves you cold beer in a bikini."

Ryan waggled his eyebrows. "Maybe tonight we could try it without the clothes."

"See? Your optimism is improving already, but don't get your hopes up." Emily winked bawdily at him.

Ryan dug out his climbing harness and was pulling it on when a woman stopped at the gangplank and called his name. He hitched the leg straps of the harness into place as he turned to see who was hailing him. The visitor was slightly taller than average height with espresso skin. She had pulled her black hair into a tight knot at the back of her head and wore a black business skirt with a matching jacket over a light pink blouse. The woman's low heels made a clicking sound on the concrete.

Emily poked her head around the corner as if on cue to see what was happening.

"Whatever you're selling, I'm not buying," Ryan said.

"I just want to talk to you," the woman said.

"Come back in six months," Ryan quipped.

"You won't be here. You'll be somewhere out on the wild blue yonder," the woman replied.

Emily walked onto the front deck to stand beside her husband with her arms crossed. "Who are you?"

Ryan noted a hint of jealousy and suspicion in her voice.

"My name is Leslie Connelly. I'm a friend of John's. You called him Jim-John Bowie."

Ryan snorted. "Now I know I don't want to talk to you. Turn around and leave. Forget my name, and I'll forget you were ever here. Even trade."

"Actually," Connelly said, "I wanted to apologize to you. May I come aboard?"

"You can send a fruit basket care of Melissa Hunt to apologize to her for making me miss dinner with her," Ryan replied.

"I don't know Melissa Hunt," Connelly said.

"She's my mother-in-law, and your shenanigans to get me to Saint Kitts caused me to miss dinner with her and for her to make frantic calls to her daughter." He hooked his thumb over his shoulder at his wife.

"I'll be sure to follow up on that," Connelly said, though Ryan doubted she would. "Now, may I please come aboard and talk to you?"

"It's your call," Ryan said to Emily.

"Leave your shoes on the concrete," Emily said.

Connelly stepped out of her heels, leaving the glossy black Christian Louboutins to sit neatly side by side at the head of the gangplank.

The three of them took seats around the table in the cockpit. Emily asked if Connelly would like something to drink. "Whatever you're having," she said.

Emily brought two ice-cold Presidente beers and a bottle of water for herself, setting them on the table before sitting down. Ryan toyed with his, rolling the bottom of the bottle around in the condensation ring. He figured he'd let Connelly say her piece so he could get back to work.

The CIA case officer cleared her throat. “I knew Dennis McGuire was dead before Ground Branch picked you up. We faked the facial recog scan by not even doing one. I figured if McGuire picked you to look into Babcock’s situation, then I needed to follow his instincts. You proved to be an excellent asset.”

Ryan knew it shouldn’t surprise him, but her admission caught him off guard. He never expected her to give him details or admit her complicity in the scheme.

“What’s the word on Blake Babcock?” Ryan asked.

“He’s being held in a secure federal detention facility for the attempted murder of his wife, failing to register as a foreign agent, conspiring to commit treason, and a host of other charges, including defrauding his wife. The only sunlight he’ll see for the rest of his life will be in a prison rec yard.”

“What about Megan’s company? Was she able to get him to sign it back over?” Emily asked.

“The FBI shut down Subsurface Kinetics, and the State Department kicked out the Iranians who were running it. No money changed hands since the FBI seized all of Subsurface’s assets, so Megan Babcock retains control of MCG. As for the rest of her corporation, her lawyers determined that she was under the influence of the drug Blake had given her. They decided she wasn’t in the proper state of mind to comprehend what she had signed, and that Blake had committed fraud. Basically, they ripped up his paperwork and threw it in the trash.”

“Couldn’t happen to a nicer guy,” Ryan stated. He wiggled in his seat, sitting up a little straighter before taking a sip of beer. Setting the bottle down, he said, “Why else are you here, Leslie? You didn’t crawl out from under your rock to apologize.”

Emily slapped her husband on the arm. “Be nice.”

Connelly chuckled. "It's okay, Mrs. Weller. He's entitled to his own opinion. But you're right, I came to ask you to work for me. I want you to be my asset. I know you're leaving on your trip, and I know what kind of trouble you can get into. I want to be your first call if you encounter something related to national security." She placed a business card on the table and slid it toward Ryan.

He made no move to pick it up.

Connelly stood and used the sliding glass door as a mirror as she straightened her clothing and smoothed her skirt. "I look forward to working together." She stuck her hand out, but Ryan simply stared at her impassively.

"Fine. Thank you for the beer." Connelly turned and walked off the boat.

Ryan shook his head at the woman's audacity. She had offered him a job and not even touched her beer.

"What do you want me to do with her card?" Emily asked.

"Leave it there," he said, then stood and went to the mast, where he hooked his harness to a line and hauled himself to the top. Seated on his high perch, he saw Connelly as she got into her car. She had balls that was for sure.

He changed the light bulb, called Emily on his phone, and asked her to turn the lights on. She did, and the little bulb glowed brightly.

After Ryan was back on the deck, he crossed the light bulb off his check list. The rest were little items he could fix while they were underway.

After a run to the grocery store, the liquor store, the hardware store, and a brief stop for takeout Chinese for dinner, Ryan and Emily returned to the boat with her Jeep packed to the roof with supplies. They spent the evening storing their provisions in the fridge and freezer, various cabinets, under the sole boards, and in the cabin they'd converted to storage and a workshop.

Every time Ryan passed the table where Leslie Connelly had placed her business card, he tried not to be angry. Still, he left it there as a reminder of what this journey meant to him—freeing himself of being a troubleshooter, all the bullshit that came with it, and the upcoming time with Emily.

Squatting in the head in front of the sink cabinet, where he was storing toilet paper, Ryan noticed a small brown paper bag lying on the bottom of the cabinet, tucked carefully beneath a bundle of cleaning rags.

Curious as to what the bag contained, he pulled it out and opened it. His eyes widened at the sight of the little white box containing a pregnancy test kit. With a rapidly beating heart and trembling fingers, Ryan withdrew the box and opened it.

Emily had taken multiple tests, and each test stick he withdrew from the box had a little blue cross in the viewing window. He stood and laid all three test sticks on the counter and stared at them, leaning forward to rest his hands on the countertop to steady himself.

This can't be happening!

Ryan breathed in and out, trying to figure out what to do next. He closed his eyes and saw images of playing catch with James in Haiti, hearing the laughter of Slater and Yasmine's son in Guyana, and holding his baby nieces and nephews. It no longer mattered if Ryan was waffling about becoming a father. He was going to be one. Hell, he was one. Ryan had planted the seed of life in his wife's womb.

"Emily!" he shouted.

"What is it?" she asked from the salon.

"Can you come down here for a sec?"

Emily came down the steps. The sound of her feet on

fiberglass thudded in Ryan's ears above the roar of his heartbeat. She entered the bathroom and saw him staring at the pregnancy test kits.

"How far along are you?" he asked.

"A month or so," she replied quietly.

"When were you going to tell me?"

"When I knew for sure."

Ryan straightened and looked at his wife, fear etched on her face at seeing his overly sullen reaction. He enveloped her in his arms, plastering a smile on his face. His mind flashed through their history together, from their first encounter at her office at Ward and Young while investigating stolen sailboats to her breaking up with him over the dangers of his job to her pleading for his help to find a missing freighter. From there, they had rekindled their relationship, and now they were starting a family.

"When would you know for sure?" he asked.

She stepped back, hands on his shoulders, cobalt blue eyes searching his face for the truth. "I wanted to tell you earlier, but we got caught up in the Babcock caper and ..."

"And you were afraid of how I would react."

Emily glanced away. "We never agreed to have children. I guess one of your swimmers slipped through. So, if you think about it, you're really to blame for this mess."

"I guess I can bear that burden," Ryan replied. "Makes me proud just thinking about it."

Emily laughed. "I think your child will be just as stubborn as you are."

He cocked his brow. "I think they'll get that from you."

Staring up at him, she asked, "Are you really okay with this?"

"I guess I have to be. At least I have a few more months to prepare."

Emily smiled. "I think it's going to be fun. You like adventure, right? Just think of it as that."

Ryan laughed.

"What's so funny?" she asked.

"I was just thinking of it as Operation Baby." He deepened his voice theatrically. "Dark Horse and Huntress bring a new life into the world."

It was Emily's turn to giggle. "Our own Dark Angel."

Ryan scoffed. "I hope it won't be as much trouble as Megan Babcock."

"Somehow, I think everything will be just fine," Emily replied.

Turning serious again, he asked, "What about ultrasounds and prenatal vitamins and doctor visits?"

"We'll figure it out. There's plenty of doctors around the world."

Ryan kissed her, pushing aside his personal demons. "I love you."

"I love you, too. Now, finish packing."

Ryan glanced down at the test kits and then back at his wife. This was uncharted territory for him, and he didn't know how to react, but he kept on smiling. "I gotta be honest, Em. I'm kinda freaking out."

"Women give birth all the time, Ryan. Everywhere in the world. Tomorrow, we're leaving. The rest will take care of itself. There's no need to worry."

But he did, and he was. Worrying came with the territory of fatherhood.

They returned to packing and finished several hours later, meeting in the master stateroom, tired but excited for the start of their new journey. As Ryan pulled the covers over himself, Emily pushed them away and climbed on top of him, initiating their lovemaking.

"YOUR MOM IS COMING, RIGHT?" Ryan asked as they stood in the galley the next morning.

"She just texted," Emily replied. "She and Paul will be here in twenty minutes. Now, help me finish breakfast so it's ready when they get here."

Ryan slipped his arms around Emily's waist from behind and held her close. "Are you going to tell her?"

"About what?" she asked, cracking an egg into a bowl.

He rubbed her belly. "The bun in the oven."

She laughed. "There's something wrong with you."

"What?"

"Have you even met my mother? If I told her I was pregnant, she would throw a tantrum about us leaving, and, as much as I love her, I'm not sticking around for that."

Ryan grinned, knowing she was right. "Have I told you yet how much I love you?"

"Every day. Now, help me, please."

Ryan busied himself with frying bacon while contemplating their voyage. The weather was perfect for sailing. The wind was out of the west and had laid the sea down into a lake of glass.

When Melissa Hunt and her son, Paul, arrived, breakfast was on the table, along with orange juice and coffee. Ryan sipped his coffee from an old Navy EOD mug. Emily handed him the business card Leslie Connelly had given him, and Ryan slipped it into his pocket when she wasn't looking.

Once they had washed and stored the breakfast dishes in the cabinets, Ryan and Emily bid an emotional goodbye to Melissa and Paul. They had come to see them off and to take Emily's Jeep back to their house to store it for the next time Ryan and Emily were in town.

After a final round of hugs, Ryan retracted the gangplank

into the hull and started the twin diesels. Paul and Emily cast off the lines, and Ryan guided *Huntress* away from the dock, turning to wave once they were in the Dania Cut-off Canal.

Emily joined Ryan at the steering station as they motored into the Stranahan River. Ryan drew in a deep breath of cleansing salt air and grinned. They were finally underway, returning to the open ocean to continue their adventure together, just the three of them.

Last night, after Emily had fallen asleep, Ryan had quietly gotten out of bed, gone to the forward berth in the port hull, and just stared in, trying to picture it covered in crayon drawings and scattered with building blocks and Legos—or maybe Barbies and unicorns. He'd have to make some changes to accommodate a baby, but they were easily doable over the next several months.

They motored past Port Everglades and turned east, following the river into the sea.

Once past the rock jetties, Ryan turned south, angling toward the Florida Keys, planning to skip the Caribbean and go straight to Panama to cross into the Pacific. He pressed the button to raise the sails, letting the electric winch unfurl the big mainsail, and then he opened the jib. With the sails set, he shut off the rattling diesel engines and listened to the sound of the wind in the rigging and the splash of water as the catamaran's hulls sliced through the sea.

"We're free, babe!" Emily said, throwing her arms around Ryan.

He kissed her hard on the lips before saying, "Thank you."

"For what?"

He grinned wildly. "Everything, babe. *Everything*."

When Emily turned to stare at the horizon, Ryan slipped Leslie Connelly's card from his pocket and released it into the wind, watching it flutter for a moment before it fell into the water.

Ryan had always believed he only needed three things to be happy—an excellent sailboat, the love of a good woman, and a worthy mission. He had them all now. And Ryan vowed that his new mission of fatherhood would be the adventure of a lifetime.

Your Free Book is Waiting

The elusive bomb maker, Nightcrawler, is targeting Coalition troops in Afghanistan. Ryan Weller's U.S. Navy EOD team is sent to find him. But Nightcrawler has plans of his own—a deadly ambush with long lasting consequences.

Get a free digital copy of the prequel *Dark Days: A Ryan Weller Thriller* here:
https://evangraver.com/free-book/

ABOUT THE AUTHOR

Evan Graver is the author of the Ryan Weller Thriller Series, the John Phoenix Thrillers, and the stand alone Liberty Brigade. Before becoming a writer, Graver worked as a motorcycle mechanic, property manager, and in the scuba industry. He also served in the U.S. Navy as an aviation electronics technician (AT) until they medically retired him following a motorcycle accident that left him paralyzed. Graver lives in Hollywood, Florida, with his wife and son. His passions are fishing, scuba diving, and writing.

To see his full biography, visit the About Section at www.evangraver.com.

While you're there, sign up for his newsletter and receive the free Ryan Weller Thriller short story, *Dark Days*.

www.ingramcontent.com/pod-product-compliance
Ingram Content Group UK Ltd.
Pitfield, Milton Keynes, MK11 3LW, UK
UKHW062305290726
14090UKWH00018B/891